T0274513

red

red

Annie Cardi

U
UNION
SQUARE
& CO.
NEW YORK

UNION SQUARE & CO. and the distinctive Union Square & Co. logo are trademarks of Sterling Publishing Co., Inc.

Union Square & Co., LLC, is a subsidiary of Sterling Publishing Co., Inc.

ISBN 978-1-4549-5130-8 (hardcover)
ISBN 978-1-4549-5132-2 (e-book)
ISBN 978-1-4549-5131-5 (paperback)

Library of Congress Cataloging-in-Publication Data

Names: Cardi, Annie, author.
Title: Red / by Annie Cardi.
Description: New York, NY : Union Square & Co., [2024] | Audience: Ages 14 to 18. | Audience: Grades 10–12. | Summary: When Tess's decision to get an abortion goes public, she is rejected and harassed by people in her community, but she soon finds solace in her music and uses her voice to end the cycle of abuse in her small town.
Identifiers: LCCN 2023001256 (print) | LCCN 2023001257 (ebook) | ISBN 9781454951308 (hardcover) | ISBN 9781454951315 (trade paperback) | ISBN 9781454951322 (epub)
Subjects: CYAC: Abortion—Fiction. | Church youth groups—Fiction. | Bullies and bullying—Fiction. | Singing—Fiction. | Self-actualization—Fiction. | BISAC: YOUNG ADULT FICTION / Coming of Age | YOUNG ADULT FICTION / Social Themes / Pregnancy
Classification: LCC PZ7.C21115 Re 2024 (print) | LCC PZ7.C21115 (ebook) | DDC [Fic]—dc23
LC record available at https://lccn.loc.gov/2023001256
LC ebook record available at https://lccn.loc.gov/2023001257

For information about custom editions, special sales, and premium purchases, please contact specialsales@unionsquareandco.com.

Printed in the United States of America

2 4 6 8 10 9 7 5 3 1

unionsquareandco.com

Interior design by Julie Robine
Cover design by Melissa Farris
Cover art by Beatriz Ramo (@naranjalidad)

To the ones speaking out and the
ones finding their voices

♩

1.

We have to drive to Maryland for the appointment. Mom got the earliest one available on a Saturday morning so she could drive me there and home and still get to work for the afternoon shift. Also, I'm not supposed to eat or drink eight hours before the procedure, which Mom says will be easier in the morning than the afternoon. "We can stop for breakfast on the way home," she tells me. "If you're hungry."

I don't know if I'll be hungry because I've never done this before. Neither has Mom, so she doesn't know exactly, either.

That's what we call it, though—"the procedure." We don't call it what it is. It's like we're afraid to say the word, like it's a curse. Maybe it is. I know that the kids in youth group would basically say as much.

This morning, they're all at Ignite, the annual fall retreat, where they do team-building exercises and share testimonials at a retreat center in the mountains. I went last year when Mom and I were new to Hawthorne. It felt good to have people take my hand and give me a hug and tell me they were glad I was there. I imagine them all there again today, playing games and praying and learning to trust each other. I remember Lily pulling me into a hug with Bri, and the weight of their arms around me felt like relief. Alden would be with them, encouraging them all to put their trust in each other and in God, because with that they can accomplish anything. When I was there last year, I expected that kind of thing to sound cheesy or disingenuous, but it didn't. The way Alden said it, it sounded real.

The car feels quiet and empty in comparison to being in that big group.

It's still dark when we leave, the sun just starting to rise as we drive through Northern Virginia and into Maryland. I wear sweatpants and a hoodie because the pre-procedure paperwork said I should wear loose, comfortable clothing, and because I feel like I could curl up inside them, warm and protected. In the cold morning air, under my hoodie, I feel small and young and old all at once.

We're lucky. That's what Mom said when she made the appointment. If this had happened back in Bloomington, it would have been a lot harder to find somewhere to do it. It would have meant a longer drive, staying in a hotel—money we didn't have. Maybe someone would have stopped us. Having to drive to Maryland, it's not so bad.

Except maybe, back in Bloomington, this wouldn't have happened.

The radio's playing pop-country songs about falling in love and broken hearts and being someone's girl. We don't change the station because that's all the other stations play too.

When I told Mom I was pregnant, she asked who the boy was. That was the way she said it: *Who's the boy, is it someone in your class, is it someone from youth group?* Which made it easy to say, *Yeah, a boy I met at a youth group thing, you don't know him, it was one time.* When she asked what his name was, all I could do was shake my head. She didn't press me, and I still haven't told her.

I don't know if I can ever tell her.

She didn't question me when I told her this was what I wanted to do—just looked up the closest places to us, found one that seemed supportive and safe. She scheduled the appointment, read through the pre-procedure materials with me, kept telling me that I was going to be okay.

"This doesn't have to affect the rest of your life," she says as we pull off the highway. "I mean, this is one part of your life. It's not who you are."

"I know," I say, even though I don't yet. I don't know who I am or who I'm going to be or who I want to be.

"No one has to know," she says, like it's supposed to comfort me.

"I know," I say again.

♩

It's a small brick building with a sign out front that reads CENTER FOR REPRODUCTIVE HEALTH in delicate blue letters. The first time we came was only a couple of days ago so a doctor could tell me about the procedure. Mom called in sick for me at school and for herself at work, and we drove out to have the consultation. I imagined a building as big as a hospital with a horde of protesters outside, waving signs with pictures of babies on them, but there were only a couple of older women. When we hustled inside, I half-expected the pavement to open up underneath me and swallow me whole.

That didn't happen, of course. I kept walking.

Now it's early enough that ours is one of a few cars in the parking lot. We wait to be buzzed into the building and are greeted by the receptionist behind a window.

"Hi, can I help you?" she asks, smiling kindly at us.

"I'm Tess Pine," I tell her. "I have an eight-thirty appointment."

She doesn't ask me to specify what the appointment is for and finds my information in her computer. Mom and I show her our IDs, and the receptionist gives me more paperwork to fill out. While I write, Mom hunches over her checkbook. I know this isn't the kind of thing we can really afford, but when I told Mom about being pregnant and that this was what I wanted to do, she didn't make me feel guilty about it. *We'll work it out*, she told me.

We don't say much as we sit there, half-listening to the receptionist taking calls and the waiting room TV playing a home improvement show. Mom sits stiffly next to me, chipping at her nails, flakes of dried red polish falling on her lap. She picks up a pamphlet off the coffee table, flipping back and forth through information about resources available for women during recovery and afterward—therapy, support groups, social workers. I'm sure she never expected to be looking at lists like that for me.

I wonder if I should tell her. She's here with me, she made the appointments, and she's paying out of her savings so I don't have to live with this for the rest of my life. So I can keep living my life. But if I tell her, it'll change everything, and all I want is for things to go back to normal. The words stick in my throat.

Even though it's early, there are a couple of other people in the waiting room too—one woman in a pale pink button-down shirt who looks like she could be Gram's age and who's flipping through a cooking magazine, and another in her twenties, stomach round and full, like she's swallowed the moon. I try not to stare at her, the pregnant woman, her face a little tired but pretty. They say pregnant women have a glow, and it's true for her. While she holds her phone in one hand, the other rests casually on top of her belly, and she looks happy.

That could be me someday. Maybe.

"Tess?" a nurse says as she enters the waiting room, holding a clipboard and looking at me. I wonder how many Tesses she's seen before, where they were from, who came with them—if any of them had boyfriends they loved or people who hurt them.

Mom stands with me, even though I'm going in alone. "You'll be okay," she tells me, her voice shaky. "I'll be right here. I'll see you after."

"Okay," I tell her, because that's what I want—for all of this to be over.

I follow the nurse down a long hall to the procedure room. The doctor went over everything with me the other day—the equipment they'll use to do it and how I'll be given medication so I won't feel anything—but I still feel like my legs aren't part of my body while I walk. My stomach knots, and I wish I could run back to the waiting room to bring my mom with me, like I'm a little kid going to school for the first time. But I keep walking, one foot in front of the other.

Even though I was here a couple of days ago, the doctor still goes over everything that's going to happen. She tells me how the procedure will go, what I'm likely to experience, and what complications, although rare, are possible. She asks if I feel safe in my current home environment, and I say yes. She doesn't ask about my relationship with the father, which is a relief.

"Do you have any questions for me?" she asks.

What I want to know is if I'm making the right decision. If this means that things can really go back to normal. If I'll ever feel normal again. If I'll be able to pray again, to feel like I'm connected to something that's bigger than me and like someone's watching out for me. I want to know if I'll be okay.

Instead, I say, "No, no questions."

While the doctor and the nurses examine me and give me medication for pain and set up an IV for sedation, I keep thinking: *When it's over, I won't have to talk about it or think about it, no one will have to know, it'll be over* . . . until it's over and they bring me to recovery.

♩

When Mom and I leave the building, when it's over, there are more protesters outside with signs. It's not a big crowd, but enough people for a Saturday morning—older people, teenagers, middle-aged women with mushroomy haircuts. They're all carrying signs with pictures of fetuses and slogans like IS THIS A CHOICE?

I scan the crowd quickly and am light-headed with relief when I don't see any familiar faces. Because I've been in that kind of crowd before—not here, but at clinics closer to Hawthorne. I've looked at the faces of women going in and out and said, "Your baby is a blessing, not a choice." I thought I was trying to help them. That's what everyone said we were doing.

Looking over the faces and posters now, I wish I could go back and tell those women, *I hope you'll be okay.* Instead, I pull the hood of my sweatshirt down and let Mom put her arm around my shoulders and walk me back to the car.

♩

At Gram and Gramps's, our home for the last year, Mom sets me up on the couch with tea, a mustard-yellow and maroon afghan, a heating pad, and Emma Thompson's *Sense and Sensibility*—my favorite movie, even though Mom thinks Austen adaptations are boring. She offers me toast and canned chicken soup, like I have a cold, but I tell her all I want is to rest for a little while. The way she looks at me, soft and sad, like I'm a little girl again, makes me want to cry more than anything else.

I could cry. Mom would hold me and tell me everything's going to be fine. But I don't want to hear that anymore. If it's over and everything's fine, I shouldn't have to cry.

It doesn't feel like sadness, not exactly. Or even regret—that's what people talked about in youth group when they talked about women who made this choice. Lying under the blankets now, I feel a strange kind of grief, a ghost ship sailing by. Someone I'll never know standing on deck, and me watching them disappear forever.

But there's also relief so deep, I feel it with every breath. I don't need to spend the next nine months and more of my life trying to learn how to be someone I'm not. Not yet. Not having to lie about who the father is, not having to go through it all alone. Guilt, too, churning through me, like I shouldn't feel relieved to have made this choice. Like I should only feel sad about it. Maybe even feeling like I lost something, and I don't deserve to be sad about it, either.

I don't cry.

Instead, I watch *Sense and Sensibility* and then *Persuasion*, only getting up when I have to change my pad. Before Mom goes to work, she makes sure I have ibuprofen and tea and my slippers. She hovers beside the couch in her jacket, looking around like she must have forgotten something. "Maybe I should stay," she says, forehead furrowed in concern. "I can call out. I should be with you."

"Mom, I'm fine," I tell her. "I'll text if I need anything."

She doesn't look entirely convinced but kisses my forehead. "Text me for anything. Seriously. I love you." We both smile a little, as if we're trying to be strong for each other.

The house feels strangely quiet when she leaves. Usually, at least one other person is home, especially if Gram has her church friends over for prayer circle or Gramps invites a few of his VFW buddies over for poker. But the timing of the procedure was good—my grandparents had already planned to visit Gram's sister, Dorothy, in Pennsylvania and would be out of town for a couple of weeks. Great-aunt Dorothy is having hip surgery, and they're going to help during her recovery.

"No wild parties while we're gone," Gramps told me with a wink, because he knew that the only parties I went to were with kids from Grace Teen Life, where we watched movies and played Codenames and the hardest beverage we drank was homemade root beer.

"I'll try," I told him. "Drive safe."

"Call us on Dorothy's phone if anything happens," Gram told Mom before she got in the car. "I don't want to come back to the house burned down."

Mom pressed her lips together in an attempt to smile. Usually, she would have given a sarcastic reply, but I was sure her mind was on my appointment and how we could never tell them about it. Not only would it break their hearts, but they would never see Mom or me the same way again.

"Love to Aunt Dorothy," Mom said, and we waved at them as they drove down the street.

Now, sitting on my grandparents' couch, under their afghan, I have an odd sense of not knowing how I got here. Like I closed my eyes and blinked and suddenly I'm not who I thought I was or where

I thought I would be. There's a before and there's an after, and I can't identify the moment in between.

I don't feel like watching another movie, so I put on my headphones and listen to music—choral music, the kind I used to sing with my school choir back in Bloomington. It's familiar and soothing and helps me remember to breathe in and out.

Every so often, I check my phone. Lily and Bri have texted me a few times: We miss you!!! and Retreat's not the same without you.

I imagine everyone at Ignite, at a retreat center in the mountains, all log cabins and dirt trails and expansive views. I inhale and exhale, as if I can smell the crisp fall air and campfire smoke. Last year, the theme for the retreat was "Living Fearlessly." Alden had us write down our fears and toss them into a bonfire, giving them up to God. "'*When I am afraid, I put my trust in you,*'" he'd said, quoting Psalms. "Let your fears go, tonight and forever, because Jesus is with you, and He's with us here right now."

One by one, we tossed our papers into the fire, watching them burn to ash. Cinders floated away from the fire and into the sky like stars. Around me, some people pressed their hands together and closed their eyes in brief prayer after watching their fears burn. A few even raised their hands toward the sky. I bowed my head and closed my eyes, and it felt like a door opening.

God, please let this be real, I prayed, even though I didn't exactly know what I meant by that. But it was what I wanted to feel—the people around me, the air, the fire, the sky, the letting go, the holding fast.

Bri leaned her head on my shoulder, and across the campfire, someone started singing. I sang along, *light the fire in my heart again*, while the flames warmed my face, and below the night sky, it felt like this was the beginning of something good.

Now they're all back at Ignite, and I'm here. I don't even know what the theme is for this year's retreat—I hadn't asked, and Alden hadn't mentioned it. I have a strange feeling of homesickness for a place I'd only been to once for a couple of days. But I miss being crowded into a room with people I was getting to know, hearing them open up about their struggles and their faith, feeling like maybe I could be open like that too.

Maybe I'll be back there next year. Maybe it'll be like this year never happened.

I send heart emojis back to Lily and Bri, saying Miss you guys too, like I'm stuck at home with the flu. I expect to get at least one other text, asking me how I'm doing, but it never comes.

♩

I don't go to church on Sunday morning. It's the first time I haven't been to Grace Presbyterian for service since we moved to Hawthorne last year. Gram and Gramps go every week, and I go with them, at first because they expected us to go, and eventually because I made friends there and sang in the church choir, and because I liked being part of a community, bound together by our faith.

Grace Presbyterian livestreams their services. It's not super high-tech, but they started doing it a few years ago for people who aren't able to get to church because they're chronically sick or older and have a hard time leaving the house. That was never an option for us, no matter how hard Mom tried to convince Gram that livestreams were basically the same as going for real, because Gram insisted that we all be there in person every Sunday.

"I know going to church isn't your favorite," she told Mom, voice clipped, our first Sunday in Hawthorne. "Lord knows we had that fight often enough when you were a girl. But it can be a good group of people around you, to support you. Plus, it's important to me and it's important to your father, and in this house it's what we do together."

"I know," Mom said tiredly. We'd arrived the night before, after packing the car and driving all day from Bloomington. "Maybe we can get a pass this once—"

"You know, Laura," Gram said, her voice even but firm, "we're happy to have you and Tess here. We are. But it's still our house, and our way goes."

I never minded going to church, not even that first day. The way Gram had described it, "a good group of people around you, to support you," sounded like something I could use. The last few years had felt so unsteady, first with losing Dad and then Mom losing her job and worrying about where we'd live, how we'd get by. A little extra support sounded like a good thing.

Now, curled up in bed with my phone, I consider logging into the livestream. No one would even know it was me watching. Even if they did, no one would question it. They think I'm a good church girl who volunteers and goes to youth group movie nights and sings in the choir and sits in a pew with her grandparents every Sunday. No one knows what I did yesterday.

Almost no one.

But I set my phone aside. Watching from a distance feels too strange, a reminder that something is different.

Maybe I don't deserve to watch. That's what some people in youth group would say, considering what I did yesterday.

Next week, I'll be back there, I try to reassure myself. Maybe I'll feel like I belong again.

I imagine everyone at church next Sunday—people from youth group with their families, my grandparents' friends, the choir huddled together. We'll be singing "A Mighty Fortress Is Our God" and "Abide with Me." I can almost hear Alden leading the group, with his clear tenor and confident piano playing. The way everyone looks to him, the way he shines in front of a group, the way he draws the light out of everyone else—it's part of what makes him a good youth minister and choir director. I fall back to sleep, repeating the lyrics in my head: *When other helpers fail and comforts flee, Help of the helpless, O abide with me.*

I still don't get any other texts asking me how I am.

♩

By Monday morning, I'm feeling better, like the doctor said I would, and plan to go back to school. Mom says I can stay home for a few more days if I want, but what I really want is for things to get back to normal, even if that means going to French class. When I check my phone, I see a bunch of messages from numbers I don't recognize.

Whore

Slut

I can't believe you!

You're going to hell for this!!!

I almost drop my phone because my first thought is: *Someone knows*. My heart is pounding, and I feel cold all over, like I've been plunged into a pool of ice water.

But there's no way anyone can know. No one I knew was at the center; I haven't told anyone, and Mom wouldn't have, either.

This has to be a prank. Some group of creeps got a bunch of phone numbers and are texting random people awful messages. I delete them all and put my phone in my pocket, trying to ignore the hard pit of anxiety growing in my stomach.

♩

When I get to school, immediately I know something's wrong. People are giving me dirty looks, or purposefully not looking at me, or not hiding that they're looking at me and whispering. Part of me wants to go up to them and ask what's the matter, but I keep my head down and rush to my locker like it's a bastion of safety.

That's when I see it—a giant red *A* spray-painted on my locker.

Only mine. No one else's has been touched. Whoever did it was careful not to get too much red paint on the lockers on either side of mine.

For a second, I stand there, staring at it, like maybe I'm seeing things. Maybe something went wrong with the sedation IV and I'm having a terrible delayed reaction. But the way other people are passing by and whispering, leaving a wide berth like the paint is contagious, I know they see it too.

I don't know who would do this. Was it the same people who sent the texts? Is it someone I know?

Behind me, I can feel people stopping to stare. *Don't cry, don't cry, don't cry,* I tell myself, even though I can feel my cheeks flush and tears begin to sting my eyes. *It'll be worse if you cry.*

Now I want the ground to open up and swallow me. Around me, people are whispering and laughing, and I'm waiting for the linoleum to shift and the earth to swallow me like I was never here. For the last year, I thought I had friends, a place, but no one comes over to me now.

No one except for Principal Bellingham.

"Tess Pine," he says firmly. "Come with me." He turns and doesn't look back to see if I'm following or not.

I could run. I could take off and run out of the school and all the way home and refuse to leave the house again. He probably wouldn't notice until I was halfway down the street. My heart thumps against my chest like I'm already running.

But everyone is still watching me and whispering and laughing. *I will not cry*, I tell myself as I take a breath, deep and diaphragmatic. In my head, I sing "Bridge over Troubled Water" as I walk back down the halls, toward Bellingham's office.

2.

"Do you have anything you'd like to tell me?" Principal Bellingham asks me once we're behind the closed door of his office. It's the first time I've been in here—I've never been in trouble before. I've never been late to homeroom, or caught without a hall pass, nothing. I wasn't even sure Bellingham knew my name until he said it in the hall. People see me as nice in the most boring way, another Grace Teen Life girl with a polite voice and neat hair. It's who I am.

It's who I was until today.

"Nothing," I tell Principal Bellingham, my voice shaking only a little. My hand reflexively goes to the thin gold chain around my neck, clasping the tiny gold cross pendant. Gram gave it to me last year, right before Ignite. It had been hers when she was a girl, a gift from when she was baptized. A few other girls in youth group had ones like it. Wearing it made me feel like I'd found something special, like I was safe and protected and loved. I'd put it on this morning without thinking. Now I wonder if I should take it off.

"You have no idea why that graffiti was on your locker?" he asks, like he already knows the answer.

In my bag, I know there are more texts lighting up my phone, telling me what a horrible person I am. I don't even want to look to see if Lily or Bri texted me again, in case they're saying the same thing.

"No," I say to Principal Bellingham. "No idea."

He studies me for a second, looking almost sad before leaning forward in his chair, his hands folded and resting on his desk. "Tess," he says gently. "I want to help you here. If you know the people who might have done this, I can make sure they're held responsible for their actions."

I close my eyes tight, as if I can stop everything from happening if I can't see it, and I shake my head. "I swear, I don't know," I say.

He sighs and doesn't say anything for a second. I open my eyes to see that he's still staring at me with a mixture of confusion and sadness. "If something's going on, Tess," he says, "you can tell me. Or Ms. Simmons, the school counselor. If you're experiencing bullying or harassment, we want to know so we can help you."

I study him back, and it seems like he's being sincere. Maybe he doesn't know me well, but he wants his school to run smoothly, and something like bullying or graffiti spray-painted on a locker isn't part of that. But if I tell him why someone might have done this to me, I'll have to tell him about my weekend, which means I'll have to tell him about what happened last year after the Spirit Light Festival. And everything that happened before. And after. About how I thought things were going to work out okay, I really did. Maybe they still can, if I keep quiet, like I promised.

There's no way I can tell Principal Bellingham any of that.

And besides, I know he's only saying he can help because he thinks I'm a nice Christian girl. The kind of person who would only get bullied because other people are jerks and want to make some innocent person's life miserable. The kind of person who wouldn't do anything wrong, who would never hurt anyone.

I shake my head again. "No, no one's been bothering me," I murmur. "Um, sorry, can I go? I'm late for French."

Now he looks more frustrated as he frowns at me, but he says, "Go ahead." He tells me that if I somehow remember anything that may be of use in this situation, to let him know as soon as possible. But we both know that I won't say anything.

When I leave the principal's office, the hall is silent, with everyone in class. I have French first period, but I don't go there right away. Instead, I return to my locker and stare at the lopsided red *A* until it doesn't even look like a letter anymore—it looks like a strange ancient symbol, something that might be carved on the wall of a cave. It's part of a language I don't know but suddenly have to learn. Distracted thoughts float through my head, like particles of dust that can't settle.

This can't be real. How is this even happening? No one else knows.

Almost no one.

I promised I wouldn't tell anyone—everything was supposed to go back to normal.

Someone must have found out. No one was ever supposed to find out.

Then I hear voices from down the hall—some freshmen headed my way. Before they can get too close, I swing open my locker, grab everything I'll need from it, and shove it all into my bag so I won't have to come back for the rest of the day. My backpack weighs a ton now, but it's better than having to stare at that giant red *A* again.

In French, everyone's already working on translating sentences from the homework. When I open the door, they all turn to me. Some people smirk, others whisper, and I wish I could back out of the room again.

But our teacher, Madame Johnson, is frowning at me from the whiteboard. "Mademoiselle Pine, le cours commence à huit," she admonishes me for being late. "Asseyez-vous."

Does she know? Her expression is stern but not unkind. Maybe not—maybe she only knows that something's wrong and I'm caught up in it.

"Sorry," I mumble as I take my usual seat by the windows, then before Madame Johnson can criticize my use of English, I add, "Je suis désolé."

It feels like a personal attack when Madame Johnson tells us to break into small groups. I turn my desk toward three others near mine, hoping that we can focus on the assignment, but one of the girls, a petite junior named Amber, is staring at me. She whispers, "Tess, did you really do it?" Like I might actually tell her the truth. Like we've said more than four words to each other since I started at Hawthorne High last year.

"Do what?" I ask, voice flat.

"They're saying you . . . you know . . ." She trails off like she's afraid to say it.

"No way," Corbin, another person in our group, says like I'm not even there. "That would mean she'd have to have sex first. Church girls don't do that."

They don't. Or they're not supposed to. In prayer group and Bible study, we talk about saving ourselves for marriage and committing ourselves to following the path that Jesus laid out for us. A couple of the girls wear purity rings on their left ring fingers, like a shield protecting them until someone comes along with a wedding band.

I can sing the songs and recite the prayers, but maybe I'm not really a good church girl. The way Corbin says it, it seems like being one is a bad thing. But not being one feels equally as bad, and I don't know what I should even want to be anymore.

I don't have to say anything to Amber or Corbin, because Madame Johnson walks over to our group to see how we're doing, and we pretend we've been reviewing ways to give directions in French. When the bell rings, I jump up from my seat and lug my too-heavy backpack into the hall. For a moment, I consider going to the nurse and asking Mom to come and pick me up, but I know she'll be worried about me and can't take another day off anyway. No, it's better to stay at school and deal with the stares and whispers. If I don't say anything, they'll get bored eventually and move on. All I need is to keep quiet for a while.

♩

Lily was the first friend I made in Hawthorne. My first day at Hawthorne High, I'd been hovering awkwardly at the edge of the cafeteria, trying to decide if I was hungry enough for lunch or if I could hide in the library for the whole period, when I felt a hand on my arm. A girl with dark blond hair was beside me, wearing a Grace Teen Life T-shirt and a warm smile. "Hey, you're the Rileys' granddaughter, right?" she asked.

She'd recognized me from church the day before—she knew my grandparents and had heard about how my mom and I were moving in with them. I hadn't done youth group back home, but it was a huge relief to have somewhere to sit for lunch. Plus, Lily and Bri and the others were the kind of people I would have been friends with anyway—friendly, involved, maybe a little quiet or dorky, but kind. I liked that they cared about something, that they believed in something. They went to the movies and had extensive text threads, but they also attended prayer groups and volunteered at church bake sales. Even if I hadn't grown up going to church or praying, it felt strangely easy to be around people who did.

Today, I don't see Lily or Bri or any of the other Grace Teen Life kids until lunch, when I stupidly head into the cafeteria like it's any other Monday. I look for our usual table by the windows. Jacob, Roger, and Emma are already there, faces solemn as they lean their heads together in intense conversation.

For a moment, I'm foolishly hopeful. Maybe I can even talk to them about what happened—not all of it, obviously, but why I had to do what I did. Maybe they'll understand. Or even if they don't understand, maybe they'll accept me in spite of everything. Forgiveness, how God is always there for you, love one another, everything Reverend Wilson talks about at church—why can't they love me despite this?

Then Roger's eyes meet mine, and I know there's no way I can go back to that table. They all stare at me, cold and judgmental, and all I want to do is shrink back into the hall and disappear inside my locker.

I'm about to run out of the cafeteria when I hear Lily behind me. "Tess," she says like it's hard for her to form that one syllable without bursting into angry tears. When I turn, I see Lily a few steps away, her usually open face hard and her cheeks tinged with red. The memory of Lily and I standing in the cafeteria last year, when I didn't know anyone and didn't have anywhere to sit, flashes in my mind, and for a second I think, *Maybe that will happen again.*

But before I even open my mouth, she says, "Is it true?"

I want to lie, to tell her that of course I wouldn't do anything like that, and I have no idea who would start such an awful rumor.

Around us, tables have quieted, and people aren't even pretending not to watch us.

If Lily notices anyone else in the cafeteria, she doesn't show it. Instead, her eyes are fixed on me like she could pin me to the wall with her stare. When I don't respond right away, she continues. "Tess. Tell me it's not true." She can't even say the word, but she sounds desperate, like she thinks there's still a chance for me.

Except there isn't. I'm not who she thought I was and maybe I'm not even who I thought I was. I'm still bleeding, still wearing a thick pad and feeling the vaguest cramps. There's no way I can deny that it happened, and I know Lily's already lost to me. "Lily" is all I can say, my voice small and choked.

She blinks at me, then shakes her head like she can't believe what everyone's saying is true. She takes a step back, then another. "I'm praying for you," she says before she turns her back on me.

♩

My first weekend in Hawthorne, Lily invited me to a Grace Teen Life social activity, mini golf and milk shakes after the Hawthorne High football game. "A lot of people go to parties and stuff after the game," she told me. "I mean, it's fine if you do that, but it's not like you *have* to. We do a bunch of social stuff that doesn't involve getting wasted in a field."

I was sure my mom would have hung out with the "getting wasted in a field after a football game" kids when she'd been a teen in Hawthorne, but I was glad that I had an alternative. I went to a couple of house parties when I was a freshman in Bloomington, and it had been both a lot (thumping music, people shouting, a fight breaking out in the backyard) and totally underwhelming (gross, flat beer, and I couldn't even hear anyone, much less have a conversation). Mini golf and milk shakes with Grace Teen Life sounded like a good way to get to know people.

At the game, I dressed in blue and white and cheered along with Lily, Bri, and a group from Grace Teen Life. Hawthorne ended up losing, but it didn't seem to matter, as everyone was still excited to go out afterward.

We piled into cars and drove to Treasure Island, the pirate-themed miniature golf course on the edge of town. Under the fluorescent lights, the paint on the giant pirate ship on the eighteenth hole was visibly chipped, and every inch of the Astroturf had been flattened by dozens of golfers' feet, but everyone cheered as we pulled into the parking lot like it was Disney World.

Before we started playing, Alden rounded everyone up for a prayer. Around me, people reached for each other's hands and bent their heads. On one side, Lily took my hand and a junior girl I didn't know took the other. I lowered my head slightly but kept my eyes on Alden as he spoke, his eyes closed and his voice warm and calm.

"Lord, thank you for bringing us together here tonight, in faith and in friendship," he said. "We ask that you look over us tonight and all weekend as we strive to do your good works. In your name, amen."

Aside from Gram and Gramps, I hadn't been around a lot of people who prayed outside of church or the dinner table. I expected to feel awkward about praying in a group in public, but instead it was the opposite—I liked the idea that something bigger was watching over us, even while we were mini golfing, and that we were all connected because of it. The way Alden said it, it felt like God wasn't just somewhere far away and separate—He was here with us, with me. I was somewhere new, and even if it was intimidating, I didn't have to feel alone.

Maybe, after some really hard years, this could be a good thing. Even if Mom and I didn't expect to be here, maybe it was where we were supposed to be.

The rest of the group echoed Alden's "amen." I repeated a second after everyone else and felt Lily squeeze my hand before she let go.

3.

I escape from the cafeteria as fast as I can before anyone else can confront me. I would go back to my grandparents' house and skip my afternoon classes, but the school would call Mom and she'd know something was wrong. More wrong, at least. She'd be pissed too—she'd march into Principal Bellingham's office and demand he find the assholes who painted my locker and who've been harassing me for a choice I made about my own goddamn body. She'd hate that we had to move to Hawthorne and that we can't move now, since she finally got a full-time job, in addition to bartending part-time, and is making money again. There's no way I can do that to her. All I need to do is get through today and hope that people move on to something else.

Instead of ditching the rest of the day, I escape to the music room. There's no chorus or band practice this period, so it's blissfully empty. Music stands and chairs are set up from the last class and I pick up a piece of their sheet music—"Variations on a Shaker Melody" by Aaron Copland, for the oboe. My eyes scan the notes and I hear the melancholic, gentle sound of the oboe in my head. I feel myself breathe in and out until I'm calm again.

I don't even notice the sound of the door opening. "Oh, sorry," someone behind me says. "Are you rehearsing?" It's a petite girl with light brown skin, dark, curly hair, and round, wire-rimmed glasses that take up most of her face. With her are two other people, a gangly boy with shaggy red hair and a girl with long blond hair pulled into a tight ponytail and a T-shirt that reads I LIKE NAPS under an illustration of a sloth. I recognize the girl with glasses and the boy as sophomores and the sloth T-shirt girl as a freshman. If they recognize me from what's going on today, they don't show it. The boy is holding a guitar case, and the sloth girl has the handle of a violin case clenched in her fist.

"We booked the room," the sloth girl says flatly. "Mr. Nelson has the form."

I quickly put the sheet music back on its stand. "No, I wasn't . . . ," I say before trailing off, because the full explanation feels like too much right now.

But the sloth girl either didn't hear me or doesn't care. "If you want to use the music room, you have to go through Mr. Nelson," she insists. "We get it every day during second period lunch, unless the brass ensemble is having an extra rehearsal for winter or spring concert."

"I get it," I say.

"I filled out the form," she says. "You have to go."

Go where, exactly? Back to the cafeteria, to sit with Lily and the rest of the Grace Teen Life people who hate me? To my next class, where people know that last weekend, I went from being pregnant to being not-pregnant? To Gram and Gramps's, where they gave us a home when we needed it and where we hold hands around the table while saying grace over dinner? To Alden's cramped office at Grace Presbyterian, hoping he'll know exactly what to say to help me survive all of this? Or back to my locker, with the red *A* cutting across it like an open wound?

No. There's nowhere left for me, and now some sloth girl is telling me I have to leave the one place that makes me feel quiet and calm. I feel my face burn as I stare her down.

"Look, I've had a *really* bad day," I snap. "I don't care if you filled out a form for Mr. Nelson or Principal Bellingham or anyone else. I need five minutes where everything doesn't feel like a giant mess, so you can go get Mr. Nelson if you want, but I'm not leaving." Before I even know what I'm doing, I grab one of the folding chairs and plunk myself down in it.

They stare back at me for a second before the gangly redhead shrugs and pushes past the sloth girl. "It's not a closed set or anything," he says. "She can listen."

The sloth girl glares at me but doesn't argue. She marches over to the other side of the room, near a large double bass, plops down in a folding chair, and begins tuning her violin.

"Ignore Mia," the gangly redhead tells me. "It comes from being a middle child. Plus, I'm the favorite."

Mia's head pops up from her violin. "Connor, don't be a dick, and you are so not the favorite!" she shouts, while Connor smirks like he's heard this all before. "Chloe's not even related to us and she's more of a favorite than you are."

"I'm definitely your mom's favorite because I help clear the table while the rest of y'all are arguing." Chloe, the girl with the glasses, nudges Connor with her shoulder as she heads to the double bass. "Come on, we've got to be out of here before brass ensemble," she says. Then she looks at me and gives me a small sad smile, like she knows how it feels not to have anywhere else to go. It's not much, but for now, I accept that little bit of kindness and breathe deeply, in and out.

I take a seat on the other side of the room from them, quietly eating my lunch and listening to the cacophonous sounds of them tuning their instruments. After a moment, they murmur song titles to each other, and Chloe counts them into the song they choose. Connor strums the guitar easily, and Chloe plays a grounding melody behind him. Mia's violin comes in after a moment, clear and bright as Connor sings in a low, gentle voice about roads and stars and a bright clear moon.

I don't play any instruments, not really—I know a little piano because of singing with choirs for most of my life, but not enough to consider myself an actual player. My dad played the guitar. He was always trying to teach me, but mostly I wanted him to play and for me to sing along. When I was twelve, he had an aneurysm and collapsed at work; he died before the ambulance could get him to the hospital. For a while, I couldn't even look at his guitar, even though Mom and I never got rid of it. Now, seeing the others play, I feel a knot of sadness and guilt twist in my stomach, and I wish I'd paid more attention when Dad tried to teach me.

But I close my eyes and my heart beats gently in time with the bass as I inhale and exhale, imagining myself on a clear road at night, going somewhere peaceful and warm and safe.

When they finish the song, they play another, one without lyrics. It's a little faster and bouncier, but with Mia's violin, there's a mournfulness behind it. I automatically try to imagine lyrics, what accompanying vocals would sound like: *learning to fly, learning to fall, no matter how far I've gone, you're still the one I call.*

Which makes me remember being in the church choir, working on songs with everyone and Alden leading us. Writing songs for the Spirit Light Festival. How I loved standing in front of the audience, lifting our voices in praise, sharing old words in new ways.

How can I go back now?

Tears sting my eyes, but the others are still playing. I focus on the gentle sounds of their instruments, their occasional break to argue about how a piece should sound. Mia's precise when she corrects her brother or Chloe—"That should have been a half step higher"—while Chloe's suggestions are more about a general sound—"That was too . . . squishy? I think we need to be less squishy"—but I love watching them work together as a band as much as I enjoy listening to their music. They really feel like a group, not just friends who play together. I pretend that I'm part of the group, too, silently sharing suggestions for where to hold a note a second longer or play a touch sharper.

What I really want to do is tell them: *Thank you for letting me be here and distracting me from everything that's going on.* Instead, when they're between songs, I say, "You guys are really good. Are you rehearsing for ensemble or something?"

Chloe shakes her head. "No, we're our own band."

"Trying to be," Mia adds.

"*Trying* to be," Chloe repeats. "We've been messing around with a bunch of folk covers and jamming together for a little while now. Connor and Mia, they've been playing together forever since their family is super musical."

Connor looks up from his guitar. "It's like the Von Trapp family, but somehow less cool."

"Connor likes people to think he's cooler than the rest of us because he plays guitar," Mia pipes up. "But he plays the autoharp, too, which is basically a grandma instrument. And he should know because he learned it from our grandma." She smirks at her brother, who tosses a guitar pick at her. She swats the pick away and looks to the girl with the glasses. "Connor and Chloe are in the same grade and started playing together in middle school band."

Chloe grins widely. "Nothing brings people together like a bunch of middle schoolers playing the *Jurassic Park* theme. And as much as we love John Williams, we branched out to more indie and folk stuff. This year we roped Mia into our sessions since she's in ninth grade now."

"Plus, I filled out the right form to get us an actual rehearsal space," Mia adds. "Speaking of, we have sixteen minutes left in this period."

Even though I'm really enjoying their music, I'm a little disappointed that Mia tries to keep the others on task—I like hearing them talk about their music and banter with each other. It's familiar and friendly, and even though it's all so far from what I'm going through right now, it feels strangely good to be around a group of people who all care about each other. I'm not one of them, but being around them helps a little.

"Right, right," Chloe says to Mia. She counts off and they begin to play a sweet, bouncy tune, with Connor and Chloe singing about Ingrid Bergman on the island of Stromboli. With Mia's melodic violin in the background, like a strange wild bird, the song reminds me of a beautiful lullaby. I want to curl up in the music and fall asleep and wake up a hundred years from now, as if I were a girl in a fairy tale. I close my eyes tight, like I can make it happen if I try hard enough. But when I open them again, I'm still here, still me, and there's still everything waiting for me on the other side of the door.

At least I have this for a little while.

They play through the Ingrid Bergman song a couple of times, and finish with an instrumental song that gets me swaying in my seat. It's loose and a little messy, but not in a bad way. The song feels like going to a field party on a late-summer night, the air smelling of sweat and smoke and peonies, fireflies dancing around as a crowd of people lifts their hands in the air.

By the time the bell rings, I almost forget that I have to go back out there, where people are talking about me and what happened last weekend. "Thanks for letting me listen," I say as I stand up, slinging my backpack over my shoulder.

"It was cool having an audience," Connor tells me. "At least, an audience who isn't part of my family."

Chloe nods her agreement. "We're here pretty much every day, if you want to come back." She sounds genuinely enthusiastic, like she hopes I do come back tomorrow. Then, gently, she adds, "Especially if, you know, you don't want to be elsewhere right now."

The way she says it, I can tell that she knows what people are saying about me. I can't imagine that she or the others missed the big red *A* on my locker, even if they didn't know exactly whose locker it was at first. For a second, I stiffen, wondering if she's going to say anything else about the rumors. Not rumors, even. About what happened, what I did.

But the way Chloe's looking at me, kind of shyly, I know that this is a small gift. She knows I have nowhere else to go and need a safe place right now, even if we're not friends and I'm not part of her band. Maybe it's because she and Connor and Mia are a little younger and focused on their music, but being with them feels safe somehow. I don't expect to talk to them about what happened, but at least I can share a space with them and not worry about them making me feel worse about everything. It's not the same as being a part of Grace

Teen Life, but for now it's something. I feel my heart swell inside me, like a balloon filling with air. I don't know what I'm going to do for the rest of the day or tonight or tomorrow morning, but at least I have somewhere to go during lunch. And maybe after that too.

"Yeah, that would be great. Thanks," I tell her.

"No problem," Chloe says. "You can tell us when we suck."

"I tell you when we suck," Mia points out, placing her violin back in its case.

"Yeah, but she's not biased," Chloe says.

"Or picky," Connor adds as he heads out of the music room and into the busy hall.

"I'm not picky. I'm *precise*," Mia argues at his back.

I take a breath and follow them into the hall, which feels noisier and more crowded than usual. But I remember the songs the trio played, and for the rest of the day, I'm singing in my head about stars and open roads and Ingrid Bergman.

4.

After that first time out with Grace Teen Life, playing mini golf and getting milk shakes, Alden gave a few of us rides home. I was the last one to get dropped off. The windows were rolled down and the night air was cool against my skin. On the car stereo, a woman with a rich alto voice, accompanied by a soft piano, sang about having nothing left to fear.

Alden tapped his fingers against the steering wheel in time with the piano. “So,” he finally said, “how’s your first week in Hawthorne been?”

I inhaled the scent of cool grass, along with something else—rosemary, maybe, and peppermint—and exhaled deeply. “Better than I expected, to be honest,” I said.

“What did you expect?” he asked. His tone was thoughtful, like he actually wanted to know the answer. Not enough people leave room for the answers. Mom was never afraid to say what she was thinking, even if people didn’t leave room for her. I, on the other hand, felt afraid to take up too much space in a conversation if it wasn’t given to me. I liked that Alden seemed to make that space.

“You know, being new,” I told him. “It’s a small town. Everyone already knows all about each other. I probably would’ve stayed home tonight if it hadn’t been for Lily.”

Alden nodded. “Lily’s that kind of person,” he said. “It’s a really good group. A few years ago, my first job out of college, I was youth minister at this parish outside of Durham. I practically had to *beg* people to come to youth group events. Eventually I was able to build up a good core group. But Grace Presbyterian, they’ve always had a very active teen life program. I feel really blessed that I get to be here, helping people become young adults in faith.”

I thought about that phrase, “young adults in faith.” It sounded like something I could be—a person who knew who she was, where she fit in the universe, who believed some greater being was going to take care of her and the people she loved.

For a moment, Alden didn’t say anything else, instead easing the car onto Sycamore. Then he drew a breath and said, “I’m going to say something, and you can tell me to shut up if you want, okay?”

I laughed a little, nervously. “Okay?” I wasn’t sure what he was going to tell me—maybe it was that I shouldn’t be at youth group activities if I wasn’t super Christian. Or that I’d said or done something wrong tonight.

But instead, he said, “Your grandma told me about your dad. I’m so sorry, Tess. That must have been really hard.”

At the mention of my dad, my body stiffened. Of course Gram and Gramps would have told people Dad had died, especially when Mom and I were moving back here after she lost her job and we couldn’t afford rent. But I didn’t expect it to come up in conversation tonight when everything had seemed so open and possible and hopeful and new.

“Yeah” was all I said to Alden.

"You've been through a lot," he continued. "More than a lot of the other kids in youth group. Losing your dad at a young age, your mom losing her job, having to move here—it can make you feel like you're having to grow up faster than everyone around you."

I inhaled the cool night air, thinking about how I felt like I had to be positive for Mom, who was already feeling so defeated by this move. I wanted to make sure Gram and Mom didn't fight too much. After my dad's funeral, no one knew what to say to me or how to be around me, and I didn't even blame them because I didn't know what to say or how to be myself anymore, either. When I exhaled again, the air in my lungs felt heavy, as if it took effort to even breathe.

"Yeah," I said again.

He slowed the car to stop in front of my grandparents' house. Inside, there was a light on in the living room and I could see the glow of the TV playing a cable news show. "In my experience, having faith—it can help with that. It can help you feel less alone. Because you're not, Tess."

That's what I wanted—not to feel alone, in so many ways. I didn't look at Alden, but I felt him watching me.

"Whether you join Grace Teen Life or not, I'm always available to talk," he continued gently, pulling his phone out of his pocket. "I can even give you my number if you want." He paused, and I could practically hear the smile curving at the corners of his lips. "Call me anytime if you need someone to talk to—or if you want a ride to Sunshine Sundaes for a milk shake."

I laughed. "Well, that's probably bad news for you, because now I'm addicted to Sunshine shakes."

He texted me his number, and I saved it to my contacts. "Thanks," I said, putting my phone away. "For—a lot. Tonight was really good."

"My pleasure," he said and patted my shoulder, giving it a small squeeze. "Take care, Tess. See you Sunday."

I smiled, thinking about how I'd be at Grace Presbyterian in a couple of days with Gram and Gramps, and how there would be people I'd recognize and could say hi to. It would feel familiar, comfortable, and I found that I was looking forward to it. "See you Sunday," I repeated.

♩

When I get home from school, the first thing I do is text Alden: Can we talk? I don't tell him what happened at school, partly because it'll be easier to explain in person and partly because I don't want to relive it all in text. It's possible he already knows. If Lily and Bri and the rest of the Grace Teen Life people know, then it's likely one of them reached out to him about it too. I wonder who it was—maybe it was even Lily or Bri. Maybe Alden tried to tell them that they didn't know the whole situation and that I should be allowed to explain before they jumped to any conclusions.

I stare at my phone, waiting for a response, even those little bubbles that mean someone's writing back. Nothing.

I set my phone aside and try to focus on my calc homework, but I only make it through a couple of problems, and I'm pretty sure I didn't even get those right. My stomach is twisting, and I feel nauseous, and I know it's not because of the procedure.

When my phone pings, I practically jump on it. I expect it to be a response from Alden, but instead it's more harassment: Burn in hell!

I drop my phone like it burned me, but after a second I pick it up again. I stare at the unfamiliar number, feeling my heart pound against my chest. Finally, I type back: Who is this?

I watch the bubbles flash and wait for the response. Baby-killer. Whore.

I feel my cheeks burn in shame and tears sting my eyes, but I clutch my phone and type: Stop harassing me. Before I can get another response, I block the number, turn off my phone, and set it aside.

My hands are shaking, and my throat feels choked. But I don't want to cry. Even if no one can see me, I don't want to admit that this bothers me. Because even if I block one number, I don't know who's behind this and how many there are. I could go to school tomorrow and find more graffiti on my locker, or worse. I don't know how I'm going to get through the rest of the year, or the rest of the week, or even the rest of the day.

I can't just sit here pretending that I can work on calc problems like it's a regular Monday afternoon and willing myself not to cry.

Before I know what I'm doing, I stand up from the kitchen table and walk into the garage. I push aside cardboard boxes that haven't been touched in months, a thin layer of grime coating all of them, until I find what I want: Dad's guitar.

When we were packing up stuff to move to Hawthorne, Mom and I didn't even question bringing Dad's guitar with us, even though I don't play and Mom isn't musical at all. Like the boxes, the guitar case is dusty when I pull it out, but the acoustic guitar inside is still shining and well maintained. I lug the case back into the house, wiping it off with a damp cloth until every inch is clean again. Then I pull the guitar out and strum a few strings, which twang sour, out-of-tune notes. It's been a long time since I tuned a guitar, and even when I was young, I would mostly make Dad do it. But I hum a low E and turn the pegs, meticulously working my way up until all the strings hit the right notes. I feel my heart beat slow and my breath steady with every strum.

My mom tells the story that, when I was a baby, I had colic and cried and cried and cried. "The only thing that calmed you was your dad's guitar," she says, sometimes tearing up when she talks about it.

Now I sit on the living room floor of my grandparents' house, stumbling my way through "Somewhere over the Rainbow" and listening to the sound of my own voice.

5.

By the time Mom gets home from work that evening, I've finished my schoolwork and started making dinner for the two of us. I don't want her to think that anything went wrong today. It'll only lead to more questions I can't answer. And besides, I only have to survive another two years at Hawthorne High. Two years is nothing in the entire history of the universe, right? I can do this.

"Mmm, something smells good," Mom says when she walks in, kicking off her work shoes and tossing her purse onto the couch.

"Chicken fajitas," I tell her. "We had some leftover stuff I could throw together."

"You're the best." She comes into the kitchen and kisses the top of my head. Then she's quiet for a moment and asks, "How are you feeling? Any pain?"

I shake my head. "Nope."

She puts a hand against my forehead. "No fever or anything?"

I brush her hand away. "No fever."

But she keeps looking at me, frowning a little sadly. "What about the bleeding? Is it too heavy? Do you think we need to call the doctor? They said if you soak through more than one pad in an hour—"

"Mom," I say, more sharply than I intended. "I'm fine. I wouldn't be making dinner if I wasn't fine."

She leans against the kitchen counter, folding her arms over her chest and studying me, like she's looking for some kind of hairline crack. "I got a call from your school today." She pauses for a moment, eyes softening. "What happened, Tess?"

I can't look at her, because I know if I do, I'll start crying and won't be able to stop. I stare at the pan of sizzling meat and vegetables, pushing them around with a wooden spoon. "It's nothing," I tell her.

"It didn't sound like nothing," she argues. "Tess." She takes a small step toward me, like that will make me look at her, but I keep staring at the pan. When she speaks again, her voice is choked, like she wants to scream and isn't sure she can stop herself. "Tess, are people harassing you because you had an abortion?"

The simple way she says it is what gets me. *Abortion.* I keep thinking of it as "what happened" or "the procedure" because I don't want to think of it as what it is. In Grace Teen Life prayer circles, we'd ask Jesus to protect the unborn and to help their mothers choose life. That was the way we always said it, "choose life," as if there were two options and the mothers only needed to realize this was the right one. It didn't feel like a choice for me. It felt like a path I was already on, and I didn't know where it would lead.

It wasn't something I'd thought much about before youth group. I knew that some girls got pregnant without wanting or meaning to, and had abortions, and that a lot of people thought it was wrong, but it always felt like a problem that was outside of my life. In my old school in Bloomington, I knew of kids who were having sex, and maybe this was more of an immediate problem for them. As far as I knew, my friends were all way more occupied with getting into honors chorus than worrying about whether they were going to get pregnant.

Then, soon after I moved to Hawthorne and started going to Grace Teen Life, one of the seniors announced a letter-writing campaign. "The state senate is going to be debating a bill at the end of the month that would protect the unborn," she said, "so it would be great if everyone could write in. We've got sample letters and envelopes and stamps, and you can say whatever you want, but I think it would make a big difference if we all wrote to support these babies."

She passed out paper and pens and address information. I read the template letter, which talked about the sanctity of life, how it begins at conception, and how the unborn needed all of us to raise our voices for them. It wasn't the kind of thing that I remembered from sex ed talks in health class, but no one seemed bothered about it. Around me, everyone started writing.

Even though I was sure my mom wouldn't have been too thrilled with me writing letters to my state senator about pro-life legislation, I picked up a pen anyway and copied the basics of the letter. It seemed harmless enough. Plus, if I was going to church on Sundays and youth group movie nights, didn't that mean I had to be one of those people speaking up for the unborn?

Now I can only nod to Mom before I start crying. She pulls me into a fierce hug, like she's both comforting me and smashing the harassers in the face all at once. We stand like that for a long time, me crying and Mom holding me, until I smell something burning and pull away.

"The chicken," I say foolishly.

Mom turns off the stove top and pulls the pan from the heat in two swift movements.

"It's ruined," I say, not sure if I mean dinner or everything else.

"Forget dinner," Mom says, ripping a paper towel off the roll and handing it to me so I can wipe the tears and snot from my face. "Who's harassing you? Bellingham said they painted graffiti on your locker?"

I tell Mom about the red *A* and how people somehow knew about the abortion. I think of Lily in the cafeteria, looking at me like I wasn't the person she thought I was. Maybe I'm not. "I don't know how they found out," I say to her. "I didn't tell anyone."

"Neither did I." Mom sighs heavily. "Well, obviously people found out and that's where we are. You know, it's nothing to be ashamed of, right, Tess? Anyone who's harassing you—*they're* the ones who should be ashamed."

I think about the alternative—what if I'd decided that I couldn't get an abortion, that I had to grow a baby inside me? People would have very quickly found out that I'd gotten pregnant. It's not like they would have all embraced and supported me then, either. They still would have wanted to know who the father was. It would have been impossible to keep secret. This felt like the only way to get my life back to something resembling normal.

Of course, now life is different anyway. I can't go back to youth group, not after they found out about what I did. I can't see myself singing in the church choir. Everything has changed. It's not exactly shame I feel, but everything feels wrong, and I don't know how to respond to Mom.

She doesn't seem to need a response. Instead, she grips the edge of the counter like it's the ropes around a boxing ring. "I swear, if I find out who's doing this—"

"Mom," I say.

"They're going to be *lucky* if all they get is expelled." She paces around the kitchen like a caged tiger. "Try to graffiti someone's locker when every finger in your hand is broken!"

"Mom, you're not going to break some kid's hand," I tell her. I put the pan back on the burner and turn the heat up.

"Okay, maybe not, but I can still key an asshole's car. It wouldn't be the first time I did that in Hawthorne." I don't doubt it. Mom grew up in Hawthorne and got in a lot more trouble than I ever have. Before now, at least.

She sighs heavily and slumps against the refrigerator. "Look, Tess, if we need to move again, I can make it work. I've got some savings now and I could find a new job and we can figure it out. We don't have to stay here."

For a moment, it seems like a great idea—we can just leave, pack up all those boxes in the garage, and go somewhere else, anywhere else. I can start over, make new friends who don't know anything about me, get a new phone number so no one would ever be able to text me anything about being a baby-murdering whore ever again. But I know how hard it was for Mom to even find a new job that paid her a decent salary, and even that was because Alden introduced her to Dr. Matten, who goes to Grace Presbyterian and was looking for a dental receptionist. Mom's finally sleeping better now that she's starting to pay down all our debt. Maybe we can move out of Hawthorne someday in the next couple of years, but not anytime soon.

"Mom, you're not going to quit your job," I tell her. "It's a few people being jerks. They'll forget about it in a month. I can deal with it in the meantime."

She looks at me hard, like she's waiting for me to burst into tears again, but I hold myself together. Finally, she says, "All right. But the minute you think you can't handle it, we're out."

"Okay," I tell her. Then, quietly, like someone might be listening, I ask, "Are we going to get in trouble?" I say "we," but I really mean her. I'm the one who got the procedure, but she's my mom, she made the appointment, she found the money to pay for it—money we still don't really have. I love her for it, and I don't want anything to happen to her because of it.

Mom pauses before she says, confidently, "No." Then she repeats it, as if she's trying to convince herself. "No. We found somewhere safe and legal. People may not like it, but no. Don't worry about that, please."

I nod, even though it's hard to push those worries away. Then I think of something else. The weekend and today have been hard but manageable because my grandparents are out of town. They're supposed to be back next week. "Mom, what about Gram and Gramps? I mean, if they find out . . ."

I trail off because I can't even bear to think of the fight that'll happen if they know what I did. From what Mom's told me, she fought with them a lot, Gram especially, when she was growing up—about what she wore, the kind of music she listened to, how late she stayed out, the kind of friends she had. She never expected to have to move back home with them, but after Mom lost her job back in Bloomington, all the bills started piling up, and she was already in a lot of debt after Dad's medical expenses and the funeral. Moving in with Gram and Gramps was the only option we had. Mom kept saying it was temporary, that after she paid down some debt and built back her savings, we could get our own place. But aside from Gram and Mom snipping at each other all the time, I didn't mind living with them—it's kind of nice to be around family, especially after we lost Dad, and I get along well with Gram and Gramps. Better than Mom had when she was my age.

But Mom never got pregnant when she was my age. Gram and Gramps definitely wouldn't expect me, someone who sang in the church choir and went to youth group movie nights and didn't break curfew, to get into this kind of trouble.

Mom stiffens, already preparing for a fight. "I'll take care of them," she says, but her voice catches like she's not sure exactly how that'll happen. For now it feels like there's a storm approaching and all we can do is wait.

♩

I'm doing laundry when I realize we're out of detergent. "Oh, damn it," Mom says. "I'm sorry, Tess, I meant to pick up more on my way home. Can it wait until tomorrow?"

I'm down to my last pair of underwear, so I shake my head. "I can go. It'll take ten minutes." When she argues, saying she can go instead, I add, "I don't want to sit at home and keep thinking about things. It's a distraction. I'll be back soon, I promise."

"Call me if you need *anything*," Mom says. Even though I still have my phone off, I tell her I will.

Mom hands me her keys, and I drive ten minutes to the grocery store. It's a clear, cool night, and it's a relief to be out and driving, the streetlights aglow overhead and the radio playing a song with a steady beat and twangy guitar and a voice like a wolf howling alone in the wild. For a moment, I think about going past the Needleman Family Market, taking a right by the barbecue stand and straight down Water Street, until I get to the on-ramp to the highway. I could keep going and never come back. I could disappear and no one would know who I really am and what I've done. I would leave this all behind.

Except Mom is still at home, waiting for me. No matter what happens with Gram and Gramps, I can't leave her here alone.

I turn into the grocery store parking lot.

Inside, the fluorescent lights feel too bright as I find my way to the cleaning products aisle. There aren't too many people shopping this late, but anytime I pass someone, I imagine that they're giving me judgmental looks, whether they actually are or not. I duck into aisle twelve, about to grab a jug of laundry detergent, when I see Bri.

She's wearing a maroon polo shirt and stocking the shelves with dryer sheets. *Shit.* I thought she only worked right after school and on weekends. Remembering how Lily reacted to me in the cafeteria earlier today, I'm tempted to back out of the aisle and pretend that the store is out of detergent.

Over the speakers, Johnny Cash covers "Personal Jesus," and my heart pounds in time with the hard guitar. There's Bri, having a normal night at her part-time job, while my day has sucked beyond belief. I imagine her sitting with Grace Teen Life people during lunch, talking about what a sinner I am and how they should pray for me. Maybe she was even one of the people who sent me those awful texts. The thought of it makes my stomach turn. Cash's deep voice resonates in my chest and my hands clench into fists, and before I can stop myself, I march over to Bri.

She turns to me like she's expecting a shopper with a question about which aisle the peanut butter is in, but once she sees it's me, she pauses. "Oh my gosh, Tess," she says.

"How did you know?" I ask her, trying to keep my voice steady. "How did everyone know?"

Her mouth hangs open for a second, her eyes darting to the mouth of the aisle like she hopes someone will appear and whisk her away. "Um . . . ," she murmurs.

I take a step closer to her. “Bri,” I say as calmly as I can. “Who told you?”

She clutches a box of dryer sheets as if she’s afraid to let it go. For a moment, I don’t think she’s going to say anything. Maybe she’ll tell me she’s praying for me, the way Lily did. But after a second, she admits, “I don’t know. Not exactly. A bunch of us got this anonymous text, a picture of you leaving a clinic. People started talking . . .” She trails off, unwilling to tell me what people have been saying.

She can’t even say the word. Maybe she has the picture on her phone right now. Maybe she even sent it to other people, has been sharing rumors. For all I know, she’s the one who painted the *A* on my locker.

“A picture of me?” I ask her, even though I don’t know if I want to see it.

She pulls out her phone to show me—and there it is, me in my baggy sweatpants and hoodie, Mom at my side with her arm around me as though she can protect me from the gaze of the protesters. One of them must have taken the picture, then sent it to someone who knows me. Probably someone in youth group.

The photo’s a little blurry, but it’s definitely me. It was only a couple of days ago, but it feels so long ago now that I barely recognize that girl. She looks so small and alone. I wish I could reach out through the camera and hold her and tell her that it’s all going to be okay, except I don’t know if it’s going to be okay. I want someone else to tell me that.

Bri slides the phone back into her pocket. “Tess,” she says. “I didn’t think you—I mean . . . what happened?” If I tell Bri what happened—all of it, not just the abortion—maybe she would understand. Maybe if she knew everything that had been going on, the reasons why I couldn’t have a baby, she’d realize that it was something I had to do. Maybe she'd sit in the parking lot with me and tell me that she's sorry about what happened, but she would have done the same, even if she didn't know whether it was the right choice or not. Maybe she would hold my hand and let me cry and tell me it would be okay someday.

But she has that picture on her phone. She didn't delete it or text back whoever sent it to her that they should mind their own damned business. She didn't find me during lunch and tell me that she was still my friend. She wants to be friends with Tess, the quiet girl who went to prayer circles and youth group retreats, not the Tess who has to deal with something overwhelming and real.

I don't tell Bri any of that. Instead, I take a breath and say, "Thank you," and turn on my heel. I barely remember to grab a bottle of detergent before I leave her behind.

♩

The last time I prayed was when I found out I was pregnant. I'd been tired for weeks, nauseated and rushing to the bathroom to gag and spit over the toilet. At the time, I assumed it was food poisoning or dehydration. It wasn't until I was at the movies with Bri and she asked if I had a tampon that I realized I should have had one on me—except I hadn't gotten my period yet.

This can't be happening, I told myself. My period could have been late for any number of reasons; I was never really that regular anyway. In a couple of days, I'd get it and feel foolish for even worrying about it. Everything would be fine.

Except it wasn't.

I got the pregnancy test from a pharmacy outside Hawthorne, where no one would recognize me as the Rileys' granddaughter. I pretended to browse the nail polish and eye shadow until the pharmacy employee moved into another aisle to replace boxes of hair dye, before heading into the feminine care aisle.

The pregnancy tests were lined up right next to the tampons and pads, which felt like a personal attack. There were a bunch of different kinds—one-step, six days sooner, and digital, even though I didn't know exactly why I needed something high-tech when I was going to pee on it. There were even ovulation tests that looked similar, but I didn't think that was what I needed. I grabbed a pink pregnancy test box that wasn't too expensive and brought it to the self-checkout counter as quickly and covertly as possible.

"Find everything?" another employee asked me while I was checking out.

"Yes, thank you!" I almost shouted, trying to block the sight of my purchase, and paid as quickly as possible. When I was done, I shoved the box into my bag and rushed out of the store before anyone else could offer to help me.

On the drive home, I felt like I had a bomb stuffed in my bag instead of a pregnancy test. Every time I stopped at a light, I glanced over at the bag, half expecting it to explode.

When I got home, I snuck by Gram and Gramps, who were doing the crossword puzzle at the kitchen table. "Tess!" Gramps called once he heard my footsteps in the hall. "What's the famous symphony by Beethoven? Is it the Fifth?"

"Sorry, really gotta use the bathroom," I replied, rushing into the bathroom and locking the door behind me.

I read the directions three times to make sure I was doing everything right—I didn't want to get a false result and have to do it all over again—but my hands were shaking, and the words seemed to all blur together. I took deep breaths, telling myself over and over that it was going to be fine. It was a precaution, and I was being paranoid, and all of this was ridiculous, and nothing was going to change.

Please, God, I prayed as I took the test, placed it gently on the floor, and set a timer on my phone. *Don't let anything change for me.*

Outside, someone was mowing their lawn. A motorcycle rode by, revving its engine. A few yards away, a group of kids were playing in a sprinkler, screaming happily as they ran around in the spray. I sat very still on the cool tile floor of my grandparents' bathroom, listening to the outside world and watching a second pink line slowly appear.

No.

No, no, no, no, no.

I picked up the test and blinked at it, feeling my pulse race and my breathing grow ragged. This had to be wrong. There were false positives, right? That happened. It was something in my system, maybe something hormonal, that was making the test show up positive when I wasn't pregnant. We didn't use a condom, but I never questioned it because I thought he knew better about this stuff than I did. Had he had sex before? I'd never even thought to ask.

Suddenly I felt sick again, but this time it was from fear. I gripped the sides of the toilet, spitting into it and wishing I could undo everything. I wasn't ready for this. I couldn't tell anyone about it—how was I supposed to do this alone?

My head was spinning, and I sank back onto the bathroom floor. I couldn't be pregnant. I went to church and prayed and sang in the choir and drove under the speed limit and did volunteer work and never did anything wrong, except now I was staring at these two pink lines that meant something was very wrong.

I didn't feel silly or paranoid anymore. I felt small and alone and like the earth had shifted and there was no way for me to steady myself.

Please don't let this be real, I prayed, picking up the test again and staring at the soft pink lines slowly becoming more visible, more real. *Please, God, don't let this be happening to me.*

After that, I didn't know how to talk to God anymore, or like I even should. It wasn't that I thought there was no one listening—it was more that I didn't even know what I could say, or why I would be worth listening to.

Someone shared the picture instead of talking to me about it. Bri and Lily too. People I thought were my friends. Maybe they were right. What could I even say to them? It's not like I wanted any of this to happen.

But I remember all the things I'd heard at church, about God's love for us even when we're alone and broken. And that's what I feel now.

As I get back in the car, I find myself folding my hands together. *I don't know if you're listening to me right now, but, God, I don't know how I'm going to do this. Please help me get through this.*

If I was expecting to see any divine signal that things are going to be okay, I don't receive it. There are no flashes of light or crashes of thunder or any other signs that God can hear me and cares about me and will help me through. But my breathing slows, and I feel my heartbeat steady, and even the feeling of my hands clasped together grounds me. I don't know if God is listening, but I know that somehow just saying the words helps.

6.

The next morning, Mom tells me I don't have to go to school, at least for the day, but I tell her I'll go anyway. "It's fine," I say, even though it's not. But if I don't go today, I'll never want to go back, and the last thing anyone will ever think of me will be how I looked in front of that bright red *A* on my locker. All I have to do is keep my head down and keep moving. I survived yesterday; I can survive today.

The graffiti is still on my locker. Even though Principal Bellingham assured Mom that he would have maintenance scrub it off, they haven't managed to do anything about it yet. I ignore the whispers around me as I get the books I need before I head to French class, where I try to focus on stilted conversations about how to catch the train to Lyon from Paris.

In chorus that morning, there are a couple of other Grace Teen Life people in the soprano section. Usually, we all huddle together, but today they all stand as far from me as possible, like I'm morally contagious. When I open my sheet music folder, I see a note tucked inside:

At seven weeks, your baby is the size of a pearl, but far more valuable! it reads, with a stock photo of a fetus beneath it.

"Sopranos," Mr. Walsh says, and all the other sopranos join in vocal warm-ups while my voice is lodged in my throat.

One of them probably did this. Someone I thought I was friends with decided to put a note in my music folder instead of asking me if I was having a hard time. And even though I slide the note to the back of the binder and stumble through the vocal exercises with everyone else, I think of what today would have been like if I'd still been pregnant. No one else would necessarily have known. I would have been nauseated, exhausted from the early stages of pregnancy and worry, and wondering if anyone could tell and, if not, how soon would they start to tell, because at some point everyone would know.

Which everyone does now.

If anyone around me is looking for a reaction, I try not to give it to them. I keep my face as placid as possible, blinking back any tears that threaten to appear. I sing "Take Me Home, Country Roads" and "Bright Morning Stars" and focus on my breathing and posture and tone, my voice merging with everyone else's.

♩

I avoid the cafeteria and go back to the music room during lunch. No one else is there yet. I find my music folder and pull the note from the back and stare at it for a moment—*your baby is the size of a pearl.* When I was anxiously googling pregnancy information, I found those kinds of fetus size comparisons, but mostly with food—at four weeks, the baby's the size of a poppy seed; an apple seed at five weeks; at six weeks, a sweet pea. I would have been eleven weeks this weekend.

But I wouldn't have felt as if I was growing something beautiful and precious inside of me—I would have felt afraid and alone and sick and weighed down, like an oyster at the bottom of the ocean.

Maybe if things had been different. If I'd been older. If I'd been more mature, like he made me think I was. If I could have told people about who the father was without worrying that anyone would get hurt. We could have gone through this together, instead of me, standing alone and pretending I could handle being a mother even though I barely knew what it meant to be myself.

I crumple the note and toss it into the recycling as Mia, Connor, and Chloe enter the room. I stiffen automatically, even though they're in the middle of an argument about whether Connor could run the Iditarod.

"I'm saying that I like the cold, and that would give me an advantage," he insists.

Mia heaves a huge sigh, like she's a tiny volcano that's built up enough frustration to erupt. "This isn't *the cold*," she argues. "This is *the Arctic*. You live in Virginia, Connor. We don't even get cold here compared to Alaska. A cold day here is probably like the Fourth of July in Nome."

"I wouldn't go *tomorrow*," he says. "I'd train and get used to it. And I wouldn't necessarily win. But I'd do better than a lot of other people who would run the Iditarod."

Mia marches over to a chair and plunks down her violin case. "We don't even have a dog!"

"I wouldn't run the Iditarod with a family dog!" Connor exclaims. "I would need professional dogs. Dogs who've trained their whole lives for this and have, like, thousands of years of dog history in running long distances in cold temperatures with a pack of dogs."

"Where are you going to find a pack of professional dogs?" Mia wants to know.

Connor slumps into a chair and puts his head in his hands. "Oh my God, Mia, I'm not actually running the Iditarod. It's *theoretical*."

"Well, you're *theoretically* going to die in the frozen Alaskan wilderness, and your final theoretical words will be . . ." Mia looks off into the imaginary Arctic distance. "'. . . *If only I listened to my sister.*'" She reaches one hand out dramatically before pretending to collapse.

Connor sits up to glare at her. "More like '*Still better than sharing a bathroom with five siblings.*'"

Chloe smirks as she tunes her bass. "Out of all of us, Mia is the most likely to survive the Iditarod." When Connor casts her a betrayed look, she explains, "Mia's always the one who gets the forms signed for our practice hour, and she makes arrangements for songs where the original version doesn't work for our group. She would totally be the one to find a dog sled team and train really hard and surprise everyone to win the race."

Mia grins broadly at Chloe before sticking her tongue out at her brother. Ignoring her, Connor frowns as he takes his guitar out of its case. "Mia can't go to the movies without taking a full-on parka, but sure, whatever, she's gonna win the Iditarod."

Chloe catches my eye and smiles, as if I'm in on the joke too. I can't help but smile back, although my lips are pressed together, in case any words escape and somehow I mess everything up again. They're being so nice to me, but I'm afraid to even hope for anything close to friendship at this point.

While I eat, trying to be as inconspicuous as possible, they play a few of the songs they worked on yesterday. I can hear small improvements each time they play—smoothing out transitions, hitting chords a little deeper, finding small variations that make the music feel that much more personal.

I used to love that kind of thing—singing in a group, working with everyone until the combined sound was in perfect unison, finding exactly the right tonality to get to the heart of a song. It feels so long ago now.

Like yesterday, every so often they stop to go over what works and what doesn't. At one point, Mia's trying to argue that Connor needs to pick up the pace in the intro. "You're playing it like it's four-four."

"It *is* four-four," Connor insists.

Mia shakes her head. "I *know* that, but that's not how it should *sound.* There needs to be a real momentum to it and you're dragging along like it's a song zombies would shamble around to."

Chloe cocks her head. "Are zombies capable of hearing? They're dead, right? Or undead. So does their hearing work?"

Connor frowns, his forehead furrowed in serious thought. "Probably not, like, full sound, but they must have some kind of baseline auditory reflexes. They know when people are around."

"Yeah, but maybe they have a heightened smell for brains," Chloe insists.

Mia exhales sharply through her nose. "If zombies burst through that door and eat you both right now, I would so not be upset about it. Can we *please* pay attention to what we're actually working on?"

"Right," Chloe says, standing a little straighter. "And I totally get what you mean. Maybe it's less of a time issue but a vibe? The intro needs to be a little bouncier. You know, like that song . . ." She scrunches her nose as if she'll remember the name of the song by sheer force of will.

"Who's it by?" Connor asks.

"What are the lyrics?" Mia wants to know.

"Guys, if I remembered that, I'd sing it. Oh my gosh, this is why I can't take chemistry before lunch, it seriously melts my brain." She shakes her head, hair bouncing around her head. "I don't remember the singer or the name or the lyrics, but it's like . . ." She hums the beat, a bright but even tune.

It's like a match striking in my head: the memory of my dad playing music with his friends in our living room, me sneaking out to listen in the hall after I was supposed to be in bed. It's both gentle and makes me want to run as though my feet could lift off the ground and fly me away. "Time to Move On," I say before I can stop myself.

They look at me like they'd almost forgotten I was there. But after less than a second, Chloe's face splits into a grin. "Yes!" she cheers. "Thank you!"

Connor raises an eyebrow at her. "I can't believe you forgot Tom Petty," he says, sounding personally offended.

Chloe rolls her eyes at him. "I told you, chemistry is melting my brain. Anyway, like that—propulsive but also soft? Upbeat but not, like, forcing it."

He nods slowly, like he's trying to figure out how to match that to the tune he's playing. "Yeah, like . . ." He plays the intro again, this time a hair faster but with a lightness that moves the song along really well. Even Mia seems pleased, and they play through the whole thing without stopping.

At the end of the period, Chloe is packing up when she says, "I can't believe you knew which song I was talking about. Are you psychic? If you're psychic, send me a telepathic message to let me know."

It takes me a second to realize that she's talking to me, and I laugh. "Oh yeah. I mean, my dad used to play it on guitar, so it just clicked." Even though Chloe doesn't know about my dad, it's strangely nice to be talking about him.

Chloe smiles. "Do you play too?"

She sounds so enthusiastic that I grin, even as I shake my head. "No, not really." A small part of me wants to mention taking out my dad's guitar after hearing them play yesterday, but I hold back, worried that it's too much all at once. Instead, I say, "I sing. I'm in chorus. I used to do choral stuff at my old school—competitions and things."

"Cool," she says, slinging her backpack over her shoulder. "I sing with this group, but I had to choose between chorus and band, and I put way too much time into learning upright bass to not get school credit for it," she says. "Anyway, see you tomorrow?"

"Yeah," I say, and it feels like something to look forward to.

♩

When I get home that afternoon, I see a package on the porch. A basket, really, the kind that might hold a nice arrangement of flowers or a picnic lunch. I freeze, remembering the texts and the red *A* and everything people have been saying. This has to be part of that. I imagine everything that could be inside, from a Bible to hate-filled notes to a plastic baby doll covered in red paint. I'd walk by it if I could, but I don't want to leave it out there for Mom to find when she gets home tonight. I steel myself and walk over to the basket, my stomach tightening as I peek inside.

Except it's not a Bible or notes or a baby doll. Inside, carefully tucked in a pink-and-white-checkered dish towel, are a pack of overnight pads, a can of vegetable soup, a bottle of Tylenol, soft, fuzzy socks, a small hot-water bottle, and a bag of mini peanut butter cups, my favorite.

It's a care package.

I dig around the basket to see if there's a card or note, but there's nothing. For a moment, I stand on the front steps of my grandparents' house, looking around as if I can spot whoever gave me this gift. But the street is quiet, except for a few elementary school kids playing basketball in their driveway and a man walking his dog.

It has to be Alden. Maybe he thought he couldn't talk to me, couldn't reach out directly, but he could leave something for me. Something to help. I hold the basket close to my chest, breathing in and out, feeling my heartbeat settle for the first time in weeks.

♩

Once I unpack everything from the care package, I take out Dad's guitar again. This time, I try to replicate what Connor played this afternoon, as if I were part of their band too. He definitely has more experience and skill than I do—my fingers keep fumbling, and the sound doesn't quite match up with the song in my head.

I set the guitar aside and flop onto the couch. This is ridiculous. I can't teach myself how to play the guitar; no one's asking me to be in their band or play at an open mic night. Where am I even going to sing anymore? There's no way I can go back to Grace Presbyterian's choir and face everyone, especially Alden. The best I should hope for is singing in Hawthorne High's pathetic school chorus.

Except I remember hearing Chloe, Connor, and Mia play and helping them figure out how their song should end. That felt like something—something really good—and maybe there's more goodness ahead somewhere.

Dad used to say *one chord at a time* when he'd try to teach me to play. I didn't have to worry about getting the whole song right, just try one chord. If that was right, try the next one. Eventually, I'd get them all, he'd assure me.

One chord at a time, I tell myself and pick up the guitar again.

It's not perfect by any means, but I stumble through what I remember of the song, and it doesn't sound entirely awful. I try it once more through, and it's sounding a little better when I hear the landline ring.

Gram and Gramps still have one, since they're so used to it. Even though they said we could give people the house number when we moved in, Mom and I still mostly use our cell phones, so I know anyone who's calling is probably trying to reach my grandparents. I let the phone ring, sitting absolutely still on the couch like the caller might sense me.

"Hello, this is Dwight and Patricia Riley," the answering machine says. "We're not able to take your call right now. Leave a message, and we'll get back to you as soon as we can."

The machine beeps, and a woman's voice echoes in the living room. "Hi, Patricia, this is Ellen Jones from the Grace Presbyterian women's Bible study. I wanted to call and let you know that I'm praying for your family and your granddaughter. I'm sure this is such an awful time for y'all, but I know y'all will help her find her way back to Jesus. Take care."

The machine beeps again as the message ends, and even though the house is silent, I'm still frozen in place.

Of course people would know about it. If everyone at school found out, of course their parents and grandparents and neighbors and coaches and Bible study leaders would know too. Of course Gram getting a call like this is all part of a normal prayer phone tree: *Please pray for Tess Pine, she strayed and had sexual intercourse before marriage and got pregnant and had an abortion, may she return to Jesus and ask His forgiveness, keep her family in your prayers.*

Gram and Gramps are going to be home in a few days. If they haven't heard about what's happened already, they definitely will once they get back. There's no way this will be the only call they'll get.

But it doesn't have to be the first one they hear.

I walk stiffly over to the answering machine and play the message again. I feel my pulse thudding in my neck, imagining Ellen from Bible study calling Gram to share sympathy, to hear gossip. I imagine Gram and Gramps on their way back from Pennsylvania, pulling into rest stops to use the bathroom and refill the gas tank, not knowing what they'd be coming home to. Everything has changed and they still have no idea.

When the machine asks me if I want to replay, save, or delete the message, I hit Delete.

7.

By Wednesday, people I've never spoken to before know my name, think they can call out to me in the hall. Guys, mostly. I'm outside of my American Lit classroom, waiting for the class before mine to finish, when I hear someone say, "That was your locker, right?"

It's a guy from the lacrosse team, a senior. Elliot, I think. A cluster of them are standing nearby, looking at me like I'm the punchline to a big joke.

"I guess" is all I can think to say in response, because from his tone, it's obvious that he already knows I'm the one everyone's talking about.

"So is it true?" he asks. Around us, everyone else goes quiet, like they're waiting to hear if I'll actually admit it out loud.

Instead, I stiffen and look straight ahead, willing Mrs. Briggs to finish her class already so I can rush into the room and hide from all the eyes on me.

Unfortunately, Elliot doesn't take the hint. He laughs, whacking his friend on the arm. "That means it's true. She'd totally be denying it and all offended if it wasn't true."

I can't even argue with him. It is true. What they're saying. Even if they don't know the whole story. My face burns with shame and frustration and tears prick the corners of my eyes. I never wanted this to happen, for people like Elliot to think they know anything about me.

Elliot's friend smirks at me. "It's always the nice church girls, man. They act all innocent, but they're into some weird shit. All that pent-up sexual frustration."

"Hey, Tess, don't worry, there's still a lot we can do that won't get you pregnant. I got a free period after this if you're interested."

People laugh and my stomach clenches, like I've been punched. The way they're talking about me, they make it sound sordid and shameful. It wasn't like that. *It wasn't.* But now they're all looking at me like I'm not a person, just a jumble of urges and body parts and shame, and all I want to do is disappear.

Breathe, I tell myself. I try to push the laughter and stares from my mind and repeat the lyrics of one of the worship songs we used to do on Sunday mornings. *I am not alone, I am not alone.* I don't even know if it's true anymore, but I make it into class without crying.

♩

That afternoon in the music room, the others are already there when I arrive. Chloe is tuning her bass, while Mia and Connor argue about whether pineapple is an appropriate pizza topping.

"It's sweet and salty," Mia says. "It's a classic combination."

"You want sweet and salty, have a chocolate-covered pretzel," her brother says.

Chloe's head pops up from her focused tuning. "That's the perfect snack!"

Connor points a finger at Chloe. "Accurate," he says. "Doesn't mean that I want my pizza to have chocolate on it, either."

"We're not talking about chocolate," Mia argues, holding her violin by her side like it's a weapon she's considering using. "We're talking about pineapple. It's not a candy. It's produce, the same as many other pizza toppings."

"No way," Connor asserts, taking his guitar out of its case. "It's a fruit. Fruit is not an acceptable pizza topping, unless it's some kind of dessert pizza, and that's basically a cookie cake under an assumed name."

Mia lowers her gaze at him. "Excuse me, the *tomato* is a fruit. If you're going to argue about fruits not being an acceptable pizza topping, you question the entire premise of the pizza itself."

Connor throws his hands in the air in frustration. "Tomatoes aren't *fruit* fruit and you know it!"

"If I had time to explain to you the botanical classification of fruits, I would, but I don't, so," Mia says, raising her violin to her shoulder. "Let's get to work. We need it."

Chloe smiles at me like she has a great secret to share. "We're working on a new song. Like our own, original, new song. Want to hear?"

I swallow a lump of anxiety in my throat. They're being kind. There's no reason to think that they're going to turn on me like my Grace Teen Life friends. If they wanted to judge me, yell at me, call me names, they would have done so already—right? Besides, all I'm doing is listening to a song. It's not like we're friends yet, or that I expect anything from them. I don't have to get hurt all over again, even if that's what they're trying to do.

But the way Chloe's looking at me, all hopeful and excited behind her wire-rimmed glasses, it's hard not to smile back. "Yeah," I finally say, setting my bag down and taking a seat close to them. "I'd love to."

"It's really new," Mia adds. "Ignore all of Connor's mistakes." Connor throws a guitar pick at Mia, who narrowly manages to dodge it.

"That's okay," I tell her. "I'm sure it's great."

And it is—what they play is upbeat and energetic, a bright song that makes me automatically sway in my chair. It's rough, but somehow that makes it feel more joyful. The piece is entirely instrumental, with Chloe's bass providing a gentle, steady rhythm, while Connor's guitar and Mia's violin find bright, playful melodies that complement each other. It makes me think of summertime and sunshine after a storm and driving with the windows down and a car filled with friends and laughter and song.

The song ends a little abruptly, but I still burst into applause. "That was so good! I love the bridge in the middle, and when the key changes a little toward the end, like . . ." I hum what I can remember of the song. "It's like fresh air and summer. And it's really fun. I know you said it was rough, but it has this playful energy that really works."

They look at each other, beaming. "Thanks," Chloe says. "That's totally the vibe we're going for. Like Brandi Carlile meets Dolly Parton meets Yo-Yo Ma, with the first day of summer thrown in."

"Definitely." I pause, looking at the three of them. "So—you wrote this?"

Chloe grins. "We did! Mostly we play covers, but we're trying to write some original stuff."

"Only playing covers at open mic nights is for amateurs," Mia adds, twirling her violin bow between her fingers.

Connor gives Mia a look. "Hey, we have to start somewhere," he argues.

"Which is why we're starting to write our own music," Chloe says smoothly. "It's definitely not perfect, but we're excited about it. And you're the first person outside of Connor and Mia's family to hear it!"

"And they've only heard it because we rehearse in our basement," Connor adds.

I smile, feeling strangely honored. Playing or singing in front of someone else, especially an original song, knowing they're listening and judging—there's a real vulnerability to it. Maybe they think it doesn't matter, since they barely know me and I'm in no place to judge anyone for anything right now. But the way they're looking at me, full of anticipation and enthusiasm, it feels like they actually care about whether or not I liked their song. I remember singing at church, arranging a song with Alden for the Spirit Light Festival, and how right that felt and how I miss it more than I expected to. This feels different, but it makes me dizzy with a strange kind of grief.

"Thanks for sharing it with me," I tell them quietly.

"Okay, so the ending," Mia says as though she hasn't heard me. "It's not good."

"It's not *bad*," Chloe says.

"But it's not *good*," Mia argues. "Not yet. Right?" She stares at me, hard, like she expects me to agree with her and is already a little annoyed with me about it.

"Um," I say, because I get what she means—the ending is fine, but it just stops instead of building to a particular finish. I replay the melody in my head, my fingers tapping gently in time against the side of the chair. A small part of me hesitates—even though they asked, and my brain is already tumbling through the tune, trying to find the right sound—I don't know if I can do this again. When I was working on the song for the Spirit Light Festival with Alden, it felt like I was where I was supposed to be and doing what I truly wanted to be doing. But everything changed and turned out so wrong—maybe that was my first mistake.

Except I keep hearing the melody in my head, over and over until I can hear possibilities, ways they can change it slightly and grow from there.

"I think it needs more of a build at the end, maybe some kind of variation," I tell them, quietly so that they lean forward a little. "What if you tied it back to the bridge, like . . ." I look around the room until my eyes settle on the piano, and before I know what I'm doing, I sit at the keys. My hands hover over middle C position. I don't know much piano, but I have enough of a sense that I can pick out the tune I'm thinking of while I accompany it with some basic vocalization. It's clumsy, but it's a riff on the melody they already have—something bright and lilting, like a bird floating on a breeze and coming to rest on a tree branch. When I'm finished, I look back up at them. "Like that?"

For a moment, they're silent, and I want to shrink in between the piano keys. I shouldn't have jumped in—they didn't ask for any advice about how to write a song, especially from someone who isn't in their band and hides out in the music room during lunch because none of her friends want to sit with her.

But instead of telling me to find a new place to hide out during lunch, Chloe nods enthusiastically. "Yeah—like that."

"Okay, what about . . ." Mia places her violin at her neck and bows the tune I played, with a different flourish at the end. Connor frowns and plays the same tune, but Mia shakes her head. "No, F-sharp minor."

"C-sharp minor," he argues, playing it again.

"That's too harsh," Mia insists.

They play it both ways, Chloe's bass providing a soothing background. Finally, Connor frowns and says, "Fine, F-sharp minor." Mia smirks but doesn't say anything else as they play it through again.

"I like that," Mia says. "I like that a lot." She looks at me like she's seeing me for the first time. "You're not in band?"

I shake my head, taking my hands away from the keys like I got caught doing something wrong. "No, I'm in chorus. I can read music and know enough piano to stumble my way through easy songs, but I don't really play anything." I don't mention my dad's guitar, or how Grace Presbyterian choir rehearsal is tonight and even though I know I shouldn't go, part of me still wants to be there as if nothing's happened because it's been like home for the last year. Even when Mom and Gram were at each other and I was caught in the middle, I could go to choir rehearsal and know that my voice would match with those around me, that we'd all be coming together to experience God with the same song. Maybe Alden could convince the others that I deserve to be there. But for now, getting to share a moment of music with Chloe, Mia, and Connor—it's not the same as choir, but it feels more comforting and familiar than I would have expected.

"You've got a good ear," Mia tells me solemnly. "And a good voice."

"She's right," Connor adds. "And Mia wouldn't tell anybody that. She doesn't even think two of our sisters are that musical."

"They're *not*," Mia snaps, like she's the one who should be offended. "Diana's pitchy and Quinn says she can play by ear but she's making it up half the time and it's annoying. But God forbid Mom and Dad tell them that when we're all trying to do 'Take Me Home, Country Roads.' "

"Because it's supposed to be *fun*, not a night at the symphony."

Connor and Mia continue to argue about whether their siblings should be held to a higher musical standard at home, while Chloe rolls her eyes at me, like we're sharing a joke. "There's an open mic night every other Thursday, in Wolfwood. It's a café, Pammy's, and they have food and a bar, but it's run by this woman who used to sing backup for a ton of country people. She got tired of life on the road and settled down and opened her own place. A bunch of really good people go, not just people who learned two chords and think they're Taylor Swift. And every so often famous people drop by to play—not a lot, but I know at least two people who have seen Alison Krauss there. Anyway, we signed up for open mic tomorrow night. You should come!"

The idea of going out to hear good music and cheer on people who might end up being my friends sounds like the best thing I could imagine right now. "That sounds amazing. I mean, I'll have to see if I can borrow my mom's car or get a ride, but otherwise yeah, I'll be there."

They go through the song a few more times, making minor adjustments to the new ending, and each time it sounds better.

I'm packing up my stuff when I notice the music binders from chorus stacked in a corner. I remember standing here earlier this week, singing beside people I thought were my friends. Whoever's doing this—they won't even come out and tell me to my face what they think of me. A few days ago, these were people who I laughed with and sang with and prayed with and trusted, and now my locker's graffitied in bright red paint for everyone to see.

What if this ends up the same way?

"Hey, Chloe," I say as she's following Connor and Mia out of the music room. When she turns, I swallow a lump of fear in my throat. "Can I ask you something?"

She tilts her head curiously and adjusts the weight of her backpack on her shoulder. "Is it about the open mic night? If you need a ride, I could see if Connor's sister has room in her car. She's coming, too, but she promised not to be too judgy about it—"

"It's not that," I say, shaking my head. I take a breath. "Why are you being nice to me?"

Chloe pauses and looks at me suspiciously, like it's a trick question. "Do you want us to be mean to you?"

"No, it's . . ." I exhale sharply through my nose because I don't want to say it. I drop my voice low, like someone could overhear me. "Everything people are saying about me. It's . . . it's not untrue. And I don't even know you and you invite me to hear your band play, and it's . . ." Tears sting my eyes because I both want to believe that Chloe and her band will let me hang out with them and listen to them play and know that this could very likely be Grace Teen Life all over again. "It's been a hard week, and if you're doing this to mess with me, well, I'd rather know now."

Chloe doesn't say anything for a moment, but keeps looking at me, her eyes sad and gentle. "You know how Connor and I got to be friends in middle school band?" she finally says.

My eyebrows knit together in confusion. "Yeah, I think you mentioned that."

"He was literally my only friend," she tells me. "Like, *no one* would sit with me at lunch. I don't even know what the deal was—one day people decided I was the person to make fun of and that was it for three years. It was like, I laughed too loud and wore dorky clothes and sometimes answered questions in class, and basically existed." She pulls her hands back inside the cuffs of her sweatshirt, like she can disappear from the memories entirely. "Anyway, in seventh grade, Connor and I were seated next to each other in band and would joke around a little and it was the best part of my day. Things have been better since we got to Hawthorne High, since it's like four middle schools in one and it's easier to blend in and there are a bunch more band geeks here. But it definitely sucked then." She smiles sadly at me, like it still hurts to think about. "I wouldn't mess with you, I promise."

She doesn't wait for me to respond, instead turning and heading for the door as the bell rings. After a moment, I follow, playing the band's song over and over in my head.

♩

I avoid going to my locker as much as possible, only stopping by at the beginning and end of the day to get whatever I need. When I open it after the last bell, a handful of wrapped condoms falls at my feet.

Of course. Like I need reminding.

Nearby, a few people laugh. "Hilarious," I mutter as I bend down to pick them up, clutching as many as possible in my fist.

It's not particularly surprising, someone stuffing condoms in my locker, but I'm surprised at how exhausted I feel. The comments, the stares, the texts, the bright red *A* painted on my locker—I feel as if I'm carrying the weight of them with me all the time now, and there's no one who can help me bear the load.

Except . . . maybe . . .

I toss the condoms into the nearest trash bin, leaving the building as quickly as possible, as if I could disappear entirely.

♩

Wednesday night is choir rehearsal at Grace Presbyterian. It's been the night I look forward to the most in Hawthorne, even more than Sundays, when we performed at services. Rehearsal has always felt like we were building something together, Alden and the choir and God too.

Driving to church feels so familiar, a small part of me wonders if the last week was real at all. Maybe it was some awful dream, and now I can join the choir again and sing with a light heart and feel safe and loved. I want that to be real so badly, I feel an ache in my chest, down my arms and legs. Maybe things weren't perfect before, but they were what I had. I wish I could close my eyes and have everything be back to normal again.

I thought everything was going to be back to normal again.

That was how I felt after my dad died. It had been so sudden, at first I didn't think it was real. And then, whenever I'd hear a song he liked, part of me thought that maybe I'd been wrong, he was still alive and I could run downstairs and share my headphones so he could hear the song too. Except he was never there, and I had to learn how to stop myself from hoping that he was.

Now I pull into the church parking lot, and I have to remind myself that everything is different. I can never go back into that church again, not in the same easy and comforting way.

Grace Presbyterian is Gram and Gramps's church. They've been going there since they were kids in Hawthorne. It was where they got married, where they baptized Mom, and where I would have been baptized if Mom and Dad had decided to raise me that way. Even though I'd only been to church a handful of times in my life before Hawthorne, I liked it right away—the sermons about faith in hard seasons, the smiles we received from other families, the surprisingly bright and energetic music. When Gram introduced me to Alden after the service my first time there, he invited me to check out the choir and youth group. It wasn't the kind of thing I'd ever done back in Bloomington, but it felt like something I could be a part of here. Like maybe Grace Presbyterian could be my church too.

Grace Presbyterian is an old brick building with a high steeple and a large sign out front that details service times and Reverend Wilson's name and full title. The church itself doesn't look like much from the outside, but inside is bright, with white walls, dark wood, and a high ceiling, making it feel bigger than it looks somehow.

I don't go in right away.

In the parking lot, I recognize most of the other cars—several people from choir, plus Alden's and Reverend Wilson's. Automatically, I park around the far side of the building, as if my car out in the open is a target.

I imagine the choir inside, Alden leading them through vocal warm-ups and the pieces they'll be singing for this week's service. "How Great Is Our God," maybe, or "Arise, My Soul, Arise." Roger's probably toward the back, with the other tenors, face solemn as he goes through the vocal exercises. Lorna was getting over a cold last week; I hope she's feeling better now, her rich alto voice grounding everyone else's. And Alden will be at the front, hands flowing gracefully over the piano keys as he accompanies the group, carefully listening for any distortions in sound and calling out directions or encouragement. When I first joined the church choir, he told me that I had a strong voice and a real maturity as a singer. It felt like the first time someone really saw me, the kind of artist and person I could be.

That's why Alden is so good at leading the choir and being the youth minister—he always knows what to say to help someone feel better, understand what they need, encourage them to be open and vulnerable and joyful with music and with God and with other people.

That's what I need now. I need Alden to tell me what to do, to tell me how to get through all of this and that I'm not alone.

That's what makes me get out of my car and walk into the church, even though I'm afraid that I don't belong there anymore. I half expect sirens to go off when I touch the door, or lightning to strike me from a cloudless sky, but nothing happens. I creep into the church foyer, as if someone will hear even the most cautious footsteps, even though the choir is loud and focused enough on their rehearsal to drown out any sounds from the lobby.

I peek into the nave, where the choir is wrapping up a song. They sound good—Lorna is back in full force, and Edwin's clear tenor is notable even from the very back of the church. Charlotte laugh-snorts when Alden makes a joke about how they could incorporate a techno remix into this week's worship.

At the front of the group, Alden is smiling and at ease. He moves from his spot at the piano to stand in front of the group, giving them specific direction about how the bridge should sound. Most of the choir are people my age, from Grace Teen Life, but a handful of adults are mixed in as well. Alden's only in his mid-twenties and has a youthful energy that makes him look more like one of the teens. He's wearing a blue-and-white-checkered button-down shirt, sleeves rolled up to reveal his forearms. Even though I can't see it from here, I've seen him in that shirt before, and I know it brings out the bright blue of his eyes. I want him to look at me, to really see me and tell me that he knows this is hard, that I won't always feel this way, that he understands why I made the decision I did.

I can't do that in front of everyone. There's no way they'll look at me like that, like I know Alden will.

I'm not going to talk to him in front of everyone else. I'll wait out here until rehearsal is done and catch him before he leaves for the night. I know that he'll stay behind, putting the music away and maybe even playing through a song or two afterward. It'll be the perfect chance to really talk to him, to feel like someone will hear me.

For the next thirty minutes, I stay in the lobby, listening to the choir rehearse and breathing in time with them. When I hear the group begin to disperse, I make sure to stay out of sight, standing as still as possible beside a rack of pamphlets with information about ministry trips, praying as a family, and finding strength in Jesus during hard times. People trickle out of the nave, chatting in small groups, and pass through the lobby without noticing me.

I stay there for a moment, waiting to make sure that everyone else is gone. My heart thuds against my chest and I'm sure that Alden will be able to hear it too.

You can do this, I tell myself, even if I don't believe it. *Just talk to him.*

I take a step forward, then another and another until I'm almost at the door to the nave.

Then I hear a phone ringing, followed by Alden's voice a second later. "Oh hey, what's up?" His voice is light and casual—it could be a friend of his from college, or maybe even Olivia, who runs the church's activities for kids in elementary school. I pause, listening to his half of the conversation: ". . . uh-huh. Oh yeah, I know . . . A little tired, but . . . yeah . . ." He laughs so fully that I imagine the smile illuminating his face.

His voice gets a little louder, until the door to the nave opens and Alden steps into the lobby, backpack slung over his shoulder and phone held to his ear.

Stop him, I tell myself. *Say something.*

Except I freeze. *Alden, please, I need to talk*, I want to say, but nothing comes out.

He doesn't even look around to see if anyone is there, waiting to talk to him. He's busy, he's distracted, this isn't the right time. He's smiling and laughing and talking and he has no idea I could even be here.

Then, in a matter of seconds, he strides casually through the lobby to the outer doors and disappears into the night. I'm left in the dark quiet of the church lobby, feeling frozen and trapped and alone.

8.

I tell myself that I'll find a way to talk to Alden later. Of course he was busy. He has a lot of responsibility at the church, a lot of people who depend on him. It'll happen. I just need to wait.

Fortunately, I have the open mic night at Pammy's to distract me. On Thursday over breakfast, I bring it up with my mom. "It's in Wolfwood," I tell her as I pop two slices of bread into the toaster. "A café called Pammy's. Apparently it's run by a woman who used to sing professionally, so they have open mic night every week. They have food and drinks, and there's a bar, but I definitely won't be drinking, and the other people I'd be with won't be either. They're band geeks, so they're not into anything wild."

"Like youth group?" Mom asks, eyeing me from over her coffee mug.

I'm surprised at how much that stings. I can't even argue with her and turn to the fridge to get the jam so she can't see how my cheeks are burning with embarrassment and shame.

She sets down her mug louder than I expected. "That was unfair. I'm sorry," she says. "But, Tess, come on, you go to youth group stuff all the time with all the 'good kids' and end up pregnant, and I know stuff happens, but when you don't even tell me who the guy is . . ."

She trails off like she's leaving space for me to tell her about what happened, even though she's asked before and I've always refused to give her any details. I know she thinks there's more to the story, but it's not something I can tell her—because if I do, I know she'll make more trouble out of it and think she's helping. *If whoever did this, if he hurt you, you can tell me, and I'll do whatever I can to make sure there are consequences.* I know she meant that in a way to make me feel safer, but it just made me want to close up even more.

"I told you," I say now. "It doesn't matter."

"Well, you can't be surprised that I'm a little nervous about you going off with—who even are these people?" She stands up from the kitchen table, leaving her coffee behind.

"Band geeks," I repeat, and the toast pops up so suddenly that I jump a little. "They practice in the music room during lunch, and unlike my youth group friends, they don't make me feel bad about myself right now." I pull out the two slices of toast and scrape jam across them. "I know you weren't exactly thrilled that I was spending all my time with church people, and now I'm not, so the least you could do is let me go to this open mic night."

"Hey," she says, her voice a little low, somehow both gentle and firm.

I raise an eyebrow at her and give her a look, daring her to argue with me.

She sighs heavily and leans against the counter. "Okay, I never exactly got why you liked going to prayer circles, but I wanted you to be happy, even if it was with a bunch of kids who organized mission trips. I *hate* that they're doing this to you." She looks at me like she wishes she could shrink me down and put me in a bottle so she could carry me with her and protect me. "I just want you to be careful with these new kids."

"They're okay," I tell her, and it feels true. Even if they're not exactly taking the place of my old group of friends, even if it's only one night out, it feels like something good. Safe, even. I had never been a youth group kind of person before moving here, but I'd always been a music person. If anything, this feels more normal. I'm not ready to trust them with big stuff, but at least I can have lunch with them and listen to their music and go to an open mic night.

"I know I haven't given you any reason to trust me over the last couple of weeks," I continue, "but the last couple of weeks have also sucked immensely, and this would actually be fun and feel kind of normal." I set my jam knife aside. "Please, Mom. I need this."

She blinks at me for a second, like she's trying to work out if she can find a reason to make me stay home. Finally, she breathes, "Fine. You can go. But you have to text me when you get there and when you're leaving, and you have to be home by ten o'clock."

"I promise. Ten o'clock." I throw my arms around her in an enthusiastic hug that almost makes me feel normal again. "Thank you. Seriously."

She kisses the top of my head. "I want you to have good things again. I really do."

I don't let go of her, instead inhaling her coconut shampoo. "Me too."

♩

The rest of the day, all I think about is going out to Pammy's that night. I get my books from my locker, which is still painted over with a crimson *A*, and I imagine the clusters of tables, musicians and friends and loved ones huddling together as they wait for their names to be called. In chorus, I think about the songs that the performers will sing or play—maybe someone will do "Ingrid Bergman," or Roy Orbison's "You Got It," which was one of Dad's favorites. While I play soccer (badly) in gym class, I think about how maybe someone else is going to Pammy's tonight for the first time, and how maybe they'll play a song that no one else has ever heard. A song that they've been writing in secret for weeks, quietly in their room, tweaking a lyric or chord until it's lilting and gentle and true. Maybe they'll take the stage with their heart beating wildly, and clear their throat and be a little rough at first, but they'll disappear into the song without realizing it, and we'll all disappear into it too. Maybe it'll be my favorite song in the whole world, and I don't even know it yet.

I'm so distracted by the idea of being at Pammy's tonight that I don't notice I almost run into Roger in the hall.

"Oh, sorry," I say automatically.

I don't expect him to apologize back, or to say anything to me except maybe a chilly *Excuse me*, but instead he takes a step toward me. "Tess," he sighs, like he's disappointed with me. "I've been praying for you."

A smile I didn't realize I had vanishes from my face, and I stiffen, thinking about how he looked at me so coldly on Monday in the cafeteria. How he probably has that picture saved on his phone right now, like Bri.

"I bet," I tell him, voice cold. "You and the rest of youth group." I'm so angry, I'm practically buzzing and have to clutch the strap of my backpack to stop myself from flying apart. "Who took that picture? Who shared it first?"

Roger clears his throat, like he's a little taken aback by my directness. "It was anonymous—everyone got a text with the picture and that's it. But I'm sure whoever did it was trying to do the right thing."

I think about what we'd talked about in youth group: following the "right" path, making "good" choices to live a godly life. It seemed like an easy thing to do at the time.

"There's nothing right about this," I say, willing my voice not to crack. I step away from him and turn to march down the hall.

But Roger meets my stride, staying as close to me as possible. Around us, people pass without noticing, or assume we're having a perfectly normal conversation. "I can understand why you're upset," he says calmly. "Were you going to tell anyone about it otherwise?"

I wasn't. I'd hoped that I could pretend it never happened. The way Roger says it, composed and knowing and helpful, I feel suddenly guilty. My cheeks burn with shame, and I pray he doesn't notice.

Roger's so good at this—turning my own words back on me so I have to agree with him. Last year, he asked me to go with him to the Snow Ball, the Hawthorne High winter dance. I'd planned to go with a group from Grace Teen Life and told him as much, trying to let him down gently. He'd asked why, if we were both already planning on going with the group, we couldn't go together too? At the time, I couldn't think of a good answer—because I didn't want to, because I wanted to go as a group instead, because I was currently seeing someone who I couldn't take to a high school winter semiformal. I felt caught and couldn't think of an excuse, and I didn't want to hurt Roger's feelings, even though it didn't feel like he was thinking a lot about my feelings in that situation. We went together, along with the rest of the group, and I had a perfectly fine time, even fun, but I felt that I'd been maneuvered somehow. That's how I feel now, even though Roger is looking at me with such a caring expression.

Roger almost sighs as he tells me, "I want to help you, Tess, I really do. I know this isn't the kind of person you are. I want to help you get back on the right path. To get back to Jesus, Tess. I know you're a good person, deep down. I've seen this happen before." He winces, adding, "Well, not *this*, exactly, but similar—Lily's sister, Alyssa, used to come to youth group all the time, and then she started spending all her time with her boyfriend. And Alyssa's best friend, Reagan, dropped out in her senior year. I don't want that to happen to you, Tess. You can find your way back to God."

For a second, it feels like maybe he could actually help me. Even if people are mad at me, it doesn't mean I can't try to make up for what happened. To pray about it, cry about it, try to get back to the girl I thought I was. Then Roger puts his hand on my arm and says, "I can help you if you tell me who the father is."

I pull away from him so hard, he holds up his hands like he expects me to swing my arm back and hit him in the jaw. Instead, I stop in my tracks and face him, my expression hard. "Leave it alone, Roger."

"Why should you have to bear this guilt alone?" he asks. "There's someone out there, and they're responsible for this too. Who is it, Tess—someone else in youth group? If they're trying to hide this, they're lying, Tess, to themselves and to everyone else and to God. Do you think I want that for you? For whoever the father is? I'm trying to *help* you."

The second bell rings, and students head into their next classes. Soon the crowd around us dissipates, but Roger and I don't move. "Roger," I say as calmly as I can. "You can help me by leaving this alone. Trust me."

He sighs, gazing down at his shoes like he can't quite look at me for a moment. Then he raises his head again and says, "How am I supposed to trust you now, Tess? Because between the two of us, you're the one with graffiti all over your locker." He shrugs and starts to walk away. "I'll keep you in my prayers."

I watch Roger disappear around the corner, and I don't move until the hall is empty and I'm late for calc. Someone may have seen me coming out of the clinic, but no one else knows what happened before then. I haven't said anything. I swore I wouldn't. There's no way Roger can find out, as long as I don't say anything. I just need to keep my mouth shut and keep moving forward.

♩

Pammy's is about a thirty-minute drive away, across town and into Wolfwood, past strip malls and homes and finally down a dirt road that makes me initially wonder if I'm going the wrong way. But the patio strung with Christmas lights and the big red sign with PAMMY'S written in swirling white letters let me know that I'm in the right place. From the parking lot, I can hear music streaming through the open door and windows—steel guitar and harmonica and a thick-voiced woman. I feel the hair on my arms stand up and my heart thump against my chest as I get out of the car and follow the music inside.

The space is already crowded with people, sitting together at tables and standing by the bar. Waitstaff dart from table to table, delivering cool drinks and plates of food with ease. At the back of the room, there's a small stage with real stage lights illuminating it, and a microphone in the middle. The group onstage now is three women older than my mom; one of them, who has long silver hair and looks like she could be Gram's age, is on the guitar. The song they're playing reminds me of a harder-edged bluegrass, as though they're all family and have been playing each other's sorrows and furies and joys for generations. I love singing, but I've never performed like that before, so free and unguarded and rough. Any performing I've done has been in choral groups or at church. Even at the Spirit Light Festival, which felt so expansive and open, it was still technically with the church choir. I imagine how it would be, to sing with a group like this, encouraging each other to dig a little deeper into a song, to try something that might not work, to be loud and raw. I stay in the back of the room while the women finish their set, swaying gently to the tune.

"Thank you, have a great night, y'all," the lead singer says into the microphone once they're finished, and they leave the stage to enthusiastic applause.

I'm scanning the audience when I hear Chloe call, "Tess! Tess, over here!" Chloe, Connor, and Mia are toward the front, huddled around a small table along with Chloe's standing bass and a girl I don't recognize. For a second, I pause, wondering who the girl is and if I should pretend I have to leave. Then I remember that Connor and Mia were going to get a ride from one of their sisters and my nerves calm. I weave my way toward them as Connor pulls up an extra chair.

"You came!" Chloe says cheerfully. "Does that mean you're a fan? Tess, you could be our very first fan!"

"I'm definitely a fan," I tell her, laughing. "When you're super famous and winning Grammys, I can say I knew y'all when."

Across the table, the girl I don't recognize holds out a hand. "Quinn Burke," she says.

"Our sister," Mia adds. Even if she hadn't told me, it would have been easy to guess—she's got the same red hair as Connor, although hers is neatly pulled into a ponytail, and the same downturned mouth as Mia.

"Tess," I say and shake her hand.

For a second she studies me closely and then something flashes behind her eyes. "Tess," she repeats, like she's remembering something, and the way she glances at her siblings, I can tell that she's heard at least some of the rumors about me. But if she has, she tries not to show it beyond that moment. "Nice to meet you, Tess," she says politely, if a little stiffly, and settles back into her seat.

I wonder how long this will last—people seeing me or meeting me and thinking, *Oh, that's the girl who had an abortion.* Not Tess who sings in the choir, or Tess who broke her arm jumping off swings in second grade, or Tess who snorts a little when she laughs too hard, or even Tess whose dad died when she was in sixth grade. I never expected the pregnancy and the procedure and everyone finding out to be a part of my life, and now it feels like it's been tattooed across my heart. I shift a little in my chair, hoping that they can't see how my cheeks are burning under the dim café lights.

"We're on around eight forty-five," Chloe tells me, which means there are at least a few other sets before them. "It's a good spot. You have to sign up online to get a slot because it fills up really fast. Mia, of course, was *on it* as soon as the form went up for tonight."

Mia beams. "I wanted eight thirty, but someone beat me to it," she admits, glancing around the room as though she can identify the offending party by sight alone.

Connor pats her on the back. "Don't worry, Mia. We'll find them after the show and egg their car," he tells her with a smirk.

Mia doesn't seem to notice the sarcasm in her brother's voice. "If their set is really good, we don't *have* to egg their car," she says, still scanning the crowd. "Maybe just glare at them on the way out."

The next set is a couple of guys in their twenties, both with shaggy hair and one with an ill-conceived mustache, but their songs are lively. After them is a tall woman with a guitar whose voice is gentle and who plays with ease. The group after that plays solely covers, which Mia thinks is great. "We'll look way more professional by comparison," she says, even though she looks like she's seriously considering egging their car. The audience applauds the group anyway, and the emcee calls up the Dog and Pony Show.

"That's us," Chloe says brightly.

"Break a leg!" I cheer, feeling my heart pounding with nervousness for them.

They take the stage, Connor helping Chloe lug her bass up. Once they're in place, Connor steps up to the mic. "Hey, y'all, we're the Dog and Pony Show. The first song we're going to be playing for you tonight is one of our original songs . . ."

Quinn lets out a big whoop of excitement, and the audience chuckles.

"Thank you, complete stranger I've never seen before," Connor adds, before counting off the song. "Two, three, four . . ."

The group plays the song I heard in the music room. It's still got the same playful, open quality, but they've obviously rehearsed since then, so it sounds more cohesive. There are a couple of moments where they seem to miss a note or hit the wrong one, but overall they're confident and bright and vibing with each other, just like at school. The ending is the slightly revised one that I heard them work on, and I'm weirdly proud that this is the version they're performing. Once they finish, I practically jump out of my seat to applaud.

"Thank you," Connor mumbles into the microphone, looking a little baffled. When he glances back at Mia and Chloe, they grin at him, like they've all survived something together. Then Mia gives him a nod, and he counts off their next song, the cover of "Ingrid Bergman" they'd been working on. The last song they play is another cover, "Keep Your Heart Young" by Brandi Carlile. Chloe takes the vocals on this one, and I'm seriously impressed by how strong her alto is. She doesn't have a huge range, but she has good breath control and a lot of heart. When they finish, the room applauds with genuine appreciation and Chloe is laughing with delight as they leave the stage.

They return to our table, where Quinn attacks Connor and Mia with a hug. "Oh my lord, y'all!" she cries. "That was so good!"

"Of course we were good!" Mia says, trying to break free from her sister's enthusiastic grip. "If we were bad, I wouldn't have signed us up!"

"I'm not even bound by blood to tell you y'all were good," I insist. "And you were *so* good!"

Even Mia looks satisfied as they all take their seats. The next performer is up, an older man with a guitar and a porkpie hat. He begins playing a slow, mournful song, and Chloe reaches for her bass's travel case. "Now that I don't have to worry about burping onstage, I'm going to get a Coke. Anybody else want one?"

I stand quickly. "I'll go," I say. "It's my treat—y'all invited me here, so it's the least I can do." They glance at each other, looking pleased, and give me their drink orders. Mia asks for cheese fries, too, which frankly sound perfect right now.

I make my way to the other side of the room, where a woman a little older than my mom is tending bar. She's got thick dark hair with visible gray streaks, and her black tank top shows off her sinewy arms. When she sees me, she nods slightly, prompting my order. "Two Cokes, two sweet teas, and a club soda with lime," I say. "Oh, and can we order cheese fries?"

She turns to the waitress at the far end of the bar. "Cheese fries for table eight," she calls. Then she looks back at me. "You're with the band who just performed—the Dog and Pony Show?" When I tell her we go to the same school, she says, "Tell your friends they're good. And I don't say that to everyone."

"Thanks," I say, even though I don't have anything to really thank her for. I wasn't the one performing, but I feel a small, warm pride for these people who might be my friends. "I really liked their set too. I've been sitting in on some of their rehearsals. They work really hard."

The bartender fills two glasses of Coke and starts to pour the sweet tea. "You play too?" she asks.

"Oh, um," I mumble, a little caught off guard by the question. My automatic response is *yes* because I'm thinking of choir and the Spirit Light Festival, how I've been singing since I can remember, and trying to learn the guitar to get my mind off things. But the real answer is *no*, since I don't know if I'll be singing anywhere outside of the school chorus for the foreseeable future. "Sort of," I finally say. "I mean, I sing."

"Me too," she says cheerfully, like we're part of a secret society, and plops a lime in a glass of club soda. "You should sign up. Open mic every other Thursday night."

I've never performed solo, and even if I wanted to, I'd have no idea what I'd sing or what kind of backup I'd need, but just the thought of standing under the stage lights, feeling like a different person, makes me smile. "Maybe," I say. "Thanks."

She lets me borrow a tray to carry the drinks back to the table, where I pass out the glasses. "Cheese fries are coming up," I tell Mia before she can ask. Then I add, "The bartender thought y'all did a great job too."

Chloe, Connor, and Mia all stare at me like I told them my head was going to explode in five seconds. "What?" I ask. "That's what she said."

"*Pammy* told you we were good?" Connor wants to know.

I glance back at the bar, where the dark-haired bartender is pouring beer from the tap. "That bartender," I clarify.

"Holy shit, y'all," Chloe says, running her hands through her hair like she has to physically touch her head to believe this. "*Pammy* of Pammy's thinks we're good."

I feel a little foolish now, not having known that the bartender was also the owner, but the Dog and Pony Show band members don't say anything about it because they're too busy squealing with excitement. When I look back at the bar, Pammy is directing a couple of the waitstaff toward the kitchen. I remember what Chloe said, about Pammy having been a backup singer who toured all over and gave it up to start this place. If I had realized it was her, when she told me she was a singer too, I would have said something like, "Oh, not for real, though, nothing like you." But the way she'd said it, as though we could have both been on the same level—for the first time, I feel like there's a whole world out there away from the church choir and I could be part of it. While Chloe, Connor, and Mia whisper excitedly about when they can sign up next for open mic night and how fast they can write more original songs, I listen to the next performers sing about heartbreak and loneliness and love and hope, and I feel like they're all singing for me.

9.

On the drive home from Pammy's, I roll the windows down and feel the cool night air on my skin and turn the car stereo up. I sing along with Neko Case and Brandi Carlile and Grace Potter louder than usual, and my heart is full, and it's like something in my voice is different. I've been singing in choirs and choruses for years—I know my register and range and how to breathe from my diaphragm. I know which notes I can easily hit and what I can stretch for. But alone in the car, driving on quiet roads, it's as if I'm hearing my voice for the first time.

I'm feeling so great that, by the time I get home, it doesn't instantly register when I see my grandparents' car in the driveway.

They're home. Early. They were supposed to be gone for at least another week. There's no way they would have come home early.

Unless . . .

For a second, I contemplate putting the car in reverse and driving off before anyone sees me. But where would I go? Chloe, Connor, and Mia all left Pammy's, so I can't go back there to hang out with them, and I don't know any of them well enough to swing by their homes.

None of my old Grace Teen Life friends are talking to me, or at least not about anything other than how I'm a terrible person. The open road seems like a great option, until I remember Mom is in the house, alone with her parents. I take a breath and make myself get out of the car.

When I open the front door, everyone is sitting in the living room, and it's as if they're clockwork pieces springing to life. Mom, perched on the edge of the sofa with her arms folded over her chest, stands up straight. Gramps is still seated in his recliner, but he straightens like a deer who's heard a branch snap nearby. Behind him, Gram stands with her hands gripping the fabric of the recliner as though she needs to steady herself.

"Tess. I texted you," Mom says, like she wishes she could send me back in time to get her warning messages.

"I didn't look at my phone. I was driving," I respond. Because usually I do what I'm supposed to.

"Tell me it's not true," Gram says. Her voice is sharp, and her breathing is slightly ragged, like she ran all the way home to hear me say it's not true. "Tess. Tell me."

I swallow hard, looking from Gram to Mom to Gramps and back again. I don't want to tell them—I don't want them to see me the way everyone from Grace Teen Life sees me. I'm still wearing Gram's cross necklace. I imagine Gram wearing it when she was my age, going to Grace Presbyterian on Sundays with her parents and football games on Friday nights with her friends. Gram has always lived in Hawthorne and has always known where she belongs. When she gave me the necklace, it felt like she was trying to give a little of that to me. Now I feel its slight weight against my neck and wish I could be that girl again, the girl she wanted me to be.

"Tess," Gram says again. She takes a step from behind the chair and strides over to me, standing so close that I can see my reflection in her eyes. "Tess, this can't be true. Tell me it isn't true. Tell me what they're saying is a vile lie, because I know you would never do anything like this."

"Tess, you don't have to say anything," Mom insists. "It's none of their business. It's none of *anyone's* business."

Gram turns to Mom like she could strike her dead with a glare. "Of course it's our business! We're her grandparents—she lives in *our* home!"

"And you never let me forget that," Mom snaps.

They look alike, Mom and Gram, although they'd never admit it. The same dark hair, although Gram's is graying now; the same stubborn line appearing across their foreheads when they argue. I've spent the last year trying to smooth things over between them, trying to make the best of things while we live with my grandparents. Now it feels strange to be caught between them in a very different way.

"Laura," Gramps says, silencing Mom. Then he lifts his gaze to look right at me. "Tess, is it true?"

I don't want to say it. But I can't live in this in-between space, pretending it never happened and assuming I can move on with my life without anything being different. It happened, and I am different, and my voice is burning in my chest because I have to say it. "It's true. I was pregnant, and I had an abortion."

It's a strange relief, saying it out loud. At least now I don't need to live with the fear of when this would happen. I can't go back. I can only go forward.

In front of me, Gram shakes her head. "No, no, no," she keeps saying over and over, her hand to her mouth like she can't control what she might say next. "No, that is *not true*."

"Gram," I say, but she takes a step back like she's suddenly afraid of me.

"*No*," she repeats. "No, Tess, not you. You're a good girl. You don't do things like this." She casts around the room, as if something on the coffee table or an old picture on the wall will help her put together the pieces of what happened. "And . . . and even if you got in trouble . . . girls get in trouble, but you manage it. We could have helped you manage it. You *know* we would have helped you."

It's true—they would have been furious and sad, but they would have agreed to help raise the baby while I was still in school. If I could still have managed school and a baby. I imagine myself, walking the living room floor with an infant at two in the morning and hearing Gram tell me what I was doing wrong and how the baby's father should have been with me, too, and somehow that makes me feel lonelier and smaller than I already do.

"I know," I tell her.

"Where would you even go to do something like this?" Gram wants to know.

"I helped her," Mom asserts. "I found somewhere safe and legal, and she got the help she needed."

Gram turns on Mom, her face hard with rage. "That shows what kind of mother you are."

"Stop!" I shout, wanting to throw myself between them, like I can shield my mom from my grandmother's harsh words.

"Who did this to you?" Gramps wants to know. His voice is low, like he wants to go throttle an imaginary high school boy.

I stiffen. "What?"

"Girls don't get in trouble by themselves," Gram practically spits at me. "Who was it?"

Mom stares at me like she's wondering if I'll finally say it. But I promised I wouldn't, and right now it would mean so much more trouble, so I steel myself and say, "I can't tell you."

"What do you mean, you can't tell us?" Gram demands. "Do you not even *know* who the father is?!"

Her comment stings, and before I can reply, Mom raises her voice. "Hey, watch it."

"It doesn't matter who the father is," I say as calmly as I can, even though my heart is pounding and tears are stinging my eyes. I need to sound like I mean it. "I made the decision. I couldn't be a parent."

Gram stares at me, a frown carved into her face. "Well, I guess I can't be a parent or a grandparent anymore." She turns to Mom. "You need to leave this house. I don't care where you go, but you can't stay here."

I glance at Mom, who never really wanted to come back here and who was just getting her life back together. Now because of me, we would be unsettled again. I never meant for that to happen. Why hadn't I thought about this before right now? My stomach knots with guilt, and for a moment I want to tell Gram that it's not true, that I'm so sorry—whatever she needs to hear to make everything go back to normal again. I want to tell Mom that I'm sorry, too, that all of this is my fault and I should have known better.

Mom takes a breath, exhaling slowly like she's stoking a fire. "Fine," she snaps, then looks at me. "Tess, start packing."

♩

Gram and Gramps retreat to their bedroom while Mom and I pack as much as we can in our suitcases and a few stray boxes that were left over from our last move. But it's still not enough, so Mom sends me to the grocery store to see if they have any used boxes they can give us. "I'll keep packing as much as I can and call around to any motel that can take us for the night."

It's strange to be in the car again. Already it feels like Pammy's was an eternity ago, and this time I don't sing as I drive. But I put on music, Hem and some Jill Andrews, and the gentle voices steady my nerves anyway.

The Needleman Family Market parking lot is mostly empty, and I don't see Bri's car, so hopefully she's not working tonight. People are going to find out that my grandparents kicked us out, but I don't want to deal with anyone's questions yet.

Inside, I head to the customer service counter. "Hi, excuse me," I say to the older man sitting behind the counter. "I was wondering—do y'all have any spare cardboard boxes?"

"Moving?" the man asks, and I nod. "Let me check in the back. We get our big shipments on Sunday, but there should be some left. Wait here."

He strolls toward the back of the store, and I hover by the customer service desk, listening to the pop-country music playing over the speaker system and the occasional mechanical beeps of items being checked out.

That's when I see him.

Alden enters the store and grabs a basket, briefly checking his phone like he needs to reassure himself that he's only getting a few groceries and doesn't need a whole cart. He's wearing his royal blue Dust and Fire band shirt under a light jacket, and even from several feet away, I can see how the blue of his shirt makes his eyes shine.

A shiver runs through my body, seeing him now, and I wonder briefly if I'm going to pass out. I want to go over to him, and I don't want to go over to him, and I feel like I'm frozen in place. Then he turns his head and sees me, and for a moment he stops, his automatic smile faltering. It returns almost instantly, but I wonder if he felt the same way seeing me.

I take a step, then another, until I'm standing in front of him.

"Hey, Tess," he says. His tone is casual, but his voice is slightly strained. He grips the basket, not moving to hug me like he normally would. "How's it going?"

In his other hand, I see his cell phone, and I dimly realize that he never texted me back. "Not great," I admit. I want him to hustle me out to his car so I can tell him everything that's been going on—how people are harassing me, how Gram kicked us out, how I went to Pammy's tonight and it made me feel better than I've felt in a long time—but he doesn't move and neither do I.

Instead, he nods and studies his shoes as though they might help him figure out the right thing to say. "Yeah, I heard—people have been saying things."

"There were protesters there. Someone must have recognized me and taken a picture. Apparently, it got shared around youth group and . . ." I trail off because he must already know what people are saying. What happened over the last few days. Even if he didn't text me back. I remember the care package left on my front porch and I want it so badly to be from him that I can't even ask about it, in case it wasn't. Instead, my voice low, I tell him, "Roger wants to know who the father is."

Alden stiffens, his eyes panicked. "What did you say?"

His question stings—does he really think I would have told Roger anything? I didn't even tell my own mother. Why would I cave for Roger? "I didn't tell him anything," I say, my tone colder than I expected. "I promised I wouldn't."

Alden visibly relaxes, exhaling deeply. He takes a small step closer, and when he speaks, his voice is soft and gentle. “Okay, good. Sorry, it’s—you know how serious this is.”

“I know,” I murmur, looking down in embarrassment. When I inhale, I smell his familiar rosemary-and-peppermint aftershave.

“It’ll blow over,” he says. I expect him to reach for me, to put a hand on my shoulder or even pull me into a hug, but he doesn’t move. “I promise. We just need to give it time.”

I think about the past week, and how it felt like months for me. What has Alden been doing during this time? Has he been smiling while praying with youth group, yet wracked with anxiety and guilt inside? Has he been watching the clock and literally wondering how many minutes he has to wait until all of this blows over? Or has it been the length of a regular week for him, as he realized that he was out of milk?

Before I can ask him any of this, I hear footsteps behind me. “Hey there, we’ve got a bunch of boxes if you’re still interested,” the customer service man tells me. “A little banged up, but they’ll get the job done. We can help get them into your car.”

Alden retreats a step from me. “Good to see you, Tess,” he murmurs. “Take care.” He doesn’t even wait for me to respond before striding down the nearest aisle and disappearing around the corner. Suddenly I feel cold and alone and like I’m about to cry under the grocery store’s fluorescent lights.

I don’t cry. Instead, I turn back to the customer service man and say, “Thanks, that would be great.”

♩

The first time Alden kissed me was last year, during Ignite. I'd spent the day listening to testimonials, holding hands in prayer, playing games, talking in small groups about the things we were afraid of and how we could offer our fears up to God. Being together with everyone who could be so vulnerable, so earnest, everything felt new and familiar all at once, and I absently thought maybe that was God.

After dinner, Alden pulled me aside and asked me to meet him back in the main lodge after everyone else was asleep. "I've got something I want you to hear," he'd said. When I asked what it was, he'd grinned and told me that would ruin the surprise.

A surprise, I'd thought. Something for me. He hadn't told anyone else.

It wasn't unusual for him to want to share something with me, not exactly. Weeks before, he'd asked me to help him with a new arrangement for the Grace Presbyterian choir, something to perform at the Spirit Light Festival. It was a big outdoor Christian music festival held every year in Hawthorne, and amateur groups like the choir had the opportunity to perform. Alden had wanted to make this year special, so he'd been working on something new. "You've got such a beautiful voice and a great ear," he'd told me. "I'd love it if you could work on the arrangement with me." I'd stayed after rehearsal for the last few weeks, working on it with him. He talked to me like I was a peer, a fellow musician and artist, not just some girl in youth group. The song was going to be a surprise for the rest of the choir, so we were keeping it a secret until we were ready to share it with everyone else. I hadn't even told Lily or Bri about it—I didn't want it getting back to Alden and have him think I was silly or immature or that he couldn't trust me. So it didn't seem all that strange when Alden asked me to sneak out during the retreat and meet him after everyone else was asleep.

That night, I listened while the girls in my cabin got into bed and whispered and laughed after lights-out, waiting for their voices to hush and their breathing to steady. Eventually I swung myself out of bed, slipped on my shoes and a hoodie, and crept into the cool night air to meet Alden back in the retreat center's main lodge.

He was already there when I arrived, sitting on an overstuffed, mismatched couch in front of an empty fireplace. A laptop was on the coffee table, and he was bent toward it in concentration, a large pair of headphones on his head. When the screen door shut behind me, he sat up.

"Hey, Tess, you made it!" he called, sliding the headphones off. He sounded delighted, like he legitimately thought I might not have come and was excited to see me. I thought of everyone back in my cabin, asleep and unaware that I was here.

I took a seat on the couch beside him and nodded at the headphones. "You wanted me to hear something?"

"Yes," he said brightly. "You've been a huge help with the song for the Spirit Light Festival, and I hope you've had as much fun working on it as I have."

I nodded. "Oh, totally." It was true—working with Alden on the arrangement for our song was the first time I'd helped write something, not just sing it. We'd taken the lyrics from the Bible, *you are the light of the world*, but the musical accompaniment was ours. We hadn't shared it with anyone yet, not even the rest of the choir, but it made me feel like we were looking at the sky for the first time, making constellations out of stars.

"Well, I never really considered myself a songwriter, but working with you inspired me," he continued, opening a music production app on his laptop. "It's still really rough, but I wanted you to be the first person to hear it." He handed me the headphones, and as I put them over my ears, music started to play.

It was primarily piano, steady and soft like spring rain, with guitar and drums playing gently in the background. After a minute Alden's voice came in, and it felt familiar and somehow unexpected, a little more gravelly than usual: *Open the door, it's right there now, let's go, let's go, we'll find it together . . .* I found myself nodding along in time with the beat, a smile spreading across my face as the song built to its crescendo.

When I turned to Alden, he was looking at me expectantly. "What do you think?" he asked.

"Oh my gosh, Alden, that's so good," I told him, pulling off the headphones. "You wrote that? All of it—music and lyrics?"

He beamed. "I did. The music program let me input the guitar and drums, so I can't take credit for playing those, but otherwise it was me. Once we started working together, I got into a groove, and this is what came out. It's a tune I'd been playing around with for a while, but everything kind of clicked."

"That's awesome," I said, and handed him the headphones. Our hands brushed and I felt a rush of warmth through my body. Before Alden could notice, I pulled my hand away, pushed a piece of hair out of my face, and mumbled, "I'm surprised it's the first song you've written. It feels really solid."

"Well, I've been playing and singing for a long time," he said, setting the headphones beside the laptop. "Like you, right? Music's always been a part of my life in this big way." He paused, dropping his voice a little even though we were the only ones in the room. "When I was little, I had a stutter. I *never* wanted to talk because of it—my older brothers would speak for me because I wouldn't say anything to people who weren't my immediate family. Can you imagine *me* not talking?"

I grinned, thinking of Alden leading youth group, guiding us through prayers and rounding everyone up for games. "Not even a little."

"Right?" He laughed. "My parents didn't want me to go through life needing my brothers to speak for me, so I did a lot of speech therapy. Part of what I learned was that music can help the brain process language and speech a little better—amazing, right? I got more confident speaking, and the stutter went away, and I found that I loved music. Even beyond the stuttering, it became a way for me to express what I was feeling and to connect with other people."

I nodded, pulling my legs onto the couch so I could look directly at him. "Yeah, I know what you mean. Like, I've *never* liked being in front of big groups. It makes me feel so . . . anxious? Like just being the center of attention is way too much."

"You're more of a one-on-one kind of person," he said, leaning his elbow on the back of the couch and turning to me.

"Exactly!" I sat up a little, like his recognition gave me energy. "But when I'm singing, it doesn't feel like that. I mean, mostly it's with a group, but even when I've had solos, it still feels different—like you don't have to worry about what you're saying or people looking at you, because everyone's caught up in the song."

Alden's smile widened. "See, I knew you'd get it." He put his hand on my shoulder and gave it a gentle squeeze.

It was a friendly gesture, I told myself, even as I felt light-headed from the slight pressure of his hand, like there wasn't quite enough air in the room.

"Is it a Christian song?" I asked, hoping he didn't notice how my cheeks were flushed. "I mean, maybe I missed it, because it's not like every Christian rock song is super obvious. But I wasn't sure if that's what you were going for."

Something about his expression was self-conscious, and he couldn't seem to quite make eye contact with me. "No, not exactly. I always expected to write songs about my faith, but this one came out differently. It, ah, was actually inspired by you." He raised his eyes, clear and earnest and beautiful, to meet mine, and suddenly it felt like we were the only people for miles. As if something had shifted, and there was a new kind of gravity in the space between us.

"Me?" I could barely manage to get the word out. My heart was racing, and every inch of my skin was vibrating with energy.

"You," he said as he reached his hand out to caress my cheek, drawing my face toward his until his lips were on mine, pressing against them with the exact right pressure and warmth. I worried a little that he could tell I didn't have much experience, but it felt more like dancing with a partner who knew how to lead—I relaxed and kissed him back, feeling warmth spread through my body as if there was a fire lit nearby.

After a moment, he broke away, breathing a little haggard as he asked, "Is this okay?"

He was so sensitive to even ask that, I thought. He must have cared about me, understood me. "Yeah, this is okay," I said, smiling.

He drew me closer, putting one hand on the small of my back and another resting on my leg. We kissed and kissed until my lips felt swollen and my head was spinning, and I felt like an electrical current was running through each of my nerve endings. *This is real, this is real, this is real*, I kept thinking.

Finally, Alden admitted that we probably should get some sleep. He was walking me to the door when he asked, "Do you think you could do me a favor?"

"Of course," I said.

"Maybe you could not mention this . . ." He pressed a kiss to the back of my hand. ". . . to anyone right now? It's just that, since I'm the youth minister, it makes things a little complicated. Other people might not get it. But I want to figure it out with you—we just need a little more time."

"Oh yeah," I murmured. "I totally get it." I did, mostly. I was sure it would make things weird with everyone else, even if half the group wanted Alden to kiss them too. And besides, Alden was a really good guy—if he said he wanted to make it work between us, he meant it. For now, this could be our secret. It felt intimate, romantic. "I won't tell anyone."

"Thank you." He kissed me once more before I hurried back to my cabin. Everyone was still asleep, and I smiled to myself as I slipped between the sheets, feeling like I'd been chosen for something.

♩

When I get back to my grandparents' house, Mom is taping up old boxes in the garage. "Oh, thank God," she says when she sees the pile of flattened boxes from the grocery store. "I already filled up the duffel bags and was worried we'd end up needing to dump things in the back of the car."

We box up the rest of our things, a surprising amount compiled over the last year. When I go through my dresser, I find a picture from last year's retreat, a big group photo taken before we all left. We huddled together, making sure everyone fit, while a few of the chaperones took pictures with about a dozen phones.

Alden managed to stand beside me in the back row, his hand pressed against the small of my back. I leaned my head toward him, smiling at no camera in particular. Now I look at my face, so happy and beatific, and vaguely remember how it felt like I'd taken a leap off the sharp edge of a cliff and expected to fly.

10.

Mom and I spend the night in the Green Forest Motel, at the edge of town. It's mostly a rest stop for truckers and road-trippers who overlook the '70s decor, scratchy sheets, and leaky bathroom faucets. In the motel parking lot, our car is packed with most of our stuff, and it reminds me of when we first moved to Hawthorne, and how I wondered if I'd make friends and whether we'd get along living under the same roof as Gram and Gramps. Now it's strange to still be in Hawthorne, under a different roof, falling asleep to the dull hum of the highway nearby.

"It's only for a few days," Mom assures me the next morning while we get ready for work and school. "I'll find an apartment we can rent, and we'll manage things until I can get a new job and we can move as far away as possible from this crap town."

I know Mom never liked Hawthorne, and right now it's not my favorite place, either. But I feel a weird pang of guilt at hearing her call it a crap town. For a little while, it felt like home.

Even though Mom's trying to be enthusiastic about an apartment and money, I know she's worried that we're going to spiral into debt again thanks to these new expenses. So after school, instead of going back to the motel, which feels too depressing, or doing homework in the library, I head to Needleman Family Market to see if they're hiring.

The woman at customer service is heavyset, with pale blue eyes and a butterfly pin on her Needleman Family Market polo shirt. When I ask about openings, she digs around in a drawer at her feet. "We're always accepting applications," she tells me. "Have you worked retail before?"

I shake my head. "I haven't really had a job before. I mean, aside from some babysitting. But I'm responsible and hardworking, I promise. And I'll take whatever shifts you have. As long as it's not during school, I can do it."

She pulls an application out of the drawer and hands it to me. "We all start somewhere," she says. "And I'd say your odds are pretty good—we're heading into the holidays, and we could use the help over the season. You didn't hear this from me, but I know that if you do a good job, chances are they'll keep you on." She winks at me and taps the side of her nose.

I take the application, smiling gratefully. "That would be great. I'll fill this out and get it back to y'all right away."

As I walk away, I scan the application—name, birthdate, Social Security number . . . present address. Shit. Of course they'd need an address. Knowing that I can't write Gram and Gramps's address on the application stings, a pinprick in my heart. What am I even supposed to write? The motel's address? To be determined? Sorry, my mom's looking for an apartment right now, I should have a new address for you in a couple of weeks, promise?

Maybe this is a bad idea. How am I going to get a part-time job if I don't even know how to fill out the application? I'm debating whether to toss it in the trash when I see Bri walk into the store, wearing her maroon Needleman Family Market polo, backpack slung over her shoulder.

As if I don't feel bad enough about how things are going, I have to run into someone from youth group.

"Tess," she says, like she has to say my name to prove to herself that it's me. "What are you doing here?"

The way she says it, *what are* you *doing here*, like she's surprised to see me out in the world, makes my skin prickle. My grandparents kicked me out, and now Bri's acting like I can't be in a grocery store? "They still let me go to public places," I mutter. "I haven't been entirely shunned from society."

"I didn't—I mean I didn't expect to see you." She glances down at the application in my hand, and her eyebrows raise in surprise. "Are you applying for a job?"

Yes. No. Maybe. I don't know what the answer is, but I hold the application tighter. "Kind of," I tell her. Then I realize that she could ruin this for me—if I apply, she could spread the word among the Needleman staff about what happened. If they don't know already. Nearby, I hear the beep of items being swiped at checkout, and the grind of old grocery cart wheels, and it feels like such a small, ridiculous thing to want, but I need to do something for Mom and me right now, and I need something to work out.

And Bri isn't looking at me like she completely hates me. She never told me that she was praying for me or cornered me in the hall to demand that I tell her who the father is. Maybe a small part of her doesn't want to shame me and destroy the life I have here. "Look,

Mom and I are trying to find a place of our own," I tell her, voice low even though there aren't any shoppers within earshot.

Her face softens a little, like she can guess what happened between my grandparents and me. "Oh," she murmurs, absently tugging on the strap of her backpack.

"I thought I could help if I got a part-time job. I . . ." I sigh, looking at her steadily. "Look, you don't have to help me, but can you not make this harder?"

She glances over her shoulder, like she's worried that the rest of youth group might be walking in behind her. Finally, she sighs. "I'm not going to get in the way of you getting a job or anything." Relief spreads through me, and I'm about to thank her, when she adds, "Honestly, I can't believe you'd think I'd try to mess with you getting a stupid part-time job. Like, what kind of person do you think I am?"

I think about the past year, going to movies and prayer groups and mini golf with Bri. Checking chemistry homework together before class. Texting each other jokes and gossip and prayer requests. Volunteering at Grace Teen Life bake sales together. Standing side by side on the sidewalk in front of a women's health clinic, imploring women to choose life. When I picture us together, I barely recognize the girl I was not long ago.

"What kind of person do you think *I* am?" I ask Bri now.

She pauses, tilting her head slightly as though she's actually thinking about it. Like she doesn't need to spit *slut* at me. After a moment, she says, "I wish I knew," and walks away.

Watching her go, I feel tears prick my eyes. This hurts more than Lily telling me she's praying for me in the cafeteria, because I know why Lily would be mad at me. But Bri saying she doesn't know me anymore, it feels even truer, hits even harder, because I don't know who I am, either.

♩

After the retreat, Alden and I saw each other as often as we could—after choir rehearsals, when we were supposed to be working on the arrangement for the Spirit Light Festival; after Grace Teen Life meetings, when he gave people rides home and dropped me off last; and on random evenings when I would tell Mom I was going to see a movie with Lily and Bri but met up with Alden instead. People trusted that I was where I was supposed to be because I'd never given them a reason not to trust me.

It was thrilling and frenetic and furtive, feeling his hands on my back and his fingers through my hair and his mouth on mine. During choir or youth group, his eyes would find mine for just a moment and we'd smile, like we were both thinking about each other and how we'd see each other later, and it felt like we were the only two people in the world. As much as I wanted to tell my friends about this new relationship, part of me liked the secrecy. It felt romantic, exciting, like things I'd only read about.

He didn't pressure me to do stuff, either. Not really. It wasn't like he tried to get in my pants the week we got back from retreat.

"I haven't done much," I told him one night when we were parked in his car after a Grace Teen Life movie night. We'd been kissing and I noticed his hands moving toward my chest. "Like, anything."

He pulled away slightly to look at me, his expression understanding and kind. "No, Tess, I totally get it. I think that's great. And I don't want to make you do anything you're not ready for. It's just that you're so beautiful and I get a little ahead of myself." He kissed my neck until I got a little ahead of myself too.

No one had called me beautiful before, not like that. Mom and Dad had said I looked beautiful before school concerts, when I had to dress up, but I'd never been called beautiful by a guy before. Boys at Hawthorne or back in Bloomington, they didn't call girls beautiful. "Hot" was a huge compliment, or maybe "pretty," or "cute," but "beautiful" felt like it was on another level. More serious, maybe, with more depth. Alden saying it felt like he saw something in me that other people didn't see.

♩

The woman at Needleman's customer service was right—I get hired almost immediately, with the intent to work at least through the holidays. They can't guarantee hours after that, but I'll be part-time, mostly after school and on weekends, through the end of the year. When the Needleman's shift manager asks if I have any hard conflicts, I tell him no.

Which means my first shift is scheduled for Sunday morning.

A strange combination of relief and loneliness mingle in the pit of my stomach as I make neat piles of apples and pears. I think of everyone—my grandparents, Lily, Bri, Alden—at Grace Presbyterian that morning, singing and praying and holding each other's hands as if I'd never been there at all.

There are other churches in Hawthorne—Methodist, Baptist, Episcopal, plus a small Pentecostal church just on the Wolfwood line. I could go to any of them, act like I'm new to town and looking for a welcoming Christian community.

But they might know me there too. I don't want to walk into a new church, only to face the same questions and stares.

Maybe someday I can find a new place. After I graduate. Maybe I'll go to college, move away, and I can spend Sunday mornings in a pew again, listening to messages of peace and love and forgiveness. For now, I stock produce and frozen foods and canned goods, trying to focus on the work instead of imagining the people and places I'm missing.

♩

After about a week, Mom's managed to find an apartment that we can mostly afford. It's closer to town than the motel, but farther from Gram and Gramps's, which might have been intentional on Mom's part. It's on the second floor, above a laundromat, so everything smells like detergent and dryer lint. "It's like having our own washer and dryer!" Mom says cheerfully as we lug our things up to the second floor. Thankfully, the apartment is already furnished, even though it's a mismatch of scratchy armchairs and wobbly tables. It's a one-bedroom, but Mom and I find an old twin bedframe and partition screen at Goodwill so I can make a bedroom for myself in a corner of the living room. I'd thought moving out of Gram and Gramps's would feel sad and strange, but as I unpack, I feel surprisingly hopeful. Even if it's cramped and has a few weird stains on the walls and smells like laundry, it's ours and I don't have to be anyone to anyone else here.

Which is what makes me feel confident to bring up the Needleman job to Mom. I'd avoided it so far, since she's been busy covering extra shifts tending bar at Custom House Pub to make enough money for first and last month's rent. But now that I'm officially hired and have managed to get through training, I have actual money to share.

"It's only a few hours a week, for now—mostly weekends, and a weeknight here and there," I tell her. "But I thought it might help."

"Tess, you didn't have to do that," she says, turning from the kitchenette, where she's unpacking our few plates and glasses left over from Bloomington. "I told you, I got this. Really."

"I know." I tuck the sheets into the bed, smoothing the top down. "I mean, my weeknights and weekends suddenly got a *lot* less hectic, so I figured I might as well make some money." When she raises an eyebrow at me, I add, "Seriously."

She still looks suspicious, but she adds another glass to the cabinet. "Fine. But you should save it—for college or a car or whatever. Don't use it on boring stuff like gas or electricity."

"I do get an employee discount," I say brightly. "Ten percent."

Mom throws a wadded piece of newspaper into the air like confetti. "Ten percent, baby! We're gonna be rolling in brand-name chips and ice cream." I laugh, and she continues, "Make sure you have a little fun too."

"I'll try," I tell her as I spread an old quilt over my bed.

♩

That night, I fall asleep by myself for the first time in over a year. It's strange not to have Mom's sleeping form in the twin bed next to mine, the same one she slept in when she was my age. Now, even though I can hear the hum of a few dryers downstairs and cars driving by outside, my makeshift room feels empty and too big somehow.

I toss and turn for a little while before taking a breath and folding my hands together.

Dear God, I pray silently. *It's Tess. I don't even know what I want to say, exactly. I don't know if I should be doing this anymore, considering. But it helps me feel less alone, so maybe, if you're listening, could you help me feel less alone?* It's still only me, in bed in the living room, unfamiliar shadows falling across the walls, but I relax and settle down more easily.

When I fall asleep, I dream that my chest has been cut open, so the interior of my heart is exposed, red and beating and vulnerable. But when I look down, I have a needle and thread in my hands. I can stitch myself back together.

11.

I make it through the next few weeks—going to school, going to work, teaching myself guitar. Whenever people side-eye me in the hall or whisper about me or loudly joke to their friends that I'm an easy lay, I keep my face stoic and my gaze fixed on an imaginary horizon. I go over chord progressions in my head: *C two three four, A minor two three four, F two three four, G two three four.*

On Thursday nights, whenever I'm not scheduled for a shift at Needleman's, I go to Pammy's for open mic night with Chloe, Connor, and Mia. Sometimes they play, and each time they're a little sharper, a little brighter, a little more relaxed. They still mostly play covers, but they work in a few new songs they've written too.

One night in late October, they play one of the new songs, which doesn't sound as good as Mia would like. "You came in late on the bridge," she tells her brother as they return to the table.

"You were rushing," Connor says, sliding into his chair.

"Y'all, it was *fine*," Chloe tries to assure them.

Mia rolls her eyes. "*Fine* doesn't get you a record deal. *Fine* doesn't get you a Grammy. *Fine* doesn't get you a sold-out show at Carnegie Hall."

"No one is booking us for a sold-out show at Carnegie Hall," Connor points out.

"Of course not, with the way you came in late on that bridge," Mia sneers, turning her back to her brother so she can face the stage, where the next act is setting up.

I lean over to Connor and Chloe, and say, "I liked it. I thought it sounded even better than the last few times y'all rehearsed it. There was this moment toward the end, when you were repeating the chorus—you added some kind of dissonance."

"Oh yeah," Connor says. "The half-step interval. I was messing around with it at home, and it sounded right."

Chloe nods, taking a big sip of water. "Yeah, I thought that worked really well. Connor tried it out yesterday, and it worked even better tonight. Like it gave the whole thing a little edge at the end."

"Right!" I say. "It was, like, a little hint of shadow in a sunny room. It gave the sound a lot of depth with only a little change."

Mia doesn't turn around, but she says, "Okay, yes, that did sound better. But watch your timing next time."

Connor and Chloe smirk at each other, trying not to laugh as the next band, a quartet of college-aged guys, begins their set. The ease with which they play together, the sparkle of humor in their eyes when they talk to each other, makes me wonder if Chloe and Connor are a couple. I remember feeling that way with Alden, when we were working on the song for the Spirit Light Festival, when we would play or sing together. When we were alone. It felt like he really saw me, the person other people didn't notice. Except we couldn't act like that around other people, the choir and youth group. Seeing

Connor and Chloe, there's a genuine warmth there, one they don't have to hide.

I ask Chloe about it later, when we're in the restroom. "You and Connor," I say as we wash our hands, "you're really close, right?"

"Oh yeah," she says. "He's my best friend. I see him more often than I see, like, half my family. My mom tells me that if I spend any more time at the Burkes' house, they're going to have to adopt me and pay for college. But joke's on her because I don't even know if I'm going to college. Like, did Dolly Parton go to college? No, and she's one of the most talented and successful people ever."

"I think you need a few more rhinestones to be Dolly Parton," I laugh, then try to gauge her reaction in the bathroom mirror without her noticing. "So, are you and Connor, like, together?"

Chloe's eyebrows go up for a second. "Me and Connor? Oh no." She grabs a piece of paper towel from the dispenser and dries her hands, wrinkling her nose as she seems to consider the possibility of her and Connor dating. "I don't see him that way." Bunching the paper towel into a ball, she tosses it into the trash and adds, "I don't see *anyone* that way."

The way Chloe says it and pauses for a second, like she's waiting for me to process what she's said, I can tell that it's not hyperbole. "Oh, are you asexual?" I ask.

She smiles. "I am! Once I realized that, it was a lot easier to explain to my parents why I love Connor like crazy and can text him all the time, but I am never ever going to date him." She cocks her head at me. "But if you're interested in him—"

I hold up my hands. "Oh no, I wasn't asking like that. I mean, Connor's great and all, but I'm not really looking for that right now." And it's true. Alden said that we need to wait a little while, let things blow over, and maybe he's right, but the more time goes by, the harder and harder it is to see us together again. At least not right now. And with everything that's happened over the last few weeks, I'm so not ready for anything like that again. Even with someone who seems cool, like Connor.

Chloe nods. "Probably for the best. He's an embarrassingly bad dancer. If you went with him to the Snow Ball, you'd be scarred for life."

I laugh as we exit the restroom and head back to the table. "I appreciate the warning."

♩

The red *A* stays on my locker through the fall, until mid-November, when the janitor gets the materials necessary to scrub it off and repaint it. Even with the same gray paint as the other lockers, mine stands out, a little brighter with its new coat. But it only lasts a few days before another red *A* is painted in the exact same spot.

I thought it was over, or at least that people were moving on. I don't get as many sidelong glances in the halls now. No one in French class asks me if I've actually had sex. Even though people from Grace Teen Life still aren't speaking to me, they've moved on to pretending that I don't exist. I'd gotten a new phone number, which stopped the anonymous texts. Gram and Gramps didn't reach out to us about spending Thanksgiving together, but I hadn't really expected them to. Mom and I are getting by. I thought I could start to move on.

Except there it was again, like it had never left. Like it would always be something I'd have to carry with me, even after I moved away from Hawthorne and met people who never knew about what happened.

This time I find Principal Bellingham to ask about the locker. "Someone painted my locker again," I tell him. "It's the same shade and everything."

He presses his lips together, staring at his computer screen and typing wildly. "Yes, I did see that. You know we just had it repainted a few days ago."

"I know," I say, mentally willing him to make eye contact with me. "And that's great. I mean, I really appreciate the maintenance team getting that done—"

"We can't keep repainting your locker every few days, Miss Pine," he tells me.

"I know," I repeat. "I thought you might know who's been doing this. Maybe there's some security footage, or—"

"Unfortunately, we only have security cameras at the entrances and exits of the school and other major student access points, not at one individual student's locker." He finally turns away from the computer, folding his hands together and setting them on top of his desk. "Besides, this seems to be a personal problem, doesn't it?" His tone is cold and clipped.

I stiffen, remembering it was only a couple months ago when I sat in Principal Bellingham's office and he claimed that he wanted to help. "It's happening on school property," I tell him, even though my voice feels small. "*To* school property."

"Perhaps you can share valuable information on who might want to do this to you," he counters, like he's waiting for me to share what everyone's wanted to know for weeks. When I stay silent, he shrugs. "Then I'm afraid it's difficult for me to help you. You can speak with the guidance counselor if you want any other assistance." He glances at the door, and I know that's my signal to leave his office and head to my first-period class.

But I don't get up from my chair. I'm the same person I was a few weeks ago, when he offered to help me and find the people who were responsible for the graffiti. Even if I can't tell him about what happened with Alden, shouldn't he still want to help me? My voice is quiet but now there's a firmness to it when I say, "Isn't that, like, your job—to help students?"

For the first time he actually looks at me, as though he's surprised to find a real person sitting in the creaky wooden chair in his office. A real person who might not be a nice, Christian girl or a murderer-slut and who might have some things to say.

Then he clears his throat, embarrassed. "My job is running this school," he mutters. "Not playing Nancy Drew for a girl who should have thought about the consequences of her actions."

I frown at him, unblinking. "Thank you for your time," I spit before marching out of his office.

♩

The week of Thanksgiving, I'm scheduled for extra shifts at Needleman's to help restock shelves. "It's the busiest time of year," the shift manager tells me. "We need all hands on deck."

"All hands on deck" means that, two nights before Thanksgiving, I'm in the stockroom with Bri, making sure we have enough cans of cranberry sauce and pumpkin pie mix for tomorrow's big rush.

So far, Bri and I have largely managed to avoid each other at work. Our shifts are usually different, and even when we have the same schedule, we're often placed in different areas—her in produce, me bagging groceries. I'm pretty sure the shift manager set it up that way, like he was worried we'd goof off otherwise.

Now Bri and I work in awkward silence, tagging cans with prices and organizing pallets for our coworkers to shelf. Every so often, I glance over at her, head bent over boxes of stuffing mix. I remember how easy it had been to talk with her and Lily, how they treated me like we'd been friends for years instead of me being the new girl, out of step with all the Hawthorne traditions and history. Their friendship had felt like a gift, God watching out for me in a new place: *Here are your people, you have a home here.*

I don't know if Bri is still my people, or if she ever was. But I miss that feeling. I miss the comfort of being with her and Lily.

After about an hour, Bri unpacks a pallet of canned mandarin orange slices and winces. "Ugh, I need to hide this," she says, almost to herself. Then, when she realizes that I heard her, she laughs in embarrassment. "We're going to my great-aunt Betty's for Thanksgiving, and she always makes ambrosia salad. I guess it's a tradition, but why would you put sour cream and oranges in the same bowl?"

I wrinkle my nose in disgust. "Yeah, hard pass." Gram didn't make ambrosia salad, but she did make a Jell-O salad with walnuts and cranberries that wasn't as bad as I'd expected. I don't know if she'll make it again this year, or who they'll be celebrating with. If they'll look around the table and wish Mom and I were there.

After a moment, Bri adds, "My cousin Jana tried to feed her portion to Penny last year." I smile, picturing Bri's long-haired dachshund, Penny, who has two great joys in life: digging into the couch cushions and food that falls on the floor.

"Did she like it?" I ask.

Bri shakes her head, giggling. "Took one sniff and refused. Which is probably for the best—I'm not sure maraschino cherries are good for dogs."

"She's got good taste," I laugh. We smile, letting the collegiality and ease hang in the air for a moment before we get back to work. I keep thinking of Bri's family, how Penny would jump up from the coziest cuddle to sit next to Bri's mom. Last year, Mrs. Miller had a partial mastectomy and spent a few weeks recovering. Gram and I brought a care package over, with food and comfortable clothing and movies to watch, and Penny didn't even get up from her spot by Mrs. Miller on the couch to bark at us at the door.

"How's your mom?" I ask Bri, my voice a little shaky and hesitant. "Is she doing okay?"

Bri nods, a sad smile on her face. "Yeah, so far, so good. She got checked last week and no more cancer so far."

"That's great," I reply. I want to add, *Tell her I'm thinking of her* or *I know that was scary and is still scary and I hope you're doing okay too.* But it feels like too much, with everything else that's gone on between us, and all I can do is repeat, stupidly, "That's really great."

"Yeah, thanks," Bri says. She picks up a can, smacking it with a price sticker. "She wants to take me dress shopping for the Snow Ball, mostly because she missed doing it last year. I'm like, Mom, there are places online for this stuff. But she really wants to go and do the whole dressing-room-movie-montage thing."

"Moms love that kind of thing," I say. Last year, I managed to avoid that scenario because Lily, Bri, and I had gone shopping with a few other Grace Teen Life girls at a department store in Wolfwood. We'd bought sparkly dresses and shoes that didn't hurt our feet too badly and celebrated with frothy, sugary coffee drinks afterward.

"Are you going this year?" Bri asks, voice both overly casual and cautious.

I remember last year, how even though I went with Roger, it had been a fun night. We'd gone as part of a big group of Grace Teen Life people. I danced and sang along whenever I knew the words to the thumping club music the DJ played. When I looked around the circle at my friends, beautiful in their dresses and suits and elegant hairstyles, moving in time with the music, I felt like I had a place with them. I can't imagine doing the same this year.

"Probably not," I tell her.

Bri nods and doesn't ask why. After a second, I'm sure she's going to go back to pricing cans of oranges, but she says, "You left early last year, right?"

It's more of a comment than a question, but I answer anyway. "Yeah."

I hadn't planned on leaving early. But seeing other couples dancing to the occasional slow song, swaying gently together, made me miss Alden. I'd told him about the dance, hinting that I wished we could go together, even though I knew that could never happen. He told me he knew it was hard, but what we had was more than a high school dance. "Besides," he added, "I didn't think you'd care about stuff like the Snow Ball. You seem so much more mature than that."

So partway through the evening, I snuck away to the bathroom and texted him Miss you.

A few seconds passed, and I saw the typing bubbles pop up. Miss you too, he replied. I bet you look gorgeous. I texted him a picture, one from earlier that night, when my hair and makeup were freshly done, and he texted back: Wow. Yeah, I was right. Then, after a moment, he added, Can you sneak out?

And I did. I pretended that I wasn't feeling well, that I'd called my mom to come pick me up. My friends said they would wait outside with me, but I convinced them that I would only be waiting for a minute and that they shouldn't stop having fun.

Because it had been fun, in a silly, school dance kind of way. As I waited for Alden outside the gym, I thought about my friends on the dance floor, waving their hands in the air and jumping even though their heels were hurting and singing at the top of their lungs together. I thought about Roger, who I didn't want to be with but who had asked me to the dance and who I'd said yes to. I thought about the after-party at Bri's, where we'd stay up late and discuss everyone's outfits and watch some terrible movie before passing out on her living room floor. I didn't want to miss out on all of that, but I also didn't want to be some immature high school girl who wanted to go to stupid dances with her friends instead of being with the guy who called her gorgeous.

I notice Bri watching me closely, even though she's pretending not to. Like maybe she's expecting me to say more.

Except I can't say more. I don't know what's going to happen between Alden and me anymore, but I still can't do that to him. It would ruin everything for him, he'd said. For us. A small part of me still wants there to be an us. Because if there will never be an us again, what were we before?

"I wasn't feeling good" is all I tell Bri now.

Bri nods, murmuring, "Right. Yeah," before turning her attention back to pricing cans.

We continue to work in silence late into the evening, everything we didn't say hovering in the air between us.

12.

Most nights, when I get home from school or Needleman's, I practice the guitar. Mom's taking extra shifts tending bar, so unless people at the laundromat are listening, no one's around to hear me. I fumble over chords and then progressions until they smooth out and what I'm playing sounds less like someone messing around and more like a real song. When I get stuck, I watch tutorials online, replaying them over and over until I can match my fingers with the instructor's. I learn "A Case of You" and "I Walk the Line" and "9 to 5" and, of course, Leonard Cohen's "Hallelujah." Sometimes, when I have a song down, I stand in front of the full-length mirror hung over the bedroom door and play and sing loud enough to drown out the hum of washers and dryers downstairs and the memory of seeing that *A* painted on my locker for the first time and everything that happened after. Even though Mom's unmade bed and clothes are scattered on the floor behind me, I almost feel like I could be at Pammy's, singing in front of my friends from the music room and total strangers and Pammy herself.

Maybe. Someday.

For now I keep practicing.

♩

It's right before winter break before I share my playing with anyone. When I get to the music room for lunch, Chloe, Connor, and Mia are already there, snacking on Christmas cookies from out of a red-and-white-striped tin and arguing about which Christmas song is the worst. When Chloe sees me at the door, she waves me over. "Tess!" she says. "Come have a cookie and tell these weirdos that the worst Christmas song is definitely 'Wonderful Christmastime,' because now it's in your head and you can't get it out."

Mia shakes her head vehemently, arguing, "Okay, that's bad, but the worst one is 'Grandma Got Run Over by a Reindeer.' Santa *murdered an innocent old woman* in that song."

"Classic hit-and-fly," Connor says, biting the head off a snowman cookie. "Still not as bad as that sappy one about the shoes."

I take a seat with them and select a snowflake cookie with delicate frosting decorating the top. "That song's awful," I admit, "but 'I Saw Mommy Kissing Santa Claus' is seriously disturbing."

Which leads Connor and Mia to argue about whether it's worse to make Santa a murderer or a homewrecker. They lean toward murderer, and Chloe says she saw a horror movie like that. "It was the cheesiest, worst horror movie, but it also made me rethink the whole Santa thing. He literally breaks into your house while you're sleeping. That's creepy!"

"So now we definitely have to prank you about Santa breaking into your house this Christmas," Connor says, grinning maniacally.

Chloe tries to kick him without getting up from her chair. "You dick, I'll murder you with a candy cane if you try it," she laughs.

We finish the cookies, and the trio plays another original song they've been working on. This one is more languid than their first, something reminiscent of a lullaby. Maybe it's the talk of Christmas songs and the promise of winter break ahead, but the song makes me think of freshly fallen snow, deep blue skies filled with stars, and feeling the soft quiet of the whole world wrap around me.

While they're playing, I notice Connor using some barre chords. I've been struggling with those, even after playing and replaying a bunch of different online tutorials. I watch closely, like I can try to pick up on what he's doing right, but it's too quick, and by the end of the song I still don't have a better sense of how I could play it correctly.

Ask him, I tell myself. *All you have to do is ask him. What's the worst that could happen?* Last year I wouldn't have hesitated, but now it feels like sharing anything will make me more vulnerable, even to people who've been nothing but kind to me. So far, guitar has been mine alone, no one else's. After everything that happened with Alden and the church choir and the Spirit Light Festival, I don't want anything to ruin this.

The period's almost over and they're packing up.

One chord at a time, Tess, I tell myself. Then, almost before I can think to stop myself, I add a small prayer: *Please, God, help me be brave.*

"Hey, Connor," I say before he can put his guitar away.

He looks at me. "What's up?" he asks.

"I, ah, I noticed you playing the F major barre chord," I say, trying to sound as casual as possible. "How do you get it to sound so natural?"

He tilts his head. "You play?" he asks. Mia and Chloe pause, turning to face me as well and waiting for my answer.

"Um, sort of," I say, fiddling with the strap of my backpack. "I mean, I just started. I've been messing around at home. I'm not, like, *playing*." I'm tempted to rush out of the room before they can ask anything else, but instead I take a breath. *One chord at a time.* "But I'm trying to learn. And barre chords are messing me up. I was wondering if you had any advice."

He nods, holding his guitar out to me. "Show me what you're doing."

I slide my backpack off and sit down beside Connor, taking his guitar. Nearby, Mia and Chloe stop packing up and watch us.

No pressure, I think and try to play the F major. The sound is tinny instead of clear, and Connor nods. "Oh yeah, I see what you mean."

"Right?!" I exclaim. "It just doesn't sound right, but it looks like I've got my fingers in the right position on the fretboard."

"That's totally normal, though—barre chords are seriously finicky." He leans forward slightly, focusing on the fretboard. "Instead of putting your index finger down flat on the low E, try angling it slightly on the side. That usually helps me."

I follow his advice and it sounds better already. "Oh wow, that does help."

"Right? It gives you better contact," he says.

"Thanks, Connor," I say, handing the guitar back just as the first bell rings.

"Don't think he's some kind of musical genius," Mia tells me, clicking the latches of her violin case shut. "It took him *forever* to learn barre chords."

"I'm trying to pass along my hard-earned knowledge, like a good person," he snaps at his sister. Then to me, he adds, "Let me know if you're working on anything else. Or maybe we could all jam sometime."

Chloe's face brightens. "Oh yes! Pizza-making and jam session. Tomorrow night. Tess, are you going to be around?"

I think about how some people are visiting family over the holidays, gathering around Christmas trees and singing carols and sharing meals and exchanging gifts, and how my mom and I will be the only ones celebrating together. How last year, Hawthorne was hit with a surprise snowstorm the day before New Year's Eve, and I spent it sledding and drinking hot chocolate with Lily and Roger and other people from Grace Teen Life. Alden had been busy that day with parish stuff, and I'd felt surprisingly excited to do something as silly and joyful as going sledding with friends. I wonder what they'll all be doing this year.

"Yeah, I'll be around," I tell Chloe.

"Perfect!" she says. "I'll text you the details."

"It's at our place," Mia pipes up. "I should be the one to invite Tess."

"Too slow," Connor says and ruffles Mia's hair. Mia shrieks and ducks away, swearing to send a murderous Santa after him. "Bring your guitar," he adds to me as he heads to the door.

"Definitely," I say. I think about how my dad's guitar has traveled with me, from Bloomington to Hawthorne, kept in a garage for a year, quiet since I was in middle school. Maybe it took a while, but now it's making music again, and maybe I can too.

♩

Mom needs the car for her shift at the bar, so she offers to give me a ride to Connor and Mia's. When I lug the guitar case out, she raises an eyebrow. “Your dad’s guitar?” she asks. She’s not accusatory—if anything, her voice is a little curious and sad, like she hadn’t expected to see it and now she’s remembering all the times Dad sang and played for us, and how he’s not here anymore.

“Oh yeah,” I say, like I forgot I was carrying it. “They’re doing, like, a jam session. I’ve been messing around with it, so . . .” I look from her to the guitar and back again. “If it’s okay. I mean, I’ll take care of it—”

She puts her arm around me, and even though her voice is shaky, she says, “I know you will.”

♩

Connor and Mia live on the other side of town, not far from my grandparents’ house. It’s strange driving through their neighborhood again, seeing houses I used to pass every day. I don’t ask Mom if she feels the same, but by the way her hands grip the steering wheel, I can imagine that’s the case.

Their house is one of the more decorated ones on the street, with Christmas lights strung along the porch, a big wreath on the front door, and an inflatable snowman in the front yard, swaying gently to the tune of “Frosty the Snowman.” When I get to the front door, I hear what sounds like a ukulele version of “Carol of the Bells,” with a clamor of voices in the background, then the sounds of a cat yowling and breaking glass.

“Damn it, Bill!” someone shouts.

I tentatively knock on the front door. After some more voices, the door opens and Mia’s there, holding a tabby cat that’s half her size. “Tess is here!” she shouts inside. Then to me, she says, “Are you allergic to cats?" When I shake my head, she steps aside to let me in. "Good. And if anyone tries to tell you that Bill is anything but the most perfect fluffy baby, they're wrong."

"Bill is a demon cat sent to cause chaos and kill chipmunks," Connor calls from the other room. "Tell her what Bill's full name is."

Mia's face is dead serious when she tells me, "William Shakespurr."

She leads me into the kitchen, where Connor, Chloe, and a few other Burke siblings are gathered, assembling toppings on homemade pizzas and cleaning up broken glass on the floor. "Watch out!" Quinn says, putting her arm out like she can block me from making the wrong move. "Bill knocked over a glass."

"Because you were trying to put a Santa hat on him!" Mia exclaims, holding Bill tight against her.

"Because he looks hilarious in it," a blond girl, perched on one of the kitchen chairs, says. She looks like she's a year or two younger than Mia and is holding the Santa hat in question.

"Your face is going to look hilarious when William Shakespurr claws it off," Mia snaps. In her arms, Bill looks more resigned than murderous.

A small woman with cropped brown hair walks into the room, bearing a broom and dustpan. "All right, y'all, out of the way. Watch out for your feet. Mia, have you fed Bill yet? Because that's probably why he's grumpy, not the hat. Also, Diana, we don't have pets just so we can put hats on them and take pictures of them for the internet. Here, take the dustpan and help me with this." She's handing Diana the dustpan when she notices me standing near the kitchen door. "You're not one of mine," she says matter-of-factly, but not unpleasantly.

"No, ma'am," I tell her.

“Which friend are you?” she asks.

“That’s Tess,” Connor chimes in. “Our friend from the music room.”

“She came to see us at Pammy’s,” Chloe adds, popping a mushroom in her mouth.

“Right, right!” The woman passes the broom to Quinn and extends a hand to me. “Tracy Burke. Mother to most of this horde. They say you sing and play guitar?”

Even though I feel like I need to qualify how well I actually play the guitar, it feels silly to say “not really” when I have the case in my hand. So I nod.

“Welcome, Tess. Always glad to have another voice in the group,” she tells me and pats me on the shoulder.

♩

The Burke family home is loud and messy and chaotic, and I love it. We make individual pizzas and eat scattered around the kitchen, then gather in the living room with various instruments. I take a seat on the floor, near a Christmas tree overflowing with homemade decorations, and gingerly take my dad’s guitar out of its case. Mia has her violin, Connor his guitar, and Chloe even brought her bass, while Quinn takes a spot at an old upright piano. Diana grabs a ukulele, while her mother takes out a banjo. “My oldest two are at school,” she says. “They’re driving back tomorrow. And my husband’s working tonight. Otherwise we’d have the full orchestra.”

“At least Nathan can’t boss us around,” Mia says, tuning her violin. “Just because he’s the oldest, he acts like he’s some kind of music director.”

"And you're bossy enough for the rest of us," Quinn adds, smiling a Cheshire cat grin.

I'm a little nervous about playing in front of all these people, most of whom have known each other since birth and have been playing together about as long. But the way they stop songs to tease each other or adjust the sound relaxes me—it feels more like being in the music room than anything else. We play some songs I know, like "Here Comes the Sun" and "Wagon Wheel," and then a bunch I haven't heard, but I mostly pick up. Chloe, Connor, and Mia play the original song they've been working on, while Diana and Quinn mess around with funny versions of Disney songs. Around me, I listen to new friends making music and watch the glow of twinkling Christmas lights and feel the warmth of the radiator combined with bodies packed together in the small room, and it feels like its own song. I start strumming without even knowing what I'm doing exactly, a gentle melody that's a little melancholic, like the best kind of Christmas songs. Like crackling fire and cold air and the darkest nights at the end of the year.

I don't notice Chloe watching me. "What's that?" she asks.

I clear my throat. "Oh, I don't know," I say. "I was just messing around."

"I like it," she says. "You should make it something."

I keep strumming, my cheeks rosy with shyness and pride and hope. "Maybe I will," I say.

13.

On Christmas Eve, I check our mailbox and there's a card from Gram and Gramps. Even before I read the return address, I recognize Gramps's handwriting, cramped but tidy. The envelope is cardinal red, and for a minute I can only stare at the names—Mom's and mine, Gram's and Gramps's—wondering what we were all doing back together in such a small space.

I don't open it for a while. I take it back to the apartment and set it on the table, like it might be rigged with some trap if I try to open it. Part of me wonders if I should throw it in the trash without even reading it. What else could they have to say to me?

But they took the time to write something, to find out our new address and send it here. They could have easily called Mom's number, even if they didn't have my new one. They could have contacted her through work, either at the orthodontist's office or the bar. I imagine Gramps carefully writing down our address, whatever message is inside, and dropping the envelope into the mailbox at the end of their street, hoping that it finds its way to us. The bright envelope, the neat writing, the stamp at the top, illustrated with holly leaves—it doesn't seem like the kind of letter they'd send if they only wanted to tell me that they still hate me.

I don't want them to hate me.

Quickly, I snatch the envelope from the table and tear it open. Inside, it's a card, the front illustrated with a giant Christmas tree in the center of an old-fashioned village, everything covered in snow. Inside, the preprinted text reads: *Wishing you and yours a Merry Christmas*. Underneath, there's a short message from Gramps: *I hope you both are well. Thinking of you this Christmas season. Love, Dad/ Gramps.*

I set the card back on the table, feeling weirdly deflated. A Christmas card? Nothing else, not really—he could have easily written that message to a coworker's family, not his own daughter and granddaughter. I don't know what I'd been expecting, but I want something more and it's not there.

I tell Mom about the card as soon as she gets home from work. I assume she'll be surprised, too, but she sighs as if she'd guessed something like this would happen. "That's your grandfather," she says, tossing the card back on the table after reading it over. "God forbid he actually talk about things."

"It's weird that he'd want to reach out like this now," I say.

Mom shrugs. "It's the holidays," she says, throwing her coat onto a kitchen chair. "It makes people feel things." She takes a deep breath, as if she needs to steel herself for what she's going to say. "I didn't know if I should tell you, but your grandma called me yesterday to ask what we were doing for Christmas. She said that if you apologized to them and, I don't even know, *atoned* or something, proved how sorry you were about the whole thing, we could all be back together."

I stiffen, imagining how badly that conversation between Mom and Gram would have gone. Imagining Gram expecting us to show up and me to apologize for everything I did so things could go back to the way they were.

"What did you say?" I ask.

"I told her what we were doing was none of her business, considering she threw us out," she says, voice rising like she's mentally reliving the conversation. Then she stops, face softening as she looks at me. "Was I wrong? Would you have wanted to go back?"

I pause, remembering when we first moved in with Gram and Gramps, how I liked all of us being together, even though Gram and Mom argued all the time and even though Mom and I had to share a room. I liked cooking dinner with Gram, playing five-card draw with Gramps, going to church as a family on Sundays. I miss them, miss the feeling of having more family around after losing Dad, miss the girl they thought I was.

Except I'm not that girl anymore. I wish we could all be back together again, but not the way Gram wants.

"No," I tell Mom, and I mean it, and it feels like saying goodbye.

♩

The next day is Christmas, just Mom and me. We'd agreed not to do too much in the way of gifts, but Mom still got me some new clothes, a couple of books, and a new guitar strap. "This was a little last-minute, but I hope you like it," she says. It's purple, with delicate red roses embroidered the whole length. It looks too pretty to stay hidden in a guitar case or in our apartment.

"It's awesome," I tell her, throwing my arms around her in a big hug. "Thank you!"

Our plan is to make pancakes with syrup and berries and bacon and coffee, stay in our pajamas all morning, and watch cheesy romantic comedies all day.

We don't go to church.

It's not new, not going to church on Christmas. I've spent most of my life not going to church on Christmas or any other day. But after last year, with Gram and Gramps and Grace Teen Life and the choir and Alden, it feels strange to spend this holiday at home instead of at Grace Presbyterian.

I wish I didn't miss it. I wish I could look back at last year and tell myself it was all a mistake, that I wasn't really a youth group person and that it was never the right environment for me. But I liked it, the songs and the prayers and the holding hands and the talking to God like He was someone who would listen. I liked the people and I thought they liked me, and I felt connected to something larger and more powerful and mysterious, and all of that feels gone now. I don't know if I left it behind or if it left me, but it's a loneliness that feels like a growing empty space in the middle of my chest.

I glance at my phone—11:05 a.m. Services would have just started. I wonder what the choir will be doing as the opening song. "Joy to the World," maybe, or "He Shall Reign Forevermore."

I could see it. Not go, exactly. But they'll be livestreaming the service. They won't even know it's me joining the feed, one of a few dozen other people. It won't be the same as being there, like last year, but maybe it will help fill that empty space.

While Mom is mixing pancake batter, I pull out my phone and put in my earbuds, sitting low on the couch to make sure she doesn't catch sight of my screen. Not that I think she'd get mad at me or tell me to stop, exactly, but she'd make a whole deal out of it. Like why would I want to take part in something when people had been so awful to me? I can't explain to Mom how the reason I want to be part of this again isn't about the friends I thought I had or even Alden. It's more than that—it's part of me, deep down, and I feel ashamed to even want it, to know that God is still there and would listen to me, even now, but I do.

I take a breath and hit Join.

The services have started. Reverend Wilson is at the front of the church, greeting everyone and wishing them a merry and joyful Christmas. The pews are packed, all the usual people in attendance, plus a bunch of others who don't attend regularly but come for major holidays. The camera is positioned in the back of the church, so it's difficult to make out individual people from behind, but I spot the back of my grandparents' heads. I wonder what their plans are for today, if they're going to celebrate with any other families from church. A few rows behind them, I see Lily and her family; her older sister, Alyssa, is with them, home from college for winter break. Bri and her family are probably there, too, but I don't see them from the way the camera's angled. In the front, the choir is listening to Reverend Wilson speak, waiting for their next song. Usually, the dress code for choir is more casual than not, even on Sundays—polo shirts and sweaters, a skirt and nice shirt at best. Alden wants people to feel like themselves when they're singing. But today, everyone is dressed up, jackets and ties, dresses and sparkly cardigans. Seated at the piano, Alden is dressed in a crisp white button-down shirt and red tie, listening intently to Reverend Wilson. Even from a distance, I can see his face is beatific, eyes bright and shining and ready to celebrate with the congregation, leading them all in song.

Which makes me feel even farther away.

I don't turn off the livestream, though. Every so often, Mom calls to me, asking if I want coffee or tea, or if I'm okay with extra-crispy bacon because that's what we have. I answer with vague *uh-huh*s and *whatever you're having*, because Reverend Wilson is talking about hope during hard times, the birth of Jesus as a light in the darkness of winter.

I know I shouldn't want that kind of hope. I'm listening to Reverend Wilson talk about a baby being born, and I made the choice not to have one. But I still hear things like *faith* and *salvation* and *love*, and it resonates deep inside, like a bell ringing a low, strong note.

I both want that kind of hope back and know that I can never have it back. Because of what I did.

Because of what we did.

It's been months, and aside from running into him at the grocery store the night Gram and Gramps kicked us out, I haven't heard from Alden. He told me that we need to keep quiet and let this all blow over, but I thought maybe he'd text or something. Even if it was just to ask how I was doing or tell me it was all going to be okay.

I watch Alden, leading the choir through "Unto Us" and "O Come, All Ye Faithful," their voices clear and joyful. I imagine him after the service, hugging friends in the parish and wishing them a Merry Christmas, and celebrating with Reverend Wilson and his family. I imagine him going back to church, to youth group, week after week, as if nothing's happened, and it doesn't feel okay.

♩

The next night, after my shift at Needleman's, I go to Alden's. He lives on the second floor of a two-family house, with his entrance around the back. It's not far from the store, so I walk, hands shoved in my pockets because I forgot gloves. I don't even know if he'll be there. Maybe he'll be at the church, hosting a winter break movie night for Grace Teen Life, or out with friends. Maybe I'll go to his door and knock and everything will be dark and quiet, and I'll feel stupid, standing there alone in the cold.

But when I get there, his car's in the driveway. From the street, I see the glow of lamps and a TV screen in his living room.

I walk around to the back of the house and climb the outdoor staircase up to his door. Inside, I hear the dim sounds of a basketball game, and Alden crying, "No, come on, terrible call!" My heart stops for a second, wondering if I'll hear anyone else with him. No other voices join his. I take a breath and knock.

The sounds of the game are muted, and footsteps approach the door. When Alden sees me, his smile doesn't falter, but his face tenses. "Tess," he says. "I didn't, um . . ." He inhales and exhales deeply. "I didn't know you'd be coming by. Is there anything I can do for you?"

"I wanted to talk," I tell him. "Can I come in?"

He glances over my shoulder, like he's expecting to see the rest of Grace Teen Life hiding in the bushes. When he sees it's just me, he sighs and takes a step back from the door. "Yeah, come on in."

I've only been inside Alden's apartment a few times. Usually, we were together in his car or in his office or any random space we could find that wasn't conspicuous. He thought it would be too obvious if I kept coming back to his apartment, so we didn't go there often. But I look around at the kitchen and the living room beyond that, seeing the dishes in the drying rack, the small Christmas tree on his table, the basket of folded laundry by his couch, the UNC-Chapel Hill banner on his wall. Ever since I told him I was pregnant, he's been living his life and coming home and nothing has changed.

I don't take off my coat as I go sit down on the couch. The basketball game is still on, but muted. In the corner of my eye, I see college athletes run from one side of the court to the other.

He sits on the couch as well, but on the opposite end. "What can I help you with?" he asks. His tone is pleasant but formal, like I'm any other person from the parish who wants to talk to him about a minor problem.

"I texted you," I tell him. "A few times. You never texted back."

He sighs, rubbing his hand against the back of his neck. "Tess, we already talked about this. You know we need to have some space right now, until things calm down." Then he laughs, shaking his head. "You shouldn't even *be* here right now. I shouldn't have even let you in."

"You'd seriously close the door on me?" I ask, imagining it. What we're doing now—Alden and I sitting as far apart as possible on the couch, me still wearing my coat, with the basketball game in the background—doesn't feel all that different from being shut out entirely. "I'm having a hard time, Alden. I thought . . ." I trail off, not even knowing how to explain what I expected from him. That we'd be together? That he'd be helping me through this? It wasn't as if he'd promised me that he would tell everyone he loved me, not yet. We didn't even expect this to be an issue, until everyone found out what I did. When I finally speak again, my voice is quiet. "I didn't think I'd be doing this alone."

He finally meets my eyes. "I know," he says softly, and for a moment I think he's going to reach out and take my hand, something. But he stays where he is. "But you know how much is at stake for me, Tess. My job, my career, the rest of my life."

"I know," I murmur, rubbing my fingertips against the rough fabric of his couch. On the TV, a player from UNC shoots and misses a three-pointer.

"You have to wait a little longer," he tells me, voice soothing even when the words grate on my nerves. I have to keep going to school, seeing the *A* on my locker, hearing about how people are praying for me because I'm such an awful sinner. Because somehow, I'm the only one who did anything wrong.

"How much longer?" I ask. My tone is sharper than I expected, and I notice him wince before he composes himself. "Like a month, six months, a year, what?"

"Tess, it's not that simple—" he starts to say.

"Make it that simple." I'm getting louder now, and I grip the cuffs of my coat. "Because right now it feels pretty easy for you and not for me."

"Can you please keep your voice down?" he asks, dropping his voice like I'm going to match his volume instinctively.

"Why?" I ask, getting to my feet, like I need more height to have this argument. "Are you afraid someone's going to hear me and ask what's going on? What would you even tell them?"

He stands up and grabs me by the shoulders. For a moment I'm not sure if he's going to kiss me or shake me or turn me out of his house, and I honestly don't know what the preferable option would be at this point. Instead, he takes a breath and says, "Tess, I know this is hard. It's hard on me, too, I promise. You think I don't want to see you anymore? It's something I've been seriously wrestling with, Tess. I miss you and I hate seeing you like this. It's absolutely killing me." He relaxes his grip and takes a step back. "But you have to trust me, we need to be careful now. If we're going to be together in the future, we need to stay under the radar about this. Keep quiet."

Keep quiet. Like I haven't been anything but quiet so far. Like I'm not the one who has had to tell her mother, her grandparents, her friends that she can't tell them anything about who the father is or how she got pregnant. Even though his tone is even and gentle, I feel frustration bubble inside the pit of my stomach.

"Tess," he says again. "Please."

"Fine," I murmur, frowning at his beige carpet.

"Thank you," he breathes, palpable relief in his voice. "It's going to work out, I promise."

"I know," I tell him, even though part of me doesn't think that's ever going to be true.

♩

I walk home alone in the dark and cold. Last year, Alden would have driven me. Now he didn't even offer.

My feet keep a steady rhythm on the sidewalk, and I listen to the sound of cold air through the bare tree branches, like a lonely, wild voice.

You say wait a little longer, you have to be a little stronger, stand a little taller. Well, what about you?

It sounds like the beginning of a song.

14.

After the new year, Kevin, my shift supervisor at Needleman Family Market, informs me that they're keeping me on, if I want to continue working part-time. "You're reliable and hardworking," he tells me one day after my shift. "I have to say, I had my doubts, considering . . ." He coughs at his clipboard, and my stomach tightens. I don't want to have a conversation about my sexual history and reproductive choices with my manager under the fluorescent lights of the stockroom. Fortunately, he keeps going. "But you've proven to be a dependable employee, and we're glad to have you on board."

He puts out his hand to shake. I take it, mumbling my thanks.

Overall, people at Needleman's haven't been worse to me than the kids at school. I got some side-eyes during my first few shifts, but once people realized that all I wanted to do was stock shelves and clean up messes and be left alone, they didn't bother me. Even Bri nods politely and says hi when we pass each other in the aisles.

Which is fine. I can handle us being polite coworkers, if not friends.

Maybe we never were.

When I think about last year, all of the good things—music, my friends, my faith—feel so far away. Like everything was washed away during a storm, pulled out to sea, never to be seen again.

One day in early January, I'm labeling boxes of cereal as "buy one, get one half off" when I hear her voice in the next aisle. "Uh-huh, thanks." Her voice is light, but there's an edge to it. I pause my sticker dispenser and listen.

"So are you new?" a man's voice asks. "I would have remembered seeing you around here before."

"Um, no, I've been here a little while," Bri replies. I can practically imagine her tight-lipped smile.

"Mmm, mmm, I don't know where I've been because I would definitely remember someone like you," the man continues.

"Ha, yeah, I guess," Bri says. "Anyway, I should get back to work—"

"Oh yeah," the guy says, his tone casual. "What time do you get off? I've got a few friends coming over, and I know they'd love to meet you. I could give you a ride if you want. I've got my truck right outside."

"That's okay." Bri's voice is high, like she's trying extra hard to be pleasant. "Anyway, have fun."

I imagine Bri in the next row, trying to stack cans of peaches while some guy is trying to get her into his truck. I can practically see the hair on her arms standing on edge, feel the knot in her stomach as she tries to figure out how to get him to leave her alone without causing a scene, because he's a customer and we're supposed to be polite and welcoming to customers, because this is a family market and we want our customers to feel like they're part of the Needleman family. And even if he leaves, what if he waits outside until her shift is over and follows her to her car?

Bri hasn't really spoken to me since before Thanksgiving. She didn't defend me when everyone found out about the abortion. She had that picture of me on her phone. I shouldn't feel like I have to protect her now.

Except she was my friend once, and no one should have to feel alone and vulnerable. I can't do nothing, not anymore.

Clutching my sticker dispenser to keep my hands from shaking, I head into the next aisle.

"Excuse me," I say, my voice louder and sharper than I anticipated. The man, who's probably in his forties and is wearing a dusty Washington Nationals baseball cap, jumps a little at the sound of my voice, quickly removing his hand from the small of Bri's back. Bri is frozen by a half-empty cart of canned peaches, but there's a glimmer of desperation in her eyes when she looks at me, like *get me out of here.*

"Do you need help finding anything?" I ask, striding over to them.

The guy clears his throat, then says, "No, I've found everything I need, thank you."

"That's good," I tell him, "because I need to snag her. Her dad's here to give her a ride home, and you don't want to keep the chief of police waiting."

He blinks, eyebrows almost disappearing under his cap. "The who, now?"

"Yeah, he's real hardcore about stuff like making sure his kids are home for family dinner, not out messing around with people on a school night, you know?" My heart is beating fast under my maroon Needleman's polo, but I try to keep my face as placid as possible.

"Ugh, he's so embarrassing," Bri sighs. "And my two older brothers are worse."

"Older b-brothers?" the guy stammers, taking a step back from Bri. "Are they cops too?'

"Oh yeah, the whole family," Bri says. "We're really close too. Anyway, I'd better go. Have fun tonight with your thing."

"I'll come with you," I tell her, grabbing her arm and pulling her out of the aisle, leaving the guy looking wide-eyed and panicked.

♩

When we reach the employee break room, we burst out laughing, half out of relief and half out of nervousness. "Oh my Lord, I can't wait to tell my dad that he's got a new job as the chief of police," she tells me, collapsing onto one of the metal folding chairs. "He's gonna be real surprised when he has to give up his accounting practice for a life of fighting crime."

I laugh harder, imagining Bri's dad, with his kind eyes and collection of math-themed neckties, kicking in doors to break up drug rings. "He's probably going to be even more surprised when he finds out about your two older brothers."

"Right? The dinner table is suddenly way more crowded." She wipes a tear away with the back of her hand. "It sucks that threatening him with big tough guys is the way to get someone like that to stop, though. Like just saying 'I should get back to work' didn't help anything." She's still smiling, but it looks more fragile now.

I take a seat next to her and watch her breathing deepen as she tries to compose herself. "What time is your shift over?" I ask. When she tells me that she's done in a half hour, the same as me, I say, "I can leave with you and make sure he's not in the parking lot or something before you go."

She nods, looking down at her shoes. "That would be great."

I tell her to stay in the break room, and I'll go finish up her work and mine before we head out. "If Kevin asks, I'll tell him that you had a family situation and needed a minute."

I'm halfway out the door when I hear her say, "Thanks, Tess. Seriously."

"You'd do the same for someone else," I tell her, even though I don't know that she'd necessarily do the same for me.

♩

It's not that I think people have forgotten. I know they haven't forgotten. Every so often, I'll be in the hall between classes and a group of guys will look at me and laugh, maybe one of them suggesting that I give him a blow job in the parking lot. I've gotten used to keeping my face stoic and my eyes straight ahead, because that's what people say to do. Don't give them something to react to. Pretend you don't hear. Don't say anything. Ignore it and they'll move on.

But one late January day, I open my locker and a pamphlet falls out. On the front is a black-and-white picture of a young woman bent over, her head in her hands, long curly hair falling across her face. Along the top, the words *Center for Hope and Heart* are written in soft white letters, with a heart illustration curved out of the *O* in "hope." *Pregnant? Scared?* delicate text reads at the bottom. *We can help.* Inside, there's information about adoption and ways to be a parent, and how counselors are available to talk to young women who need help.

On the back of the pamphlet, on top of the address and hours and contact info, someone's attached a sticky note. *For the future.*

It's Lily's handwriting. I recognize it from notes she took in class, from youth group volunteer sign-up sheets, from posters we took to women's centers to try to convince people to make another choice.

It shouldn't be a surprise. Lily hasn't even spoken to me since that day in the cafeteria. But seeing this note makes my eyes prick with tears and my teeth clench. *For the future* . . . When I think of the future, I don't think of pregnancy centers or that awful, panicked feeling when I saw that second pink line. I don't even think of Alden, not in the same way I used to, the two of us dating in secret until I graduated, and we could tell everyone we'd fallen in love. When I think of the future now, it's hazier, but I know that I don't want to go through this ever again.

If Lily thinks that I'd want any of this to happen again, for it to have happened at all, then maybe she never knew me.

I almost crumple the pamphlet and hurl it in the trash, but I stop. If I throw it away, Lily will assume that I got it and maybe even kept it and considered it in case I ever decide to unexpectedly get pregnant again. I want to throw the pamphlet in her smug face, but instead I march over to her locker and slide it inside.

Down the hall, I see Roger standing by his locker, watching me with a quiet curiosity. If he wants to tell Lily that I was at her locker, he can do that. They can start a prayer chain about how ungrateful I am for their helpful advice.

I turn on my heel and walk the other way, holding my shoulders back and my head high and breathing in and out, deep from my diaphragm. In my head, I can hear the hard twang of a guitar and drums that match the beat of my footsteps.

♩

I keep playing the guitar, mostly in private and occasionally with Chloe, Connor, and Mia. By mid-February, I've got a handful of covers down, so I don't feel embarrassed playing in front of other people, and I've been working on a few original songs too. I haven't shared any of those with anyone else—not with my friends from the music room, not with my mom, no one. They feel too personal, even though I shy away from writing anything that feels too close, too specific. I have to wait until Mom's at Dr. Matten's office or at the bar to practice them, like I'm afraid she'll ask about them. Even hearing my own voice, singing the words I wrote makes me feel too exposed.

I want to say I'm doing just fine, I want to say I've never thought about what might have been, except when I see you standing there and it all washes over me again.

But I keep doing it. I keep hearing new melodies, one chord following another, and new lyrics floating around my head like bees around sweet tea. It's scary and exciting and I'm afraid for anyone else to hear me, but I don't stop doing it. Everything that's going on, everything I'm still feeling—the only way I can process any of it is through songs, other people's and my own.

I remember being at Pammy's and feeling like all the songs were for me. I imagine standing on that stage, playing and singing and giving that feeling back to someone listening.

So I do it. I sign up for an open mic night.

Mia sends me the info on how to do it. "You need to be at a computer or phone or whatever *exactly* when the sign-up list opens. The good time slots fill up so fast. You don't want your first time playing to be the very first or the very last." I follow her instructions to the letter, partly because I trust her and partly because I know that if I mess up, she'll never let me live it down. I enter my name and contact info and don't let myself hesitate before hitting Submit.

I get the confirmation email almost immediately: *You're on the list!* it reads, along with info on when to arrive and what to bring with me and suggestions for how to prepare. I text Mia, telling her I'm booked in my preferred time slot and thanking her for her help.

She replies: Good! Now go practice.

♩

I practice every free minute I have before the open mic night. When I'm at school or at work or brushing my teeth, I repeat the lyrics in my head while my fingers twitch with the memory of the chords. Even though Mia definitely side-eyed me for it, I'm only going to be playing covers. Nothing I've been working on feels even close to ready for public performance. And besides, I'm not looking to sign a record deal or anything—all I want is to give this a try.

Mom wants to come, but she's working that night. "Let me see if I can find someone to cover my shift," she tells me. "I bet Connie will swap with me—she's got Saturday night, and that's the UVA-Duke game. There's no way she's going to want to deal with that crowd."

"Mom, it's fine," I tell her. "I'll feel more nervous if you're in the audience. Strangers don't have any expectations."

"Strangers also don't cheer enthusiastically no matter what," she points out.

I imagine my mom in the audience, applauding loudly and aggressively after I fumble my way through the set and glaring at anyone with less than her level of enthusiasm. Not exactly the vibe I want to go for during my first solo performance. "Chloe and Connor and Mia will be there, so I won't be all sad and alone. I bet Chloe will cheer enthusiastically no matter what. Mia will tell me everything I need to work on, but that's Mia."

She frowns but doesn't try to argue. "If you're sure . . . ," she says.

"I'm positive," I assure her.

By the time I get to Pammy's, I'm less sure. Even though I've been there a few times since my friends first performed and it's a slightly slower night than usual, the room feels louder and more crowded, and the air feels thicker, making it harder to breathe. I watch the first couple of performers—a bearded guy with a keyboard and a trio playing bluegrass—and feel as though I'm shrinking smaller and smaller in my seat, like Alice in Wonderland. When a server drops a glass and it shatters, I visibly jump.

"Nervous?" Chloe asks gently.

"Me? No, I'm great. I'm cool. I'm very ready to do this," I say, voice tight and shoulders tense. I try to take a sip of water and end up spilling half of it down my shirt.

"Oh yeah, you seem really chill," Connor deadpans.

"Did you practice?" Mia asks. When I nod and tell her that it's basically all I've been doing, she shrugs. "Then you'll be fine."

I wish it was that simple. Even though I've practiced the songs over and over until I can practically play them in my sleep, the idea of standing up in front of all these people, people I don't even know and who don't care about me and probably only came to hear someone mess up—and I've messed up so much lately—it's so much harder than I thought it would be, just to sit here and wait for my name to be called.

Finally, they call my name.

Even though I'm pretty sure my legs are going to give out on me, I manage to stand and make my way to the stage. I barely hear Chloe shout, "Go, Tess!" as I take my spot in front of the mic. The lights are brighter than I anticipated, and I have to squint at first. From the stage, it's hard to make out individual faces.

"Hi, everybody," I murmur, worried that I'm either going to be too quiet or too loud. "I'm Tess Pine. I'm going to play a few songs for y'all tonight." Oh my gosh, of course I'm going to play a few songs, like everyone else here for open mic night. Someone in the crowd coughs. "Okay, thank you. I'm gonna do it."

In all the years I've been singing, I realize this is the first time I've ever been in front of an audience all alone. No choir to sing along with me, not even to back me up when I had a solo, not even someone playing accompaniment. Memories of singing along with Alden rush over me, and suddenly I feel so alone and foolish and vulnerable. What am I even doing, pretending like I have anything in me that anyone else would want to hear?

Except I'm already here and everyone's looking at me and waiting for me to start. I take a breath. *Focus, Tess*, I tell myself. *One chord at a time.* And then, I send up a small prayer: *Please, God, help me through this.*

I fumble my way through my set. My first song, "Wildflowers" by Tom Petty, is definitely the shakiest. It's supposed to be sweet and heartfelt and a little wild, but I'm stiff and my voice sounds shallow. I mess up a few times on the guitar and it feels like each missed note echoes through the room. "Walkin' After Midnight" is a little better—I don't mess up too much on the guitar, but the whole time I'm thinking, *Seriously, Tess, who the hell tries to outdo Patsy Cline their first time out?!* The last one I do is "Middle Cyclone" by Neko Case, and it's gentle and melancholy and I find my way into the music. For a moment, everything slows down. I hear the sound of my own voice and my heartbeat steadies. I feel less small and more solid, and I hope someone out in the audience feels that too.

"Thank you," I say into the microphone, and I mean it.

When I find my way back to my table, my friends are smiling encouragingly. "You did a really good job!" Chloe says as I sit down.

"You were kind of shaky," Mia admits. "Especially in the first half."

"But that was your first time," Chloe counters. "And you never have to perform for the first time ever again!"

I'm so relieved to hear that, I laugh out loud.

♩

Later, when I'm driving home, I send up another prayer. *Dear God, it's Tess. I know it's not the same as singing in the church choir, but thank you for being with me tonight anyway.* On the radio, a young country star sings about heartbreak and missing what he had, and I realize that this is what I miss—those moments when I felt like I had faith in something greater than me, that God was listening even when I felt small and foolish and quiet. I miss it more than I want to admit. Joining Grace Teen Life and the church choir wasn't about finding friends and a place to go on weeknights. It felt like I was discovering a part of myself, and now that was gone. *I miss you*, I add to the end of my prayer, not even knowing what that means exactly, but maybe whoever's listening does.

15.

"No. Not her."

It's a warm, rainy afternoon in mid-February, and I'm at Needleman's, replacing a coworker at checkout, when I hear a customer speak up. Her voice is sharp and sour, and when I look over, I see the next woman in line shaking her head. She's a little older than my mom, with short blond hair and a pink-and-white button-down shirt under a yellow raincoat, and she's frowning at me. My stomach clenches and I freeze, halfway to replacing the register tray.

If my coworker Cheyenne notices the woman's tone, she doesn't show it. "Excuse me, ma'am?" she asks as pleasantly as possible.

The woman keeps shaking her head, pointing at me now. "I don't want this one to check me out."

"I'm going on my break," Cheyenne tells her smoothly, "but Tess'll get you checked out real fast." She pats me on the shoulder and rushes off to her smoke break before the woman can argue again.

The woman, however, isn't satisfied by Cheyenne's assertion. Now, instead of shaking her head, she's glaring at me and pointing with her index finger like she wants to use it to poke a hole right through my chest. "I know you," she practically spits. "I know you from Grace Presbyterian. You're the one who had the abortion." Her voice drops to a whisper when she says the word, but her eyes stay fixed on me, cold and hard.

"Um," I murmur. "Ma'am, if you'll just put the rest of your items on the belt—"

"You got yourself in trouble and took it out on that innocent life," she continues as if she didn't hear me. "Well, you listen to me. All life is precious, and God knows what you did."

Blood is thumping in my veins and in my ears and all I can do is stare back at her. "I know," I tell her, because I want this all to be over. Because it's more complicated than that, and I don't want to argue with a woman in the Needleman Family Market checkout line about it or tell her anything about what happened. My face is hot and my eyes sting, and around me people have stopped to watch us. All I want to do is escape, but I feel frozen in front of my register.

Then I hear another voice: "Is there a problem here?"

Bri is suddenly standing beside me, voice calm and face placid. I stay still, not sure if I should even breathe.

The woman nods. "Yes, I want you to replace her. I don't want her touching my things. I want a different checkout girl."

"Well, I'm sorry, ma'am, but no one is going to replace her," Bri says evenly, mouth set in a determined line. "Tess is perfectly capable of getting you checked out. And maybe you should think about your own sins before you start casting stones around here."

The woman bristles. "Excuse me. I don't like your tone, miss," she hisses. "I want to speak to your manager."

"He's not available right now," Bri tells her, even though I know that Kevin's in the back, going over the orders for the week. She puts her hand on my back, as if she can help me stand a little straighter. "If you're not comfortable with my friend here, then I'm afraid I'm going to have to ask you to leave."

The woman glares at both of us for a moment before muttering a *humph* of offense, slamming her basket onto the belt, and clutching her purse to her chest. "I'll be writing a very stern letter," she announces before she marches toward the exit.

In the checkout lines around us, coworkers turn back to their registers and customers pretend to focus on their items.

"You okay?" Bri asks me quietly.

Even though my heart is still beating fast and my cheeks are still flushed, I nod. "Yeah. Yeah, I'm good," I tell her, placing my cash drawer down slowly.

She gives me a half smile and heads back to produce, where she'd been arranging lemons in a neat pile. *My friend*, she'd said. Maybe that was still true after all.

♩

Last year, Grace Teen Life people arranged a pro-life protest at a women's clinic a few towns over, near a local college. It was the first week of February, early into the college's spring semester but weeks away from spring break, so students were on campus. When I thought of protests, I thought of people marching in the streets, crowds and speakers, maybe the cops trying to break it up, but Lily assured me it wouldn't be that intense.

"We're not going to, like, get arrested or anything. It's mostly going to be us, plus a few other people from church," she'd said. "And we don't go and call people murderers or anything. We'll stand on the sidewalk with some signs and pamphlets and try to help people." She had given me one of the pamphlets, which had a picture of a baby in utero on the front that looked as if it was floating in space. I scanned through paragraphs about how even in the very early stages, babies feel pain, how the procedure can be dangerous for the mother, and how after, the mother is at greater risk for depression and self-harm. I didn't ask Lily about where the pamphlets or the information inside had come from.

We're trying to help people, I told myself as I signed up.

I didn't tell Mom about the protest. When I mentioned I was going to an event with Grace Teen Life that weekend, all I said was that it was a volunteer thing. I'd done other volunteer stuff with the group before—bake sales to raise money for retreats and mission trips, Christmas carols at the senior center, and cleaning up a local park—so it wasn't a surprise to her that I was busy with something like that. But I got the feeling that protesting at an abortion clinic might not be something she was cool with, so I left that part out to avoid a potential fight.

We met early in the Grace Presbyterian parking lot on a Saturday morning. Alden brought coffee and donuts, and we ate them while he organized the group into various cars.

Before we left, Alden gathered everyone up for a prayer. "Lord, we ask for your courage today as we try to change hearts and minds and save innocent lives. We know that, as you laid down your life for us, every single life is precious from the moment of conception. Please help us take your strength and your love into our work today. In Jesus's name, amen." His voice was solemn but hopeful. I stood beside him in our prayer circle, and when the rest of us echoed "Amen," he caressed the back of my hand with his thumb.

We caravanned to the clinic, about an hour away, arriving just before it opened for the day. It was a plain white building on a busy but unassuming street—a tire shop across from it and a Starbucks a block away. A white sign outside read PRETERM WOMEN'S HEALTH SERVICES in black letters.

We parked along the street and gathered on the sidewalk, several yards away from the building. Paige passed out signs she and other Grace Teen Life people had made that week. They read A LIFE IS NOT A CHOICE and STOP ABORTION NOW and CHOOSE LOVE, CHOOSE LIFE.

It all sounded good and kind and uplifting. We were there to help people make a different choice. To choose love and life.

But it felt strange to see women pull into the parking lot of the clinic and duck their heads to avoid looking at us. Some of them looked like they were students at the local college, others like they could have been my mom's age. I wondered if they were doctors or nurses or receptionists, or patients. If they were coming here today because they felt like they didn't have any other choice, or maybe they were afraid of what their lives would be like otherwise. If they had anyone at home who would help them afterward. Looking at their faces, their hair, the clothes they wore, they could have been anyone.

"God loves you and your baby!" Lily called to them, her voice so kind that she might as well have been talking to someone from church.

"Please, you don't have to do this. Turn to Jesus," Alden pleaded. "Make that step. We can help you."

"Your baby is a blessing, not a choice," I shouted, wanting to sound sure of myself. Wanting to help those women the way Lily had talked about.

Even though we said things that sounded supportive and hopeful, no one came over to us for more information or to ask questions or to tell us that they'd changed their mind and wouldn't be going through with a procedure that day. After a few hours, we packed up the signs and drove back to Hawthorne.

I rode in Alden's car, sitting in the passenger seat. A few other Grace Teen Life people—a couple of freshmen and a junior—were in back, watching funny videos on one of their phones. When Alden asked what I thought about my first pro-life protest, I admitted, "It didn't seem like we really did anything. No one changed their minds."

He nodded thoughtfully. "That's true. But that doesn't mean it was a waste of time. Maybe some of the people we saw were only there to get a preliminary checkup or other information. They could go home, think about what we said, and make a different choice. Someone could really be wrestling with this right now, because of you."

He reached over and patted my upper thigh before anyone in the back seat could look up from their phone.

"Maybe," I said, but I was thinking of those women from the parking lot. I imagined them going home and putting away groceries and changing the sheets on their beds and texting their moms and living lives that I didn't really know at all.

♩

By the end of my shift, the rain has stopped and the skies are a deep expanse of stars. Mom texted me to say that things are busy at the bar, so she'll be late picking me up. No worries. Get those tips! I text back, even though I'm ready for this evening to be over.

I slide my phone back into the back pocket of my jeans and hug my arms around my chest, thinking about the woman from earlier. I didn't recognize her from Grace Presbyterian, but she obviously recognized me. Maybe she's friends with Gram and Gramps. I haven't seen my grandparents since they threw us out, but I can imagine Gram hearing similar things from her friends in Bible study or small group. *That's not the Tess I knew,* Gram would tell them. *I don't know what happened to her. I never should have brought her and her mother into my home.*

It stings to think about. I wish I could think *good riddance* and try to move on, like Mom, but I can't. I remember saying grace at dinner together, and Gram asking about my day while she helped to fold my laundry, Gramps singing along to oldies while he gave me a ride to choir practice. I wish I didn't miss all of it, but I do, and I know I'll never be able to tell them.

"Tess?" Bri sees me while she's leaving Needleman's for the evening. "Are you waiting for someone?"

"My mom," I tell her. "She's running a little late."

She pauses for a second, holding the strap of her backpack before she asks, "Do you want a ride?"

♩

I haven't driven with Bri since she first got her license in August. She still drives carefully, going exactly the speed limit and checking both ways multiple times before going through a stop sign, even though there's barely any traffic out on the road now. Her phone is connected to the car's speaker system, playing an upbeat Christian rock song about how God's love makes us flawless in spite of everything.

"Thank you," I tell her. "For helping me today."

She doesn't respond at first or even look at me, staring through the windshield at the damp roads. Her lips are pressed together, and her eyebrows knit in thought. Finally, she says, "She shouldn't have said that to you," so softly that I'm not sure if she's speaking to me or to herself.

"A lot of people think that," I mutter, imagining the woman and Gram and other people at church, gathered together and talking about what a terrible person I am.

Bri glances at me for a split second before turning her attention back to the road. "It's not everyone," she tells me. "I don't think everyone thinks that."

"What do you think?" I ask tentatively, because even though I'm afraid of her response, I genuinely want to know.

She's quiet for another moment, while in the background a guy sings about how God knows all the stars in the heavens by name. "I don't know, Tess—it was like all of a sudden we found out what happened, and we didn't even know you were having sex, much less pregnant, much less . . . you know. It was just like a *shock*, you know? Like at first, I didn't even believe it. You never talked about stuff like that. It wasn't like you were dating someone and, you know, things happened. Because things happen to people in Hawthorne, youth group included, even though they don't talk about it. But you didn't tell anyone you were dating someone. You haven't even told people who the guy is."

She pauses, like I might fill in the gap for her. And I want to—Bri defended me today and it's been months and I haven't told anyone. Maybe Bri would understand, even keep my secret. But she's still going to church and youth group, and I can't risk this getting out. Alden said it would seriously destroy his career and his life. No matter what happens between us, even if we can never go back to the way things were, I can't do that to him. He's a good guy—he doesn't deserve that.

All I can do is murmur "I can't."

She doesn't try to argue with me about it. Instead, she pulls the car into the laundromat parking lot and parks in one of the empty spaces. The laundromat glows, stark, fluorescent light reflecting off the white tables and machines.

"I don't know what I would have done," Bri tells me. "I don't know if I would have made the same decision or not. But I don't think you're a bad person." She offers a small smile. "I miss you, Tess."

I feel a lump in my throat, even as I smile back. "I miss you, too, Bri."

16.

That Sunday, I decide to go back to church.

It's been months since the last time I was at Grace Presbyterian, a little less than a week before the procedure. I had sung in the choir and prayed along with everyone and tried to listen to the sermon, but I spent the whole time feeling like I was made of glass, fragile and transparent. If Alden felt the same, he never showed it—he kept singing and praying as if nothing was wrong.

But now I keep thinking about what Bri told me: *I don't think you're a bad person.*

I don't know what kind of person I am, but I also don't think I should feel like I can't go back to church.

I text Bri from my new number: Hey, it's Tess. Maybe I could join you for church on Sunday? I hit Send before I can second-guess myself, and for a moment, I feel nauseous with anxiety, wondering if I made a mistake. But then Bri texts back: Definitely! You can sit with my family.

I stare at my phone, smiling to myself, happy that I'll have somewhere to sit, people to sit with. In my head, I repeat the lyrics from

"Amazing Grace": *'Tis grace has brought me safe thus far / and grace will lead me home.*

When I tell her about my plans for Sunday morning, Mom tries to convince me to stay home. "Those people were so awful to you. Why would you want to put yourself back there?" It's hard to explain it to her, but it's not about them. It's about finding myself again, and part of that is faith, even if it's hard for me to know what that means right now.

"Besides," I say, "I'm going to be with Bri and her family."

Mom seems unmoved. After a disgruntled exhalation, she relents. "Fine. But I'm coming with you."

When we get to Grace Presbyterian that Sunday, my stomach is a knot of anxiety. But I know if I don't go in now, I'll never work up the courage again. In the parking lot, I recognize other cars—Bri's family's sedan, Lily's mom's minivan, Gram and Gramps's Buick. I imagine them inside, going to church like any other Sunday, while here I am, trying to psych myself up in the passenger seat.

"You got this," Mom tells me. She puts her hand on my back as we head into the building.

Inside, nothing has changed since I was here months ago, since I used to come every Sunday for services and on Wednesdays for choir practice. The way the light filters through the tall windows, how the sound of the piano carries to the back of the room, the air smelling faintly of old paper—I feel both at home and on edge.

I glance at the crowd, trying to spot my grandparents in their usual pew. A few rows from the back, Bri turns to see me. She gives me a little wave, moving over in the pew to make room for my mom and me.

"You made it," she whispers when we sit down.

"Somehow," I say, still tense, as though I'm waiting for an alarm to go off. But Bri's mom leans over to smile at me, too, and reaches out to squeeze my shoulder. It's been months since I've seen her, and she looks good—healthy. Her cheeks are pinker than the last time I saw her after her surgery, and she's gained some weight.

Beside me, Mom seems to relax a little, seeing Bri's and her mom's welcoming reactions. But I notice her eyes keep darting left and right, as if she's expecting someone from the congregation to stand up and try to physically throw us out.

No one does that. Instead, Reverend Wilson talks about living beyond the moment and obeying God's word even when it seems difficult. It's hard to see him from where I'm seated, but at the front of the church, I can hear Alden and the rest of the choir. They sing "Thy Word" and "Christ Is Mine Forevermore," and I feel a strange out-of-body experience listening to their voices mingling without mine. I should be up there with them. If only one or two things had happened differently, I would have been there, singing along and looking out at the congregation and helping them feel God's love through song and feeling right about my place in the world. Now, sitting beside Bri and Mom in our pew near the back of the room, I murmur the lyrics, my voice thin and shaky.

I make it through the service.

While other people stay behind to mingle, Mom and I head to the door as quickly as possible. I know that Mom wants to avoid Gram and Gramps, and even though I doubt that they'd start something in church, in front of Reverend Wilson, I don't want to chance it, either.

"Laura, Tess," I hear someone say. It's Dr. Matten, mom's boss from the orthodontist's office. She's a tall, slender woman with deep brown skin and close-cropped hair. Her voice is pleasant, if a little surprised. "I haven't seen you here in a while."

"We thought we'd give it another try," Mom says, trying to keep her voice bright while laying a protective hand on my shoulder.

Dr. Matten smiles warmly. “Well, I’m glad you’re here,” she says. “Take care, and I’ll see you tomorrow morning.”

I breathe an internal sigh of relief. Even though I noticed people eyeing me suspiciously during the service, no one says I should leave. Maybe Bri was right. Maybe there are some people who don’t think I’m a bad person, who wonder if there’s more to the story than whatever they heard through the prayer phone tree.

On the way out, I see Lily from a distance with her family. She’s laughing about something with her mom when we make eye contact. My stomach drops, and I feel the blood rush from my head, remembering that day in the cafeteria and wondering if she’s going to call me out again here. But she looks more confused than angry, blinking at me with her eyebrows knit together. I’m too far away to hear, but I can read her lips when she opens her mouth to speak: *Tess?*

Her mom looks over as well, smile twisting into a concerned frown. I hurry away before either of them can tell me to leave.

♩

I don’t see Lily again until a few days later. That morning, while I’m pouring myself a bowl of cereal, I get a text from her. Tess, it’s Lily. I got your new number from Bri.

When I texted Bri on Sunday, I hadn’t expected her to share my number with anyone else. For a moment, I stare at my phone, at that familiar number, wondering if everything actually has blown over, just like Alden said it would.

Meet me in the auditorium after last period? she asks.

Why? I text back.

Please, it’s important, she responds.

I take a bite of cereal and chew slowly. The way she looked at me at church on Sunday, it wasn't with hatred or anger. Maybe Bri said something to her. I imagine us all together again, going to Sunshine Sundaes for milk shakes this summer and getting our hair and makeup done together for junior prom and maybe even going to the Ignite retreat together next fall. It fills me with hope and longing, and I text her back: Okay.

The rest of the day, I feel like my nerves are raw wires, sparking at the slightest provocation. In French, Madame Johnson asks me to translate a sentence about shopping at a fish market, and I practically jump out of my seat when she calls my name.

After the last bell, I walk stiffly to the auditorium. *If she yells at you or calls you a murderer, you can leave*, I remind myself. *But maybe things will be different.*

When I open the door, Lily is already there, but she's not alone. With her are Roger, Paige, and a few other Grace Teen Life people. They're gathered near the stage and turn to me when they hear the door open.

I freeze in place. "What's going on?" I ask.

"Tess, you came," Lily says, all relief.

"Why are all of you here?" I ask, looking at the faces of people I used to think were my friends. *Why didn't Lily tell me it was going to be a group of them when she texted me?* Probably because she knew that I wouldn't have shown up. I take a small step backward.

"It's because we care about you, Tess," Roger tries to reassure me, taking a step forward. His hands are folded together like he's about to make a speech.

"We're not here to shame you or judge you. We want to help you," Lily adds. Her voice is calm, and her face is friendly, if a little sad. "Please, will you stay? Give us five minutes—I promise, we're all coming to this from a place to help you and support you, and if you don't want to hear what we're saying, you can leave."

Their faces are open and hopeful, and I feel foolish rushing out now. I slowly walk toward them. "Five minutes," I say.

Lily reaches out a hand to me as the rest of the group members grasp each other's hands in prayer. "Dear Lord, thank you for bringing us together today. We strive to bring your grace and love into our conversation, and to help our friend, your daughter Tess Pine, during this dark time. In Jesus's name, amen."

"Amen," the others repeat. It's so familiar, I find myself echoing along with them.

Lily turns to me, hands pressed together in front of her mouth. After a moment, she says, "Tess, I can only assume that these last few months haven't been easy for you. And I want to apologize for that. I was not the friend I should have been. I felt confused and betrayed and I lashed out, and that was my sin. I sinned against you, and I sinned against God. I'm sorry, and I hope you can forgive me."

It's what I wanted to hear, but it sounds slightly distorted, like playing a familiar tune with one of the notes gone flat. "Um, thank you," I murmur.

She smiles shyly. "When I saw you at church the other day, I had a realization. I shouldn't be waiting for you to find your way back to the light and to Jesus's love and forgiveness. I, well, we"—she gestures to the others—"need to be here for you. To bear witness and help you find your path to redemption."

I stiffen, looking from face to placid face. "Excuse me?"

If Lily notices my hesitation, she doesn't respond. Instead, she reaches into her backpack and pulls out her Bible, sticky notes peeking out of several spots. She opens to a page and reads, "Proverbs 28:13 says, 'Whoever conceals their sins does not prosper, but the one who confesses and renounces them finds mercy.' " When she closes the book, she looks at me with such hope and excitement that my mouth drops open a little in shock. "It's right there—no matter what you do, no matter what your sin, if you confess and come to God with your open heart and admit that what you did was wrong, you can find forgiveness. You don't have to be alone. You can repent and find God's love again."

She reaches out to take my hand, but I pull away from her. After months of ignoring me and treating me like an outcast, she thinks she can talk about redemption and forgiveness? About not being alone? Suddenly I feel both cold and hot at the same time, my fists clenched at my sides. "What if I don't want to repent?" I say.

"Tess," she sighs. "I saw you at church the other day. You obviously want to have a relationship with God."

"Yeah, but that doesn't mean I would change what I did," I say, and as I'm saying the words, I realize it's true. I want to reconnect with the faith I had, to talk to God again and be a part of something larger than myself. And I don't know if what I did was right or wrong, exactly. But that doesn't mean I would go back and make a different decision. Even if my relationship with Alden hadn't been a secret, even if he'd been okay with everyone finding out, I still wouldn't have been ready to have a baby, to carry it for nine months and then be a mother. Maybe one day, but not now, not even if things had been different between Alden and me.

Roger cocks his head at me, like he doubts I know what I'm saying. "Come on, Tess. You have to know that what you did was wrong."

Lily holds up a hand toward him. "We're not here to judge. We're here to help Tess find her way back to God."

"I don't need you for that," I snap, feeling the anger smolder right in my diaphragm. "How can you even talk to me about this? You have no idea what I was dealing with." My voice is rising, bouncing off the walls of the auditorium as if this was a concert, and my fists are still clenched like I'm ready for a fight. "And you know what, maybe if you'd come to me with all of this talk about *mercy* that first day, I probably would have agreed with you. But I'm finding my own way back, and I don't need any of you to pretend to help me and make yourselves feel better."

Lily winces a little, like I actually hit her. "Hey, that's not fair."

"Oh, it's not fair?" I spit back. "Is it fair that you confronted me about this in the cafeteria? Or that I had to get a new phone because I got a bunch of anonymous texts calling me a slut and baby murderer?"

She pauses in confusion. "What? Tess, I didn't know anything about that."

"What about the big red *A* on my locker?" I snap. "It's hard to not know about that. Maybe you were even the one who sent the picture around in the first place."

"I don't know who did any of that, I swear," Lily says and holds up her hands in defense. "All I want to do is help."

"Oh yeah? Like putting that pamphlet for the crisis pregnancy center in my locker? That was really helpful." Her forehead furrows, like she has no idea what I'm talking about, and I want to knock the sticky notes out of her Bible. "Oh, come on, don't lie to me. I saw your note. I know your handwriting, Lily."

"Tess, I don't know what you're talking about. I swear, I don't," she tries to argue.

Roger takes a step forward, like he can physically interrupt our argument. His voice is smooth and calm as he says, "Whatever happened, the point is that we're trying to bring you back to Jesus."

But Lily ignores Roger's petition. Her eyes are focused on me as she continues. "Tess, can we please talk about this—"

The door opens, and Bri rushes into the room. I stare at her hard as she makes her way toward us. “Lily, stop,” she says.

I turn toward Bri, remembering how she’d given Lily my new phone number. She’d told me she didn’t think I was a bad person, and yet I was still someone who needed intervention to get back to God instead of actual compassion and support. “Did you know about this?” I ask.

“Tess, I had no idea, seriously,” she says, and I want to believe it’s true.

But it doesn’t matter, because whether or not Bri was a part of it, I’m done. “Whatever. Pray for yourselves and leave me out of it,” I tell them, turning on my heel and marching out of the auditorium before anyone can stop me.

17.

The next day, at my shift at Needleman's, Bri catches me in the break room. "Tess, can we talk?" she asks. Her voice is hopeful, if hesitant, and she eyes the two other coworkers who are on their break, scanning their phones. Even though they don't seem to notice us, she adds, "Maybe in private?"

I remember Lily asking the same thing, if we could talk, and stiffen at the memory of how that turned out. "I don't think there's anything to talk about," I say.

Bri's right behind me when I march out of the break room, toward the snack food aisle, where I'm supposed to be restocking eighty different kinds of pretzels. "I want you to know I'm sorry," Bri says. "Really, I understand if you don't want to speak to me again. But I'm so sorry, and I never thought Lily would do anything like that."

I hadn't either. Even with the pregnancy center pamphlet, and her being so mad at me that day in the cafeteria, I thought she'd genuinely wanted to reach out now. I don't turn to look at Bri, but I feel myself soften a little, because maybe I made the same mistake. A small part of me worries that I'm going to do the same with Bri—trust that she wants to be my friend and then get hurt again. But Bri's here now, trying to apologize and make things right. Maybe that's something.

I stop in the middle of the snack food aisle, next to the pallet of pretzels ready to be shelved. Bri pauses a few feet away. When I start to shelve the bags, she helps without me asking her to.

After a moment, I say, "What did you think she was going to do?"

Bri shrugs. "I seriously thought she just wanted to talk to you. Maybe apologize for how things have been or at least listen to your side of things. That's why I gave her your new number. I only heard about it because Kayla told me that she and some other people were going to try to help you—that's the way she said it." She pauses, like she's not sure if she should continue, before adding, "I think Lily thought that's what it was—her trying to help."

I remember standing in the auditorium, hearing people who were supposed to be my friends judge the choice I'd made without knowing anything about how it happened. Without even asking me how I felt about any of it. "It wasn't helping," I snap.

"I know," Bri assures me, her voice soft and contrite, even though she had made an honest mistake by sharing my number with Lily. She hadn't been the one trying to redeem me. I think of being at church with Bri and her family, feeling welcome again, at least in a small way. Maybe Lily should have tried that approach instead.

"Thank you," I say to Bri, and I'm not sure if I mean for her apology or for inviting me to sit with her at church or for helping me restock pretzels. Maybe all of it.

Bri shakes her head and says, "Thanks for hearing me out." But her voice is tense, and I know she's thinking of something else.

Even though I'm afraid of what she might say, I ask, "What is it?"

An older man holding a half-filled basket turns the corner of the aisle and sees us standing there. “Where do y’all keep the pancake mix?” he calls.

“Aisle seven,” I shout back without taking my eyes off Bri. The man disappears in search of pancake mix, and for a second I’m afraid that Bri will shake her head again and tell me it was nothing.

But she doesn’t pretend it’s nothing. Instead, she inhales and exhales deeply, like she’s trying to find the right way to say it. “Yesterday, in the auditorium, you told Lily something about texts and a pamphlet with her handwriting?” She doesn’t have to wait for me to reply. “That people had been harassing you? And your locker?”

I go very still. “Yes,” I say carefully.

“Lily didn’t know anything about that,” Bri insists. “And she was really confused about how you’d gotten anything like that with her handwriting on it. She wanted to know who would do something like that, who would send you texts and stuff and who sent the photo to everyone. So Lily asked around, and she kind of figured out who it was.” She pauses and glances over at me before returning her gaze to the bag of pretzels in her hand. “It was Roger.”

I feel like I’ve been dunked in ice water. Roger, who asked me to the Snow Ball? Who claimed that he wanted to help me get back on the right path? Who wanted me to tell him who the father was so he could help him too? *Murderer, slut, baby killer.* I feel like I can see those texts all over again, making me sick to my stomach. I always thought Roger was a little self-righteous and judgmental, but I didn’t think he’d be vindictive enough to organize something like this.

“I can stop,” Bri assures me, holding a bag of honey-mustard-flavored pretzels like it’s a bomb that might go off if she moves wrong. “If you don’t want to know any more.”

I remember how, after the procedure, I wanted everything to go back to normal. To pretend nothing ever happened. I know different now. "I want to know."

Bri tells me how Roger found out about me being at the clinic from his cousin, who was among the protesters that day, and to him it felt like it was a personal attack. He'd asked me to the Snow Ball, been nice to me, and then he found out that not only was I into someone else, I was having sex with them. Why hadn't I picked Roger, who was a nice guy and who wouldn't have pressured me that way? Like he was entitled to me because he'd been nice and I'd been new. But attacking me in person wasn't Christlike, so he decided to spread the word about what I'd done and text me about what a terrible person I was, all while pretending that this was a way of guiding me back to the "right path."

"But I know his cell number," I say. "And I got the texts from a bunch of numbers."

"Apparently he found some app that can disguise your number," Bri explains, "so it could look like you were getting them from a bunch of different people instead of him. Plus, he convinced a few other people to do it too. Then, once word got around, things kind of took off from there."

I shake my head, like there's too much conflicting information rattling around inside. "But what about the pregnancy center pamphlet? That definitely had a sticky note from Lily on it."

Bri sets down the bag of pretzels on the shelf and picks up another one. "That sticky note was from something totally unrelated—it was from like a youth-group-fundraiser thing. Lily had organized some flyers and had a bunch to save for the future, and I guess Roger just snagged one of the notes without her noticing."

A small part of me is grateful that Lily hadn't been involved. But I imagine Roger, singing in the church choir and leading discussions in small group and acting like he's so godly, trying to hurt me when I was already hurting. He was probably the one who spray-painted my locker too.

"Maybe I shouldn't have told you," Bri says.

But I shake my head. "No. You should have," I insist. Even if I don't know what I'm going to do about it, at least now I know. Because Roger can walk around pretending he's being a good person and acting like he wants to help redeem me, when really, he's just another sinner.

♩

I keep going to church. I sit with Mom and Bri and her family, and I pray and sing along, if a little quieter than before. Even if some of my former friends from youth group want to redeem me, even if their parents think I'm a bad influence and don't deserve to be there, even if Gram refuses to look at me whenever I'm within a ten-foot radius, I show up every Sunday. It feels strangely better than staying home—people can think I'm a sinner, and maybe I am, but when I'm at Grace Presbyterian, I feel like I'm still a part of something bigger than myself. I deserve to be there too.

Just before I turn seventeen, at the end of March, I'm leaving church when I see a note under the windshield wiper of our car.

Mom notices it, too, and moves to grab it before I can. She must assume that it's some kind of hateful message and wants to stop me from seeing it, but I'm a second faster and snatch it.

Except when I read it, it's not a hateful message telling me what an awful person I am.

It's from Gramps.

Dear Tess, it reads. *I would like to take you out for your birthday. Please call me at work to discuss.*

Mom's deeply suspicious about the offer. "Oh no," she says on the drive home. "My parents just want to attack you again. Or maybe it'll be like your so-called friends from church who tricked you into meeting up with them so they could save you from eternal damnation, or whatever the hell they wanted." A car takes a second too long at a light and she honks the horn at them.

"Then why did Gramps sneak this note to me?" I ask. It feels different than the Christmas card he sent months ago—that had been a one-way communication, maybe something to make himself feel better. This feels like him actually reaching out. "They could have come up to me after the service," I say, turning the note over and back again to see the familiar script. "And it doesn't sound like he wants Gram to know."

Mom presses her lips together before muttering, "True."

I hold the note gently in my hands, like it's a bird that might fly away if I move too quickly. I remember Gramps giving me rides to choir, sharing ice cream late at night, telling me I got my musical skill from my dad like it was something I should be proud of. Maybe it was naive or foolish, but I wanted to hope that things could change between us again. "Let's give him a chance," I tell Mom.

So I do. When I call the hardware store where he works, we have a brief conversation about where and when to see each other. We plan to meet at a diner in Wolfwood on the morning of my birthday, where Gram's friends are less likely to see us. It feels strange to be so covert, especially after all the sneaking around I did last year, but I get the sense that Gramps will feel better if we take things slow.

He's at the diner before I get there, sitting in a booth with a giant menu in front of him. "Tess," he says, standing up unsteadily. He pauses, like he wants to give me a hug but isn't quite sure what to do. "You made it."

"Hi, Gramps," I say, sliding into the booth across from him.

He sits back down, smiling sadly. "Have you been here before?" he asks. When I shake my head, he tells me that he comes here sometimes with some of his buddies from the VFW post. "The coffee's pretty good, and the blueberry pancakes are made with fresh blueberries."

A middle-aged waitress comes by to take our order—pancakes and coffee for both of us—and when she leaves, we sit in silence for a minute. Gramps bunches the thin paper napkin between his fingers and says, "Happy birthday. Seventeen. I can't believe it. I couldn't let the day go by without, you know . . ."

I study him for a moment—the salt-and-pepper hair and craggy face, the hunched posture and restless hands, the mouth ready to smile. But here we are, at a diner in the next town over to make sure we avoid Gram getting word of us even having a conversation. I want to go back to the relationship I had with my grandparents where they loved me and were excited to celebrate my birthday and thought I was a good person. But there's no way back to that, not anymore.

"Gramps," I sigh. "You can't take me out for breakfast and pretend nothing ever happened."

He shrugs, staring down at the speckled laminate tabletop. The waitress comes by with our coffees, setting them down gently.

"Things are different now," I tell him. "You and Gram, you wanted us to leave. You threw us out."

"That was a mistake." He adds two creamers and one sugar to his coffee, stirring it intently, like it's a magic pool he can look into and see a different past. "Your grandmother, she was upset and confused and hurt. We both were—we never expected . . ." He trails off, unable to say the words.

I let everything unsaid hang in the air between us as other patrons talk and dishes clink together in the kitchen.

"We already missed so much with your mother," he finally continues. "I don't want that to happen with you too." When he looks up at me, his eyes are shining with tears.

We eat pancakes and drink coffee. He asks how Mom is doing and how school is going and if I've been singing. I ask how work has been and how his friends at the VFW post are and if he thinks he'll grow green beans in the backyard this summer. We're not where we used to be, but maybe this is the path to somewhere new.

♩

That morning, after breakfast with Gramps, I have a shift at Needleman's. I'm stacking oranges in a neat pile when someone bumps hips with me. "Happy birthday," Bri says, holding out a card.

I take it, opening it to see a drawing of a corgi in a party hat, shaking its stubby tail. *It's your birthday! Dance your butt off!* it reads.

"This is adorable," I say, grinning. "Thanks."

"Are you doing anything special?" she asks, stacking oranges alongside me.

I'm supposed to go out with my music friends later to celebrate my birthday. When Chloe found out about my birthday, she insisted we do something. "Leopard Hat Red Jacket is playing at Pammy's. They're like, Tom Petty meets Patty Griffin with a little Irish folk music thrown in. My sister goes to Vanderbilt and heard them in Nashville, and she said they were awesome. We should go!" Mom has to work, so it feels like the perfect excuse to get out and celebrate a little.

I think of last year, when I spent my birthday at a Grace Teen Life prayer group. Bri and Lily had brought cupcakes, and at the end of group, they said a special prayer for me and the year ahead. A small part of me wishes someone would do that for me for this year.

Instead, I tell Bri about going to see Leopard Hat Red Jacket. "That sounds awesome," she says. "Have fun."

"Thanks," I say, adding another orange to the stack. As Bri's starting to walk away, I turn. "Do you want to come?"

♩

"You don't play anything?" Mia asks Bri, like she might as well be asking how Bri manages not to breathe air. We're all crammed into a small table at Pammy's. Saturday night is a little more crowded than the usual open mic Thursday evening, but we managed to snag one of the last tables in a corner.

Bri shakes her head. "Nope. My parents signed me up for piano when I was little, but I was so bad and hated it so much, they decided it wasn't worth paying money for it."

Mia nods thoughtfully. "And you don't sing?"

"I mean, I do, but not well," Bri laughs. "Like I can make sounds come out of my mouth, but they're not sounds people want to hear."

Mia studies Bri for a moment, a tiny worry line appearing between her eyebrows. After a moment, she asks, "So what do you do with your time?"

"Normal people things," Connor admonishes his sister. "Not everyone's a giant nerd like you."

I mouth *sorry* to Bri—I'm used to Mia's bluntness, but I forget that not everyone might like it. Thankfully, Bri only smiles and shakes her head as if to say it's okay. A waitress comes by to take our order and Chloe makes a point of mentioning that it's my birthday.

"Happy birthday! How old are you?" the waitress asks.

"Seventeen," I tell her.

She puts her hand on my arm and sighs softly, as if I've told her I was a newborn kitten. "Oh, honey, that is exactly the right age to be. You've got everything in front of you."

And that night, it feels like it. Leopard Hat Red Jacket, a trio of guys in their twenties, takes the stage and they're just as good as Chloe's sister said. We sip Cokes and sweet tea and snack on cheese fries, listening to their rough but mournful songs. Their sound gives me an idea for a new song, one with a little faster melody, and I play it over and over in my mind so I don't forget it when I get home. Connor and Bri bond over their mutual hatred for their gym teacher, and Chloe realizes that she and Bri were on the same youth soccer team in elementary school. Toward the end of the night, Chloe leads a loud and enthusiastic rendition of "Happy Birthday" that gets the rest of the crowd to join in. It's not the same as last year, but hearing all the voices around us come together in love and kindness and hope, it feels strangely like its own prayer.

♩

The next night, Mom suggests we go to Sunshine Sundaes for a belated birthday celebration. I used to go all the time with youth group but haven't been here since the summer. Now that it's getting warmer out, it feels like the right time to make the trip back. "I mean, why only celebrate your birthday once when you could celebrate for the whole week?" Mom asks. "Maybe we should get you one of those plastic tiaras to wear all month."

I put my face in my hands. "That's not celebration, that's torture."

Fortunately, the Sunshine Sundaes milk shakes are the opposite of torture. They've just reopened the stand for the season, and even though the evening is a little chilly, Mom and I sit at one of the picnic tables outside, sipping our milk shakes—mint chocolate chip for me, cookies and cream for her. "How about this summer, we come here at least once a week?" Mom suggests.

"Twice a week," I counter.

She nods and takes another sip. "You're right. Ice cream has dairy, which has calcium, which is good for your bones."

"I like that kind of parenting," I laugh.

Mom tells me the story of how she gave birth to me, which was almost in the car on the way to the hospital, after being a week and a half late. "Your dad was so chill," she says. "Like, I was yelling at him that the baby was basically going to come out of me right then, and he was all 'Okay, yes, I hear you, we're going to make it.' And of course we did, but they barely had any time to put me on the hospital bed before you popped right out."

I wrinkle my nose. "Ugh, gross. Don't talk about your womb and popping."

"Well, that's what you did," she says, taking a long sip of her milk shake. "You might have been a little hesitant to be in the world at first, but once you decided you were coming, *you were coming*."

I swirl the last of my milk shake around with my straw, imagining myself in my mom's position. If I hadn't ended the pregnancy, I would have been super pregnant by now, almost full-term. I wouldn't have had Alden by my side to drive me to the hospital, trying to keep me calm, like my dad had done for my mom. I would have been so afraid of the whole experience—sharing a body with a baby I didn't even know yet, anticipating labor and delivery and the pain as my body took over, the fear of what would happen next when I was responsible for this whole new person who needed everything from me. But what would I have known about them from the very first moment? Years later, could I have told them something about themselves over milk shakes? Even if I wouldn't change my decision, I remember that feeling I had after the procedure, of a ghost ship sailing past, and I think it's something that will stay with me forever.

"You ready?" Mom asks, standing up from the picnic bench.

I nod and take the empty cups over to the trash while she goes to start the car. From my position around the side of the ice-cream stand, I notice two people at the front of the line, about to place their order.

Alden. And a girl from youth group—Kayla. She's a year younger than me, a sophomore. She has long blond hair and a wide smile that lights up her whole face.

There isn't anything inappropriate about what they're doing. They're in public, ordering milk shakes from a popular spot in town. It could easily be that she's having a hard time and needed someone to minister to her. But the way he's smiling at her, the way his hand briefly brushes against the small of her back, how he leans down slightly to whisper in her ear . . . Something is wrong, something I recognize now but couldn't understand when it was happening to me.

I freeze, unable to tear my eyes away from them, feeling like the ground underneath me is shifting and I'm the only person around who realizes it. My stomach lurches, and I grip the side of the trash can, wondering if I'm going to throw up or pass out. Because it feels like everything that already happened is happening all over again, and there's no way for me to stop it.

18.

That night, I can't sleep, thinking about Alden and that girl. Kayla. I wonder if he's told her that she's special, mature for her age. Alden used to say that to me, that I was smart, beautiful, creatively mature. That he could talk to me about things—music, songwriting, faith, life—that he couldn't talk about with other people.

I wonder if Kayla likes music too. She wasn't in the choir last year, and I don't remember seeing her singing the last few weeks when I've been at church. I picture her at Sunshine Sundaes with Alden, her bright smile and open face—she's only a year younger than me, but I think, *God, she's so young.*

Maybe her family has fallen apart in some way. Maybe she feels like no one has really listened to her before, no one has really seen her, and suddenly here comes Alden, with those beautiful eyes that could see her and with a patience that suggests he's really listening to what she's saying.

Maybe I'm wrong. I hope I'm wrong.

After all, I have no evidence that anything's happening. Nothing but this feeling that I need to stop whatever it is.

You're jealous, I tell myself as I turn over in my bed. Outside, cars pass, their headlights streaking across the wall. *You miss Alden and you saw him with someone else in a probably totally normal way, and you're imagining things.*

Except this small part of me knows it's not jealousy. Because Alden, he's never going to be with me again. Not really.

Which hurts more than I expected it to, after everything. It's a bitter kind of grief, knowing that this thing I imagined will never come to pass. Maybe not even because of what happened and how everyone found out. Maybe it was never going to happen, and this only made me realize it more quickly. If Alden had ever cared about me, he wouldn't have made me go through all of this alone. He said so many things that made me feel like he cared about me, like he saw me and heard me for who I was, but maybe that was all a way to get what he wanted.

He should have known better.

I'm starting to know better.

Kayla. She might not know better.

I inhale and exhale, the faint scent of detergent and dryer lint from the laundromat hanging in the air, and turn onto my back, staring up at the ceiling. Kayla probably has friends who can help her. Lots of friends in youth group. Maybe she has parents or siblings who will notice that something's not right.

Except I had friends and family who could have noticed too. Everyone thought—thinks—that Alden's a good guy.

I thought he was a good guy.

Everyone will keep thinking he's a good guy, unless someone does something.

I clasp my hands together and close my eyes. *Please, God, I don't know what I'm supposed to do. Help me know what to do.* When I drift into sleep, I still don't know what to do, but I have the feeling that I won't be alone in this.

♩

The first time Alden and I had sex was last April, on the last night of the Spirit Light Festival. When Alden told me about the festival, I'd imagined it like the choral festivals and competitions I'd been to—lots of groups performing together over a few days, sharing music. But all of those had been more formal settings, at nearby college auditoriums or, a couple of times, at the Bloomington Symphony Orchestra. The Spirit Light Festival felt more open, brighter, messier but more exciting, like summer camp. From Friday night to Sunday evening, hundreds of people camped out and prayed together and listened to performers and felt connected to God and each other. I stayed up late to dance and sing under the stars, woke up with the sunrise, sprinkled my hair with dry shampoo and slathered sunscreen on my skin, and lifted my hands to the sky in praise.

And then, on Sunday, I got to sing with the Grace Presbyterian choir.

Most of the performers were professionals, but on Sunday, after a giant nondenominational morning service, the festival included a handful of amateur singers and groups like ours. It was a chance to connect with the community and include everyone's voice, Alden had told me.

The crowd gave us a modest but enthusiastic round of applause when we took the stage. I spotted Lily and Bri toward the front, near stage right. "Tess!" Lily shouted, waving wildly, like I might miss her otherwise. "Woo, go, Tess!"

In front of us, a few mics were set up to help carry the sound over the crowd and wide field. Nearby, Alden took a spot at a piano and counted us off: ". . . two, three, four."

We opened with a cover of "Indescribable," followed by "I Could Sing of Your Love Forever." It was the first time I'd performed in front of a crowd, outside of Sunday services, in over a year. I felt a little shaky and pitchy at first, but after a moment I relaxed into the songs. Around me, the other members of the choir seemed to feel the same, and our voices joined together joyfully.

When Alden played the first notes of our arrangement, I felt a surge of anxiety. I'd spent months working on it with him, a surprise for our choir—something new to sing at the festival. Working on that song was what brought Alden and me together. If the audience hated it, would that make Alden think less of me?

Trust, I reminded myself and started to sing.

"You are the light, the light, the light of the world . . ."

Singing at the Spirit Light Festival, with the voices of the choir around me, seeing my friends in the audience, that's what I felt like—radiant with love and support and faith. I was here, a part of something.

"Let your light shine, you will shine. Take my heart, take my hand, all that's yours and mine . . ."

Around us, the stage crew turned the lights up slowly, a warm glow washing over us. Our voices lifted, hitting every note perfectly. We sounded better than we ever had before, even in our best rehearsals.

". . . we will shine."

Our voices held together on that last note, hovering in the air in a perfect crystallization of sound. Alden held up his hand and closed his fist, guiding us to the end. The audience burst into applause, and I even heard a few cheers of "Woo, Tess!" from the Grace Teen Life crowd.

I helped make something, and all of these people, they liked it.

My smile was so wide, I thought my face might crack open. When I caught Alden's eye, he grinned, applauding lightly in my direction. *Thank you*, he mouthed, and it felt like *I love you*.

♩

When the festival ended, it felt like I'd spent the weekend in a whole other universe and now I was supposed to get back to my normal world. So when Alden asked if I could help him take a few things from the festival back to his place, I said of course.

I hadn't been to his apartment before. Alden told me that he wished we could spend time there together, but it would look too conspicuous if neighbors saw me going there all the time. It was neater than I expected, especially considering he'd been so busy the week before the festival and he was a single guy in his twenties. Even though it was a simple apartment—kitchen, living room, and a bedroom beyond that—it seemed so grown-up. He had his own place, made his own meals, cleaned up after himself, did whatever he wanted. He didn't have to go home to his grandparents' house, where he slept in a twin bed in his mom's childhood bedroom. Being in Alden's apartment made me feel more mature too.

He told me he wanted to share another original song he'd been working on. It was a little rough and didn't have any lyrics, but it made me think of bonfires and fireflies and slow kisses. When he stopped, he looked at me with an intensity in his eyes. "I can't stop writing music that reminds me of you," he said, voice low and throaty. "You sounded so amazing today, and you're so beautiful . . ."

He reached for me and pulled me into a deep kiss. I felt flushed and eager, kissing him back like if I stopped, the day might end and I'd have to go back to normal life. Kissing Alden on his couch, in his apartment, I felt like this was what the future might be—us, sharing an apartment together, writing songs and singing, sharing faith and love and making a life for ourselves.

His hands moved under my shirt, down my pants, tugging at them gently. "Is this okay?" he asked.

"Mm-hmm," I murmured. It wasn't farther than we'd gone before, but it felt different, being somewhere private where no one else could disturb us. Dimly, I remembered conversations in youth group about how couples should set boundaries and help each other stay pure. But Alden would know better than I would about any of that, and maybe it didn't really matter if we were supposed to be together.

When he pulled away, I expected him to say we should stop. Instead, he rose from the couch, took me by the hand, and led me into his bedroom.

I had never been naked in front of someone like that before. I'd barely kissed anyone before Alden. But he pulled off his shirt and unbuttoned his jeans so casually, I found myself doing the same. I trusted him and laid down on the bed beside him and kept kissing him and touching him and let him kiss and touch me. Even then, feeling the warmth of my body against his, I didn't know how far we would go.

"Tess," he moaned.

I didn't stop it. I didn't say no.

It wasn't that I didn't want it to happen. Not exactly. Maybe I thought my first time would be different and that I would be able to talk about it with friends afterward. But it felt right at the time, the weight of his body against mine and his mouth on my bare skin. I wanted him to feel good, and I trusted him to make me feel good too. I wanted to be the kind of girl he would always write songs about.

♩

I barely sleep that night, thinking about Alden and Kayla, what he might have told her. What they might be doing together. How far it might have gone already. When I do fall asleep, I dream about a giant comet streaking across the sky, turning everything orange and purple and red, waiting for it to fall to earth and destroy everything.

The next day after work, Bri gives me a ride home. All day, my stomach's been in a knot of anxiety and my muscles ache, like I've literally been carrying around a weight on my back. When we get in the car, Bri notices that I've been a little quiet. "Are you okay?" she asks. "You seem . . . I don't know, tired? I know people say *you look tired* and it's a way to say *you look bad*, and I don't mean that."

I laugh lightly. "Thanks. I didn't sleep well last night."

As we drive, Bri tells me about this SAT prep course she signed up for. "I'm taking the test in June, so I've got a little time, but now I'm supposed to do all these practice tests every week, and I meet with a tutor and study group once a week. It's not even like you're learning any new math or anything—it's basically learning the right ways to take the test. And I feel like a good score could help me get a good scholarship, but oh my gosh, it's a *lot* of time. I had to skip small group for the past few weeks, and Alden said they'd pray for my SAT results, which is either a good use of divine intervention or really unfair for everybody else."

At the sound of Alden's name, I tense. Bri is focused on the road, so she doesn't notice. She has no idea. There's no way she'd know. She thinks Alden is a good person, like everyone else. Maybe I'm the only one who knows, and if I don't tell her, if I don't tell anyone, no one else will ever find out and maybe someone else will get hurt. The words are building inside me, and I have to say them, I can't not say them.

"Bri." My voice is soft but insistent. "It was Alden."

At first her eyebrows furrow in confusion and she opens her mouth to ask what I mean. Then I see the realization on her face. Her mouth hangs open and her eyes go wide, and she pulls over to the side of the road, stopping the car right there.

"Are you serious?" she asks.

I nod. I've carried this secret with me for over a year, knowing that I could never tell anyone about my relationship, or whatever it was, with Alden, because it could hurt him. Now that I've said it, I feel a little lighter. I can practically see the words, each letter, floating in the air around me.

"Alden?" she says, not exactly like she doesn't believe me, but as if she's trying to wrap her head around how this could be the same person she's known for years. "Alden-from-youth-group Alden?"

"That Alden," I say.

She sits back in the driver's seat, exhaling deeply. "Shit, Tess." Then she looks at me. "How? I mean, I don't need to know any of the details, but—he's, like, Mr. Church Guy."

I tell Bri about how we worked together on the song for the Spirit Light Festival last year, spending more and more time together. How he first kissed me at the retreat. How he'd drive me home from choir and youth group stuff and use that as an excuse to be with me. How no one thought anything of it because he was Mr. Church Guy. How I thought he cared about me and that what we'd had was real. How I couldn't tell anyone about it, even before I found out I was pregnant, because he said it would put his position in the church and in the community at risk.

"Except I think he's doing it again," I add, telling Bri about seeing him with Kayla. "I don't have any proof of anything, but I feel like something's wrong."

Bri's quiet, looking through the windshield at the road ahead with such intensity that she might as well be driving. "Maybe you're wrong," she finally says, and I think she's going to argue with me. Then she says, "But if you're not . . . what are you going to do?"

"I don't know," I tell her. "But I can't do nothing."

♩

When I found out I was pregnant, Alden was away on a youth group mission trip in Texas. It was an annual summer trip, and he'd wanted me to go, too, but with travel it was too expensive, even with the fundraising that Grace Teen Life did. He was out of cell service range for most of the trip, so I spent weeks nauseous with anxiety and morning sickness and trying to pretend that everything was okay.

The morning he got back, I asked if we could meet. Soon would be great, I texted. I didn't mention anything about needing to talk or the fact that I was roughly seven weeks pregnant at that point. Every day, I held a vague hope that I'd get my period after all and it would be a giant fluke and I'd never have to mention it to him or anyone else.

I can't wait to see you, he texted back. I've missed you.

It gave me some small comfort, imagining that, while I was here, alone, worried about what was happening inside me and what I was going to do, he'd been missing me.

I met him at his office after the rest of the parish staff had gone home for the day. He'd gotten a nice tan while he was away, making the blue of his eyes fluorescent against his skin and light gray T-shirt.

When I arrived, he got up from his desk to shut the door behind me. "Hey, come on in," he said casually, as he would to any other person in Grace Teen Life. Once the door was safely locked, he pulled me closer for a fierce kiss. "Tess," he breathed. "I missed this so much."

"Ah, me too," I mumbled, stiffening slightly as his lips started to trail down my neck. I didn't want to have sex again, not right now, not in his office when I needed to tell him that maybe we shouldn't have been doing this in the first place. "Um, can we talk?"

He chuckled softly and took a step back. "Yes, oh my gosh, of course. Sorry, I got ahead of myself."

"Yeah," I sighed. "That's kind of the thing."

His forehead furrowed as he noticed that something was different about my tone and posture. "What is it? Are you okay?" he asked, leaning back against his desk.

"Yes," I said automatically, then realized that wasn't true at all. "I mean, not really. Like soon after you left, I started feeling kind of sick and I noticed that I hadn't, um, gotten my period when I should have." I flushed with embarrassment, talking to him about my period, even though we'd had sex—it all felt so strange and uncomfortable. I wasn't ready for any of this. "So I took a test and it was positive." My stomach lurched and it wasn't from morning sickness, it was from having to say the words, like that would make it real. But he was frozen, as if any sudden move would put him in harm's way, and I knew that I was going to be the one who had to say it. "I'm pregnant."

Alden's face fell, and for a moment he closed his eyes tightly, like he could block out everything that was happening right then. "Shit," he finally said, cradling his face in his hands.

I stood very still in the middle of his office, half wishing the floor would open up and swallow me, and half wishing that Alden would put his arms around me and tell me we would figure it out, that it would all be okay somehow.

He didn't do that. Instead, he straightened up, took a breath, and asked, "Does anyone else know?"

Not *how are you?* Not *that must have been so hard to deal with alone.* Not *I'm sorry I wasn't here for you.*

"No one else knows," I murmured.

"Good," he breathed, "that's good. Sorry, this is a lot to process. I'm just—I'm wondering how this could have happened."

I was a little confused. "Well, we . . . you know," I said.

He pursed his lips and exhaled sharply through his nose. "No, I know. But I thought you were on the pill or tracking your cycle to make sure you weren't ovulating. That kind of thing? I mean, I couldn't have done that. We have pamphlets about it somewhere around here."

"Oh," I said, suddenly feeling small and deflated. Maybe I should have been more careful. I thought he was taking care of any precautions we needed. Was that my responsibility? Why hadn't I thought more about this? How was I supposed to be responsible for another person, one who would need literally everything from me, when I didn't even know I was supposed to ask about stuff like this?

"What are you going to do?" he asked, and I honestly didn't know how to respond. I hadn't even thought that far—I kept hoping it would go away, or at least that once I told Alden about it, he'd have a plan. Something to help me get through this. To get back to the way things were. Except now he was looking at me expectantly, as though I was the only one this was happening to.

"I don't know. I haven't thought that far," I admitted. I didn't want it to be real, and thinking about the next few steps made it seem more real. All I wanted was for this to never have happened.

"Look," he sighed, sitting back on the edge of his desk. "I don't want to tell you what to do, but there's no way I can be a part of this"—he waved toward my stomach—"right now. I mean, if people found out about us, about how we'd been together, I'd be in serious trouble. I'd lose my job. I could get in legal trouble. This could ruin my life, Tess. Seriously and permanently ruin my life."

It was something we'd talked about before, the reasons why people couldn't know about our relationship. Before, it felt furtive and romantic. Now it made me feel afraid and alone.

I didn't think to ask him, *What about my life? What if that's already ruined?*

"I've put so much at risk to be with you," he told me. "I can't do this too. You get that, right?"

I didn't necessarily want it, either—not now, at least. I'd imagined someday, after we could be together in public, maybe we'd get married and have kids. But that was never what I wanted for us, for myself, right now.

The way Alden was looking at me, it was like he was afraid that I could hurt him instead of the other way around. "I know," I finally said.

"Good," he exhaled. "Good. I can trust you to keep this, us, quiet, right? Whatever you decide to do. At least for now."

"Yeah," I said, digging the toe of my shoe into the faded carpet of his office floor. "You can trust me." Then I told him that I should go, and he let me leave without touching me again.

♩

"It's not enough, those things you say, but after a while, I'll be okay." I'm at home, working on a new song while Mom's working late at the

pub. I'm mostly messing around, playing with what lyrics and chords sound right for this feeling that's been hanging over me. It's rough, but just the act of making music makes me feel better.

My phone dings—Bri.

Hey, she texts me. I've been thinking about what you said and watching Alden with Kayla. Maybe it's because now I'm looking for something there, but I feel like you might be right about them.

I feel my pulse race, even though I stay very still.

It's not even anything specific, she continues. Like a weird feeling all of a sudden? How he keeps being near her. I don't know . . .

But it's weird, right? I ask. Because I remember him doing that to me too—not anything right out in the open, but the fact that he was always there, paying attention to me. At the time, I thought it was because I was new and quiet, and he wanted to help me fit in.

Definitely weird, she agrees. I can't stop thinking about it.

She promises to talk to Kayla, hint that maybe Alden isn't such a good person to be hanging out with like that. But I worry that Bri saying something isn't enough—it's too easy to dismiss one voice of concern. Then I remember what Bri told me about Roger, how he'd used an app to disguise his number so he could text me hateful messages. I don't want to do anything like that to Kayla, but maybe I could send her an anonymous text about Alden.

Do you have Kayla's number? I ask Bri.

She finds it in an old youth group text thread and sends it to me. Even though I doubt Kayla has my number, I download an app that'll keep my message anonymous. Before I can overthink it, I type, Please be careful around Alden. He's not as trustworthy as he seems.

Text bubbles pop up, and almost immediately there's a response. Sorry, who is this?

I want to tell Kayla that it's me. That I'm warning her because I know what Alden's doing and I realized it way too late for me but it's not too late for her. But I worry that, if I'm honest, she'll think I'm crazy or jealous or evil, that I'm trying to get in the way of whatever Alden's convinced her they have together. For now I reply, I'm just trying to help. Please stay away from him.

After a minute, my phone pings again, but this time it's Bri: Also, it made me think about this girl who used to come to youth group, Reagan? She was really good friends with Alyssa. Then she stopped coming all of a sudden. That was before you moved here. Something might have happened to her too.

I remember Roger mentioning Reagan a while back and how she'd been so close with Lily's older sister, Alyssa. I'd always assumed that Reagan got interested in other things, maybe started dating someone and dropped out of youth group. But the suddenness of it raises my suspicion.

I check Alyssa's social media profiles to find anyone named Reagan. One is a pretty girl with dark, wavy hair and freckles across the bridge of her nose. In her profile picture, she's wearing sunglasses, standing with her back to a wall graffitied with butterflies, arms raised slightly like she's summoning them to fly.

I take a breath and send her a message: Hey, I'm a friend of Alyssa and Lily's from Hawthorne. Could I ask you about something?

19.

Reagan is in her first year of college at the University of Michigan, studying engineering. “I think I want to do environmental engineering, but I’ve been talking to some of the upperclassmen and biomedical also sounds really interesting, so I don’t know. I’ve got to get through the core requirements first, and my physics class this semester is seriously going to kill me,” she tells me. We’re FaceTiming, me from our apartment and her from her dorm room. Behind her, I see star charts and nature photographs taped to the wall, along with a string of twinkle lights. I wonder where I’ll be in less than two years, how I’ll decorate a dorm room and what kind of roommate I’ll have, what kind of people I’ll make friends with. Right now, my corner of the apartment feels so small and temporary. A spring storm has rolled into Hawthorne and rain patters against the window while I listen to Reagan talk.

She’s bright and friendly, chatting about her freshman year classes and friends. “For spring break, I signed up for this volunteer trip, doing this river cleanup project. It was tiring, but also really fun.”

“Did you do it through a church group?” I ask carefully.

She pauses, smiling sadly. "No, I don't do a lot of stuff like that anymore," she admits. When I reached out to her initially, I mentioned wanting to ask about her experience in Grace Teen Life and why she left. She'd been casual about it, saying she didn't fit in anymore. When I mentioned that I was wondering if it had anything to do with Alden, she suggested we talk.

Now she goes on to say that she used to be really into Grace Teen Life and church stuff when she was growing up. "My parents both grew up in Hawthorne, so we'd been going forever, and it was a given that I'd be involved in youth group. Then when I was a freshman, Alden got hired as the new youth minister. He was young and cool and engaging, you know?"

I remember how Alden could make you feel like he was really listening, how he could draw in a room full of people or just one person. "I know," I say.

Reagan talks about how she was into nature and hiking, so Alden offered to take her to some good trails near Hawthorne. "It started off as a youth group thing, but he said he wanted to go on harder trails and that I was the strongest hiker in the group. So eventually, it was only the two of us. My parents never asked about it, because he was such a nice guy and it seemed totally safe. Plus, my brother was having problems with drugs at that point, which took up a lot of my parents' time." She pauses, looking off camera, as though the right words might be somewhere nearby. "Alden kept telling me that I was special, beautiful, mature. It felt good that someone else was paying attention to me."

"I know," I say again. I hate hearing that Alden said the same things to someone else, that he never meant any of it, but it's also a strange and awful relief to know that it wasn't just me.

Reagan was sixteen when Alden first kissed her, one day while they were hiking alone. "It felt like this natural thing at the time," she tells me, "but now I think he'd been planning to for a while."

They were secretly together for the next several months, until Alden wanted to go farther physically, while Reagan was frustrated that she couldn't go out with him on normal dates. "Other girls, their boyfriends take them out for their birthday. For my birthday, we hooked up in his car near some hiking trail. It's stupid, but it made me feel like this wasn't what I wanted." So she broke up with him and stopped going to Grace Teen Life altogether. "I was really focused on doing well in my science classes so I could get a scholarship to a good engineering program. My parents were disappointed that I wasn't doing church stuff, but concentrating on school seemed like a good excuse to not go to youth group anymore."

"You never told anyone?" I ask, imagining Reagan studying after school, alone, while her friends got to live their lives. While Alden got to live his life. "About Alden?"

She shakes her head. "Nope. I mean, he's the youth minister. Everyone loves him. Who was going to believe me?"

♩

I wonder who will believe me now.

Bri. Mom. Chloe, Connor, Mia. Maybe Gramps.

The women's health clinic—they had pamphlets about resources, counselors, people you could talk to if you'd been hurt somehow.

So many people have been hurt. People who couldn't get help.

I hate that Reagan felt so alone when everything happened to her. That I've felt that way, too, for a long time. That Alden made us feel like we were alone.

Maybe there are others who feel alone right now.

When Reagan and I finish our call, I can't stay in the apartment. I need to move, to walk somewhere, even if I don't have a particular destination. It's stopped raining, but drops are still falling from trees and making me wish I'd grabbed my jacket. Instead of going back, I dodge puddles, increasing my pace to match my heartbeat.

It wasn't just me. He made me feel like what we had was special, that I was special, but that was never the case. I wasn't the first and I'm not the last, because he knows what he's doing. Because he's charming and kind and talented and friendly. Because he works with teens, so why would it be weird for him to be hanging around a bunch of teenage girls? Because of course people would listen to him instead of us.

Instead of me.

My head is pounding, and my heart is racing, and without even knowing exactly what I'm doing, I find myself walking right to Grace Presbyterian.

There are a few cars in the parking lot, but otherwise it's a slow evening. Behind the church, the skies are clearing, streaked with deep red and orange and purple as the sun sets. The air is thick and cool, and from a distance I hear voices singing together, a piano playing gently behind them.

Of course. Wednesday. Choir practice.

I imagine all of them, coming together as usual, practicing the hymns for services on Sunday, Alden leading them and offering minor adjustments to help their sound. Maybe they're even preparing for this year's Spirit Light Festival, getting ready to perform new songs in front of hundreds of young people of faith. Maybe Alden's convinced one of them to write a new adaptation with him this year too—in secret, not even telling the others that he had help with it. I clench my fists so tightly that my fingernails make tiny half-moon indentations in my palms.

He gets to keep on living life. I defended him and protected him, and he gets to move on without anyone knowing anything about who he really is.

I want to go in there right now and yell at him about how I thought I loved him, and I thought he loved me. How I trusted him. How he used me and, when I proved to be a liability, threw me away so he could move on to the next girl. How he's the reason I had to get an abortion in the first place. How everyone still thinks he's some good, godly person, when I've been harassed since the day it happened, and how I've been alone through all of it. I want to light a match and burn the whole building to the ground, thinking about how this all started there.

But I don't. Because even if I go in there and yell at Alden, how many people will believe me? They'll think I'm some unhinged teenager looking to cause more drama and take down some poor innocent guy because of my own selfish mistakes. Maybe there will be some gossip, but he'll keep being the youth minister and leading the choir on Sundays, and eventually, they'll all forget anything I said about him. I need to figure out a way for as many people as possible to listen to me. For them not to look away.

Which gives me an idea. It's going to take a lot of work and a lot of people, but maybe this will be something. Something that will help people believe me. That will help them believe each other. And for the first time in a while, I think of Alden and I smile.

♩

As soon as I get home, I check the Spirit Light Festival website—specifically, the amateur performer application section. *We are excited to include local individual and group music artists in this festival. Please fill out this application and submit it as soon as possible. The deadline is April 2.*

That's three days away. Good.

I calmly but efficiently scan the guidelines and fill out the application—solo performer, guitar and vocals. Experience: multiple years of music performance, mostly in choral groups, including state competitions and solo experience at local open mic nights. Previous years performed at the Spirit Light Festival: one.

I hover over the Submission button and, for a moment, second-guess myself. The Spirit Light Festival is a lot of people. What makes me think any of this will work? That anyone will want to listen to me?

Help me be brave so maybe someday someone else won't have to, I pray and hit Submit.

♩

Alden finds me on Sunday after services. I'm leaving church when I hear him call my name. "Tess, hey, Tess!" When I turn, he's dodging through parishioners to catch up with me.

It's the first time he's tried to talk to me since I told him I was pregnant.

"Hey, Mom, can I meet you at the car?" I ask.

She raises an eyebrow, looking between me and Alden, still approaching us. "You sure?" I haven't told her about Alden yet, because I need to make sure I have my plans in place first. Otherwise, I'm pretty sure I'd have to stop her from ramming a car through his office.

"I got this" is what I tell her now.

Alden reaches me as my mom walks toward our car. "Hey, Tess, you got a minute?" he asks. His voice is light and pleasant but tight, like there's an invisible knot around his throat.

I keep my tone as cool as possible. "What is it?"

He pulls me aside to a corner of the church parking lot where there aren't too many people. "I saw that you submitted an application for the Spirit Light Festival," he says, then narrows his eyes slightly. "Are you sure that's a good idea?"

"Why wouldn't it be?" I ask, feigning ignorance.

He takes a sharp breath. "It's, you know, how things have gone for you this year. Maybe this isn't the best time to perform at such a big event like that. If you want, I can take the application out—no harm, no foul."

How things have gone for *me* this year. Not for him, not at all. "Oh wow," I drawl. "You'd do that for me?"

He smiles, for a second thinking that I'm being sincere, but stops when he sees the hardness in my eyes. "Tess, come on," he murmurs. "This is a big event, and I don't know if you're ready for something like this."

"I'm not?" I say, and instantly a wave of doubt hits me. I've managed to get through performing at Pammy's a handful of times by now, but that was for a few dozen people, not over a hundred at a big outdoor festival. It would be me, onstage, all alone.

"You've got a great voice," he tells me, tone low and soft, "you really do. But you haven't been playing the guitar long, right? I'm saying this because I want the best for you, and I don't know if you're in the right place for this right now."

My eyes narrow, remembering he's the one who put me in this place. "Really?" I say. "Why wouldn't I be in the right place for this right now? Is there a particular reason why you'd want to stop me from performing? Something you wouldn't want people to know about?"

His whole body tenses. "Tess—"

"No, really," I say, my voice growing louder. "If you think that there's something you want me to hide, why don't you let me know right now exactly what that is? Because if you're fine, I'm fine, and I should probably get a slot at the festival. To prove that we're both fine."

For a moment, his mouth hangs open like a fish as it flaps around helplessly on a dock. Then he clears his throat, recovering. "No, nothing. Everything is perfectly fine."

"Perfect," I say, grinning. "See you at the festival." Before I spin away and head back to the car, I add, my voice low and sharp, "And stay the hell away from Kayla."

20.

When Mom and I are driving home from church, I notice that she's way quieter than usual. Her hands grip the wheel and her mouth is set in a thin line as she stares at the road ahead. My stomach drops—I have a feeling what she's going to say, but I wait for her to actually say it. On the car stereo, a woman sings a slow, gentle song about wishing that things were different.

"Tess, I supported you through all of this," Mom finally says, not looking at me. Her voice is slow, like she's trying to choose her words carefully. "I'm not upset about that—I love you and I want to support you, but, honey . . . I need to ask you something and I need you to tell me the truth."

I swallow a lump of anxiety in my throat. "Okay."

"When you were talking to Alden just now. The way he was talking and looking at you—I . . ." She takes a breath, exhaling slowly before speaking again. "Was it him?"

I wish I could tell her that it wasn't. I want to lie again, say it was a boy I met through youth group, and pretend that it was a one-time mistake. But it was so much more than that, in so many awful ways, and I don't want to protect Alden anymore.

"Yes," I tell her.

Mom's quiet again, her grip on the wheel tightening until her knuckles are white. "Is that why you've been quiet about this?"

"Yes," I say again. I feel a weird pang of guilt, like I should be embarrassed both about being with Alden and about keeping it a secret, even though that isn't what Mom's suggesting. But now, sitting in the passenger seat, I feel like I should have known better—I was a smart girl, even though I was in a new place. Mom had taught me not to put up with guys being creepy.

Except it hadn't felt like Alden was creepy. When it was happening, it felt like he cared, like he really listened to me and saw me. Like he loved me. Now, even knowing that he'd done this before, that he was trying to do it again, I feel small and foolish because I'd believed him.

We pull into the laundromat parking lot, but Mom keeps the car running. "We need to go to the police. What he did, it's not right."

"I know," I say. "But, Mom, please—"

"It's *illegal*, Tess. You were, what, fifteen, maybe sixteen when he—" She exhales sharply, like she can't even say the word and has to expel the air itself from her mouth. Then she continues. "When I think about everything you've been through, the things people have said and done—he deserves to be prosecuted for this." Her voice is rising, and I have a feeling that Mom would like to drive right over to Alden's house, drag him out, and throw him in jail herself.

"Mom, I know," I say. "But all those people who said things about me and harassed me—that's not going to change. They still think he's a good person. And I'd have to make a statement, and we'd have to get a lawyer . . ." I trail off, thinking of everything that would be involved in pressing charges. I doubt we could even afford a good lawyer to help us.

Mom seems to realize that too. She turns the car off but doesn't move from her seat. Her eyes are shining with tears and her voice is choked when she says, "I'm sorry, Tess. I should never have brought you here. I should have realized something was wrong. I was so excited that you had an outlet for music here—I never even thought . . . I'm so sorry, Tess."

"It's not your fault," I tell her, and it's true.

It wasn't my fault, either. And I need to make sure that everyone knows that.

"I need to tell people what happened," I say calmly, "but I need to do it my way. Maybe after, we can talk about going to the police or moving or whatever. But can you trust me to do this first?"

After a moment, Mom nods. She wipes away tears as she says, "I trust you. But you need to be honest with me, okay? No more secrets."

When I told Mom I was pregnant, she didn't pressure me to tell her who the father was or what had happened. Instead, she pulled me into a hug and whispered into my hair, "You're going to be okay. Whatever happens. Whatever you decide. You're going to be okay." I wanted that to be true then, and it feels like it's becoming true now.

"No more secrets," I tell her, and I mean it.

♩

I start to tell people about what happened.

Bri helps me reach out to some youth group people, including Lily's sister, Alyssa. After hearing about what I had planned, Reagan reached out to her as well, explaining how Alden had groomed and abused her and that was why she'd left youth group. Alyssa and I schedule a phone call for after school one day so I can talk to her too.

"Wow, screw that guy," Alyssa says, furious, after I tell her. In the background, I can hear people nearby, and I imagine her sitting on the library steps at college, watching people play Frisbee. "Like, what he did to you and Reagan, while telling us all to save sex for marriage—just wow, fuck him."

I almost laugh at Alyssa swearing like that. Lily can barely say "damn," let alone "fuck." "Thanks for believing me," I say.

"Of course," she says. "I mean, after talking to Reagan—both of you wouldn't make something like this up, you know? And like, I loved youth group, but things in real life can be complicated. I love my sister, I would die for her, but I think the way youth group people treated you when they found out about the abortion was really shitty."

It's a relief to hear her say it, and I ask, "Do you think you can help me talk to Lily too?"

Alyssa and Bri reach out to Lily first. They explain that I want to talk to her, and that it's serious. Bri assures me that Lily knows this isn't an opportunity to bring me back to Jesus. "Trust me, after how the last attempt went, I think she gets it."

Bri drives all of us to Sunshine Sundaes, a neutral ground with ice cream. We sip milk shakes and sit on a picnic bench far from the stand, Lily on one side and Bri and me on the other. For a moment, it reminds me of when I first moved to Hawthorne—the three of us, sitting in the fresh air, chatting about classes we were taking and what shows we'd been watching. Lily has the same bright smile, the same cheery voice, even as she seems shier around me now.

Finally, I take a breath and start. "I know you don't agree with what I did," I tell Lily, "but I hope you can understand why it happened."

Lily nods, sitting forward slightly, like she's really listening. "What happened?" she asks.

I tell her everything—how Alden started grooming me at choir and youth group; how he kissed me on the retreat; how things escalated until I got pregnant; how he'd done almost the same thing to Reagan; how I'm afraid he's going to keep doing the same thing to other girls. Lily is quiet during most of it, but her eyes are wide and her face pales, making her look a little sick as all the pieces come together.

Finally, when I'm done, she says, "I can't—it's Alden."

"I know," Bri says solemnly.

"I mean, we *know* him," Lily continues. "He doesn't seem like that kind of person. Like, he's a *nice guy.* He seems so godly. But . . ." she trails off, trying to make sense of all of it.

Bri takes Lily's hand, giving it a tight squeeze. "I know," she repeats.

"Do you believe me?" I ask, and I'm a little afraid to hear the answer.

Lily takes a breath and, after a moment, nods. "I think so. Between you and Reagan . . ." I feel a knot release in my stomach, but Lily continues. "Even if what Alden did was wrong, why didn't you tell us sooner? We could have helped you, you know, so you didn't have to . . . make the choice you did."

I know Lily means it. She would have wanted to help, even if she'd been shocked at the time. She would have looked up adoption resources or figured out ways for me to have the baby while still going to school, carried my bag at school when it got too heavy, prayed for my baby. She would have meant well. But she wouldn't have been the one to carry the baby, go through labor and delivery, and live the rest of her life knowing that things could have been different. That they weren't supposed to be this way.

I knew what she thought the right choice was supposed to be. I was supposed to spend nine months growing and carrying the baby and either raise it myself or give it up for adoption. I would have been seventeen by the time I gave birth, not even a legal adult at that point.

A baby is not a choice, we had shouted when Grace Teen Life protested at the women's clinic. But a baby wasn't a punishment, either.

The whole time I was pregnant, people would have been talking about me, how I seemed like a nice church girl but was impure, a chewed-up piece of gum. They would have said, *Of course, look at her mother, she was wild when she was a girl too.* They would have wanted to know who the father was—how could I have spent the rest of my life dodging questions about who the father was?

I can't do this, Alden had said.

I couldn't do it either.

I'd thought that if I didn't have a baby, things would go back to normal. Maybe not at first, but after some time. Alden and I could keep sharing music and seeing each other. Eventually, things would be okay between us. I could keep going to school and Grace Teen Life and singing in the choir. I didn't want to lose any of that. Nothing had to change; no one had to know.

Except it didn't work out that way. Everything changed. Everything needed to change, but not for the reasons I thought at the time. Even if Lily can't understand why I did what I did, it was always going to be the choice I had to make.

"I couldn't" is all I tell her. Maybe Lily and I will never be friends like we were before, but for now she can accept that I'm telling the truth.

♩

When I put together my plans for the Spirit Light Festival, it starts with the red *A* on my locker.

Every day at school, staring at it like an open wound, I thought it stood for the choice I'd made, the way people were judging me for it. Now I realize I could make it mean something else. Because *A* might be on my locker, clear and red and remarkable, but it could also be something that too many other people carry around with them as well. I think about Bri getting harassed by the guy at the grocery store, girls getting catcalled by guys driving by when they're just trying to walk down the street, guys thinking they have a right to a girl's body because they take her out to dinner; about people who are hurt and feel like they can't talk about it because, somehow, it's their fault when it's not.

It's not our fault.

I call the Center for Reproductive Health and ask about resources available. "I was there in the fall," I mention, "for an abortion. I remember seeing some pamphlets about people to talk to, if you'd been hurt by someone." The person on the phone asks me if I'm safe and I say yes, it's for a project I'm organizing here in town. They give me information about therapists and counselors and social workers in the area who can help individuals and who can do presentations and workshops for groups. I take down all the information and make more calls, mostly about group events. But I also keep the names of therapists who have experience working with survivors of sexual assault and share them with Mom. We check who's covered by her insurance and who's fairly close and accepting new patients. After keeping secrets for so long, it feels good to try to find someone to talk about things with. Someone who's trained to help.

That's what I want. To help other people. To connect them to people who are trained to help. To make sure they all know they're heard. To give them space to speak up.

Bri, Lily, Chloe, Mia, and Connor help me spread the word about my plan—slowly, through conversations at school and texts and messages on social media. *Join the Scarlet Support Project! If you've been sexually harassed or assaulted or abused, meet at Pammy's at 2:00 p.m. on Saturday to learn more about a project to raise awareness and share support.*

"Oh my gosh, no one's going to show up," I complain to Mom on the way to Pammy's that Saturday. "It's going to be me and my friends and I'm going to be seriously embarrassed."

"People are going to show up," she assures me. "And if they don't, so what? We'll figure it out. You don't need a big group behind you to speak out."

"Yeah, but it feels a lot easier." Now I feel a little ill driving on the back roads to Pammy's and I know it's not from motion sickness.

Chloe had asked Pammy if we could reserve the space for a private gathering, even though the restaurant wasn't technically open during that time. She'd agreed, partly because Chloe was so charming and enthusiastic, and partly because Chloe estimated that it would be a dozen of us and nothing rowdy would happen. When Mom pulls into the parking lot at Pammy's, I see more than a dozen cars.

"Okay," Mom breathes, surprised.

Inside, there are more than thirty people, some seated around tables and some standing by the bar, even though it's closed. Near the entrance, I meet Stacy, a tall woman with short black hair and warm brown eyes, the counselor and social worker who's going to help facilitate today's conversation.

"Thanks so much for being here," I tell her.

"I'm glad I can help," she says. "It looks like a great group."

I scan the room, recognizing a lot of people—a bunch from school, a handful from youth group, a few more from church, and others I only vaguely know by sight from around town. Most are teen girls or young women, but there are a few guys mixed in as well. I see a few people from the Hawthorne High jazz band and the Queer Student Alliance at a table with Chloe, Mia, and Connor, while Bri is sitting with Lily and a few other girls from Grace Teen Life. Bri's mom and my mom take a seat at the bar, Pammy coming by to ask if they need anything.

At first, I'm excited that so many people showed up—I seriously thought I'd be here with my friends and have to scrap my idea for the Spirit Light Festival. Maybe Bri was right when she said that not everyone at Grace Presbyterian hates me.

But then I see all the faces in the room, imagining how they all have lives and stories and people who love them, and they're here because someone hurt them. Or because someone they love has been hurt. There are too many people here, too many people who have been hurt. Maybe no one listened to them before, but they want someone to listen to them now. A slow anger builds inside me until it's time to walk up to the stage and call everyone to attention.

"Hi, y'all," I say, and the conversations pause. "My name's Tess Pine. If you don't know me personally, you probably know me as the church girl who had an abortion last fall."

I pause, glancing around the room to see if anyone's going to react negatively. Even Lily and others at the youth group table stay seated.

"Thanks for being here today—seriously. But I'm sorry that you have to be here. I spent the last year, more than a year, thinking that I had to keep quiet to protect someone else, even when that person was harming me. Even after it was made public that I'd had an abortion, I thought I couldn't share my experiences with anyone, even the people who loved me. But staying quiet didn't help me, and it won't help any of us. It only helps the people who want to take advantage of others and feel entitled to our bodies and hurt us."

I pause again, looking around at all the people here today. They're watching me carefully, some with sadness in their eyes, like they're remembering the harm done to them. Some with determination, like they want things to change, starting now. Some with both.

"I think there's a big problem with silence in this town," I tell them. I take a breath, because it can't just be me doing this. It's not my town—it's all of ours. "And I think we can change that—together. We're fortunate to have Stacy Millis, a counselor and social worker at the Wolfwood women's center, with us, and she's going to be leading today's workshop on sexual assault awareness." I motion to stage right, where Stacy is sitting at a nearby table. "But first, in the spirit of doing this together, maybe we can start with y'all talking to each other and, if you're comfortable, sharing why you're here today."

There are a few seconds where everyone looks around at the people at their tables or standing nearby, then soft murmuring begins. I wander around, catching snippets of people's stories—getting groped while waiting tables, being pressured into giving head after the Snow Ball, getting called a slut because they had a D-cup by sixth grade, getting attacked by a guy they thought was a friend. In the back of the room, I see Mom talking to Mrs. Miller and Pammy and a few other women. Pammy is talking about how she got pregnant when she was young, barely out of school and trying to make it as a musician. She'd had an abortion then too. "I was in Tennessee at the time—not the easiest thing to find, but at least it was legal," she said. "I wouldn't have started this place and had my son now if things had been different." Near the stage, Mia is leading a frank discussion with her band friends, while a few tables away, Lily is speaking softly as if in prayer. All around the room, people are sharing with each other. Some stories are hard to hear and hard to share, but people keep talking, even the ones who need to take breaks as they speak. It feels important, all of us being together, sharing our experiences and telling each other we're not alone.

It's a start.

♩

After the workshop, people thank me on their way out. They share email addresses and phone numbers on a sign-up sheet Mia created so we can let them know about more conversations, more events. They want this to keep going and so do I.

"This was awesome," Bri tells me as she and her mom are leaving.

"Stacy did such a great job," I say. "I really liked what she said about consent not being a binding contract and how you're allowed to say no even if you'd said yes before." It was something I hadn't thought of when I was with Alden. Once, after choir rehearsal one night, we'd hooked up in his office at the church, and I'd felt strange about it. But I didn't say anything because I didn't want him to think I was being naive or immature or that I wasn't into him. He didn't notice anyway. Now I wish I could go back to last year and tell my past self that I'm allowed to say no, that Alden had been trying so hard to avoid hearing me say no.

Bri nods. "Oh yeah, seriously. But you did a great job too. You put this together."

I look around the room, where a few small groups of people are still talking, like they don't want to leave yet. "Thanks. It feels good, being here together like this."

"It helps to not feel alone," Mrs. Miller says, her expression soft and knowing. I remember Gram and I bringing food for Bri's family after her mom's mastectomy, how it felt like such a small thing, but it was our way of showing that we were there for them during a hard time. And then I remember the care package left for me on my grandparents' front steps, right after everyone found out about the abortion. It had been full of things that were meant to help me recover, to let me know that someone was thinking of me and wanted me to feel okay during a hard time. I thought it had been from Alden.

It had never been from him. Of course it hadn't.

"Did you leave something for me?" I ask. Mrs. Miller's forehead furrows in confusion and I continue, "When I was recovering."

Recognition flashes across Mrs. Miller's eyes and she smiles sadly. "It was so small," she says. Beside her, Bri's eyebrows rise—I guess she didn't know her mom had done anything for me. But if Mrs. Miller notices her daughter's surprise, she doesn't show it. "I wish I'd done more. I didn't want to impose on you and your family in a private situation, but . . ." She trails off for a moment, sighing. "I know it would have helped if I'd been more open with my support."

I glance at the rest of the room, where the last groups of people are moving toward the door, and beyond that, where people are hugging and sharing goodbyes in the parking lot. "I think that's what we're doing now," I tell her, and it feels like a good thing.

21.

Over the next couple of weeks, the Scarlet Support Project meets a few more times. We keep sharing stories and resources, talking about what problems we see in Hawthorne and where people could make changes. A group of kids from school wants to change the school dress code, which states that girls can't wear tank tops in case their shoulders distract boys. A group of older women talk about ways to support victims of domestic abuse and how to get them safely to women's shelters. A few people start a letter-writing campaign to elected officials about reproductive rights policies and resources. We meet in living rooms and coffee shops and parks. New people keep coming. Almost immediately, it feels bigger than me, in a good way.

Not everyone's happy about the group, though. I'm in the Needleman's parking lot one evening, about to walk home after my shift, when I see Gram walking toward me.

Aside from seeing her from a distance at church, when she studiously ignores me, I haven't interacted with her in months. I remember when she would look at me with such warmth and joy. Now her mouth is set in a hard, thin line and she's clutching the strap of her handbag like she's afraid someone might snatch it from her.

"Gram," I say, "what is—"

"Why are you going around making trouble?" she asks, her voice a sharp whisper.

"I'm not—"

"Having all those meetings?" she interrupts. "Talking about things that don't need to be talked about. It's not appropriate and it's not godly. You were such a good girl—I don't know what happened. Why are you doing all of this? All you're doing is stirring up trouble in people's homes and schools and businesses."

I open my mouth to argue that people *want* to talk about these things, even if they're difficult. That they *need* to talk about them. But looking at Gram, I see fear shining behind her eyes—maybe because she's afraid of what could change in her community, or because she's afraid to admit that someone has hurt her too. Despite everything that's happened between us, when I look at her now, all I feel for her is sadness.

She goes on to rant a little more, until it seems like she's tired herself out. "You need to get yourself right with the Lord," she finally tells me. "I'm praying for you and your mama."

"So am I, Gram," I tell her and walk away.

♩

I keep writing new music, tinkering with the songs I have, practicing over and over. I want it to be right, to say and sound exactly how I feel and how I want others to feel. Alden told me that he didn't think I was ready for a crowd like this, not solo, and I want to make sure he's wrong.

The week of the Spirit Light Festival, people from the Scarlet Support Project meet behind the laundromat, everyone instructed to bring a plain white shirt. Mia, Connor, and Chloe bought as much red spray paint as they could find within a twenty-mile radius.

"The last place we went to had one can of red and three cans of cranberry. They tried to argue that cranberry was basically the same thing, which is the most absurd thing anyone's ever said about spray paint," Mia mentions, while Chloe and Connor unload canisters from the trunk of Chloe's dad's car. "I told them that cranberry was absolutely unacceptable, and they should have their eyesight evaluated if they want to be a successful paint supply store."

"Thank you for striking fear into the hearts of local merchants," I say, trying not to laugh.

Throughout the afternoon, people come by with white T-shirts. We spread out sheets of newspaper and hand out cans of spray paint while people draw red *A*'s on the white fabric. Seeing the red paint spread across white fabric over and over, I keep thinking about "Snow White," the Grimm version, and how Snow White's mother wished for a daughter after seeing drops of her own blood on the clean, white snow. How every drop of paint feels like a different wish for the future.

"Hey, what are y'all making?" a woman going into the laundromat asks.

"Armor," I tell her.

♩

When Bri picks me up to go to the Spirit Light Festival that weekend, I'm nauseous with anxiety. She opens the trunk of her car for me to load in my stuff, and she must see how nervous I am, because she says, "You don't have to do this, you know. You can change your mind. No one would be mad at you."

Part of me wants to hear this. I want an out, the option to avoid conflict entirely and keep quiet. People have been judging me for months now—why should I put myself in a position for them to judge me some more?

Except it's not just me anymore. It never was.

I put my guitar case in her trunk. "Let's go."

The crowd seems bigger than last year, even though I doubt that's true. While Bri and I unpack our things and head toward the field, I notice a few people eyeing us, and I brace myself for any confrontation. Fortunately, most people seem interested in making sure they have all their supplies, so we make it to our spot easily.

Connor, Mia, and Chloe are already there, setting up a couple of tents. Connor and Mia's family go camping on most vacations, so they had all the gear we needed.

"Y'all, this is so exciting!" Chloe squeals. "We're at an actual music festival!"

"A Christian music festival," Connor points out. "Hand me that stake?"

"Probably why it's a music festival my mom would let me go to for a whole weekend," Chloe replies, passing him the stake. "All weekend, y'all! Tons of bands, outdoor bathrooms, snack food—it's the dream."

I'm glad that Chloe and the others are so excited. Having a little supportive group around me makes me feel better about the whole weekend, not to mention performing. I want this to be a good experience for all of us. As we set up camp, I send up a little prayer.

Dear God, it's Tess. Please help us all find strength and joy and comfort this weekend. I think we're going to need it.

♩

The first couple days of the festival pass without incident. We listen to solo performers and bands, some of whom I remember from last year and others who are totally new to me. Mia is particularly impressed by a quartet that includes a mandolin player, vowing to learn the instrument herself over the summer. I catch up with Lily and a few of the Grace Teen Life people, who are camping not too far from us.

I don't run into Alden.

It's not surprising, considering he's behind the scenes for most of the festival. I know that I'll have to see him before I perform, but at least I can spend the rest of the weekend focusing on listening to music and being with my friends and reminding myself that I deserve to be here too.

Wearing my red *A* T-shirt on Sunday helps remind me of that.

Because it's not only me—Bri and Chloe and Connor and Mia and Lily and other people from Grace Teen Life wear theirs. Other people from school or church or in town join the festival for the day, wearing their shirts. In the crowds of people, it's hard to avoid seeing them.

Whenever someone asks me what the shirts are about, I tell them they're part of a project to raise awareness for sexual assault and abuse and body autonomy. I ask if they want a pamphlet with info on resources for support groups and women's centers and reproductive rights, if they or someone they know needs support. "There are a lot of us," I say, "but we want to change that."

Early on Sunday morning, I'm getting in line for the bathroom when I see Roger. When he notices my shirt, the red *A* painted boldly across my chest, he freezes.

For a moment, I stare at him, remembering how he was the source of the rumors about me, hateful text messages, the painting and repainting of the *A* on my locker to let people know that I should be ashamed of what I did. Except I'm not ashamed.

"I know it was you," I tell him, my voice firm and even.

I don't need to expand because he doesn't try to argue. Instead, he clears his throat and says, "I was trying to do what was right. I was trying to help."

"No, you weren't," I insist, more calmly than I would have expected. I don't need to prove anything to him, and I don't have to protect his feelings, not anymore. "If anyone needs help, it's Alden."

I watch his face as he puts it all together, eyes widening and mouth opening slightly in realization. He can't even say anything except a mumbled "I'm sorry" as he wanders off.

♩

There are a handful of amateur performers this year, including Grace Presbyterian choir, Alden among them. Roger is conspicuously absent, but otherwise the group is all there, Alden leading them in a prayer. I feel a twinge of sadness, wishing I was still with them.

Instead, I gently strum my guitar. I can practically hear my dad's voice: *One chord at a time.*

"Hey, Tess," Alden says as he walks over. There's a friendly smile on his face, but his steps are careful, as if he's trying to avoid springing a trap. The sharp white of his button-down shirt makes his eyes seem both a brighter and colder blue than usual. "I wanted to say break a leg out there."

"Thanks," I say stiffly. "You too."

He nods, stuffing his hands in his pockets, and glances at the crowd. "I heard you were the one organizing the T-shirts today. I think what you're doing is great—really admirable. Helping other people find resources and support. That's great, seriously."

Even though what he's saying is complimentary, I can hear the slightest shakiness in his voice. "Helping *other* people," I echo.

"Well, you know, what we had . . ." He clears his throat and looks around the backstage area, unable to meet my eyes. "If you ever misunderstood something, or maybe I unintentionally said or did something . . ." He takes a breath and meets my gaze, his eyes shining with what I previously would have assumed was earnestness, but now I can see is pure veneer. "I never meant to hurt you. I cared for you, I really did. I still do, Tess."

"Tess Pine, you're up next, Tess Pine," one of the tech crew calls.

"I need to go," I tell Alden, turning from him.

He takes a step forward, reaching for my arm. I pull away.

"Tess," he says, freezing for a second. He tries to smile in a genuine, charming way, but it comes across as forced, panicked. "Whatever you're going to do out there—you don't have to do it. If you—we'll never be able to go back to the way things were before."

For so long, that was what I wanted. I remember lying on my grandparents' couch, under their afghan, bleeding and telling myself that I could go back. I think of the girl I was then, and I want to hold her and tell her things are going to be okay, someday, if she keeps moving forward.

"Tess Pine," the techie calls again.

"Tess," Alden says, voice insistent. He's not smiling anymore.

"I don't want to go back," I tell him before I turn and head toward the stage.

♩

The stage feels bigger than it actually is, like I'm shrinking as I step up to the microphone. Lights readjust slightly, centering on me, and for a moment I wish that the amateur performances were scheduled for nighttime, because it would mean I could look into the audience and not see everyone's faces. Instead, I see some people look a little taken aback, and people start murmuring when they see me take the stage. Then I catch sight of Bri, Chloe, Connor, Mia, Lily, and other people in the crowd. They smile up at me, cheering enthusiastically. Beyond them, I see more people in white T-shirts with red *A*'s painted on, all waiting for me to start.

"Hi, y'all," I say, feeling like my voice is too small, even with the microphone. Then, quietly, I count myself off.

My first song is a cover of "Better Is One Day," which has a soft intro, but the chorus has a great rhythm that gets me centered in the song. The crowd settles in, too, rocking gently along with the beat. I fumble a chord in the bridge and a split second of panic rushes through me. But I keep going, remembering that this is my dad's guitar, that my mom's guitar strap is around my shoulder—I can do this, one chord at a time.

"Thank you," I murmur after I finish the first song and the audience gives me a smattering of applause. "You might recognize the next song, in a couple of slightly different contexts."

It's my own creation, a mash-up of "Amazing Grace" and "Everything's Alright," from *Jesus Christ Superstar.* After working on the

"You Are the Light of the World" adaptation with Alden, I wanted to do something similar for one of my songs this year, except now people would know that I wrote it. I kept going back to "Amazing Grace," but I remembered Mary Magdalene's quiet, gentle song from that musical, and the words kept flowing together. Now I feel like I'm talking to myself as I sing, "*I once was lost, but now I'm found, everything's all right . . .*"

The crowd's a little more engaged this time, and after I'm done I hear a few more whoops of appreciation.

"Thanks, y'all," I say, gazing out over the crowd. My heart is full and it's beating, and this is where I'm supposed to be. "This next song is an original. It's been a rough year for me, and it's taken me a lot to get back to music and get back to God. I'm still trying to get back to God, to be honest. For a while, I felt like I didn't deserve to be heard at all. But I came to realize that that was only what some people wanted me to think—that I should be silent. That I didn't deserve to be listened to. I'm not saying I haven't made mistakes, and I'm still wrestling with a lot of things, y'all, but I don't think God wants us to feel alone and ashamed, especially if we've been hurt and abused. The people who hurt you, they want you to stay silent. They don't want you to find forgiveness from God, from yourself. But you deserve that grace and that comfort, and you deserve to be heard."

I take a breath, feeling the red *A* on my chest burning brightly. "Someone tried to make me think I didn't deserve to be heard. So, Alden, this song's because of you."

I don't pay attention to the murmur that goes up among the crowd or my friends cheering from the front. I ignore Alden, off in the wings, going pale. All I focus on is the sound of my guitar and my own voice as I start to sing:

"Someday, years from now, maybe things will be different. Maybe I'll be stronger, a little braver, and no longer afraid to reach

out. I know that You'll be there, Lord, waiting for me, and You know that, no matter how hard I've fallen, no matter how long the road is, I'm always enough . . ."

When I'm finished, I murmur "Thank you" one final time into the microphone. Mine wasn't the best or most professional performance of the weekend, or even that unique or amazing of a song, but it's what I needed to hear.

I look out over the crowd, at everyone wearing a red *A* on their shirt. Maybe one of them needed to hear my song too. And I hope that when they're ready to speak, someone is ready to listen.

22.

Nothing is different and everything is different.

I don't see Alden again after that. The next time I hear about him is a few days after the Spirit Light Festival, once word has gotten around about my performance and Alden, and people make the connection between us. Bri texts me on Tuesday evening, when she's supposed to be at a youth group prayer circle: Alden's gone. He left town. Check the church's Facebook page.

When I do, I see a vague post by Alden, saying that he'll miss everyone in the community but it's time for him to look for new opportunities elsewhere. He thanks everyone for their love and support as he continues to serve the Lord. I stare at his profile picture, all smile and blue eyes, and for a moment I don't know what to feel, exactly. The person in the picture was the person I thought he was—kind and funny, a good listener, a gifted musician, someone who wanted to help other people grow in their faith. After everything that happened, I feel stupid for missing the person I thought he was. But the real Alden, the person who made me feel like he was the most important person in my life, like I had to shield him from harm, he's the one who ran away. Who was always ready to run as soon as someone figured out who he really was.

I'm still here.

Bri found out that Alden disappeared Monday after work, as soon as Reverend Wilson confronted him about some "troubling rumors" he'd been hearing about Alden's behavior regarding some teenage girls in the parish. Alden had tried to brush it off, assuring Reverend Wilson that none of it was true and someone was out to tarnish his good reputation. But the next day, Alden never came to work, and all that was left was the farewell post.

I drive by Alden's apartment that night. I don't expect to see him there; even if he was, I wouldn't have anything else to say to him. But I want to see it for myself—the lights off, the empty driveway. I park Mom's car on the street and walk up to his house, the back entrance dark. When I peek in the windows, I see that much of the furniture is still there. I'd assumed it was Alden's. Maybe the apartment had come pre-furnished, like ours had, or maybe Alden had decided it was better to leave as much behind as possible. But his books, his albums, his keyboard, everything that made the space feel like him, are gone.

It's not like I spent a lot of time there. Only that first time we had sex, plus a handful of other occasions. Now, when I try to remember being here with him, it's like I see all of it through dark water, hazy and distorted.

When I leave, I walk quietly down the stairs to the driveway, hearing the solid sound of my own footsteps.

♩

On Sunday, Mom and I go over to Gram and Gramps's for dinner. Gramps called to invite us over earlier in the week. He and I had continued to meet for breakfast every so often, so getting a call from him wasn't unusual. But he brought up all of us getting together at their house, and I knew he'd heard about what happened at the festival, too, even though he didn't say as much.

"Just the four of us, nothing fancy," he'd told me. "A chance for all of us to be together."

I paused, remembering how Gram had confronted me after work, how she thought I'd been stirring up trouble. "How does Gram feel about this?" I asked.

Gramps sighed and I could imagine him absently rubbing the back of his neck as he tried to figure out what to say. "She wants to see you. Both of you. She's coming around."

I thought about that day in the Needleman's parking lot, the sadness and fear behind her eyes. "Okay," I said.

It's the first time Mom and I have been inside Gram and Gramps's home since the night they kicked us out. Nothing has changed—same water stains on the coffee table, same faded family pictures on the walls, same smell of pine-scented cleaner and old newspaper. I see the couch against the wall and remember lying there, thinking that everything was going to go back to normal, when really nothing had been normal for a while.

Gramps meets us at the door and gives us both a big hug. Gram hangs back for a moment, worrying her hands together like she's not sure what to do with them. She and Mom exchange polite but tense nods of hello. When she looks at me, I see hesitation there. There didn't used to be any—I was a good girl, her sweet grandchild who sang at church and had nice friends and was so helpful around the house. She doesn't know who I am now. She doesn't know I'm still that person, even if I made choices she didn't agree with or understand. But the way she's holding back, she looks like a spring about to pop—she wants to reach out. Maybe she wants to get to know me again.

"Hi, Gram," I say, soft and gentle, like I'm talking to a scared animal.

"Tess," she says and takes a step forward. When she pulls me into a hug, it's a little stiff and sudden, like she's not sure how her limbs work. But it feels like a cloud has been lifted, and we all move deeper into the house.

For dinner, we have roast chicken and baked potatoes and salad. When we compliment the meal, Gram tells us she tried a new recipe for the chicken, butterflying it and roasting it on a rack. Gramps tells us about the fundraiser he's doing with the VFW to help recent vets who have been injured in the line of duty that will cover the cost of rehab and prosthetics. I talk about studying for finals, how I'm going to take the SATs this summer. The conversation is pleasant, if a little superficial, but it feels like this could have been any evening last year, until Mom starts talking about how work is going.

"Between the orthodontist's office and the pub, I'm keeping busy," she says.

"You work a *lot*," I chime in, like my grandparents won't be convinced otherwise. "She works really hard."

Mom shrugs, taking a bite of potato. "At least we're getting out of debt again."

Gramps coughs into his napkin and mutters, "Well, you know, if rent is an issue and you . . . well, want to save some money . . ." He and my grandmother exchange a glance, and I can tell this is something they've already talked about. "We have the space."

But Mom shakes her head fervently. "We're fine where we are."

Gram frowns, her mouth a thin, straight line. "You don't have to cut off your nose to spite your face," she says. "Save the money."

"We haven't done anything with your old room, since . . ." Gramps trails off, like he's afraid to mention why exactly we left.

But Gram takes a breath and continues. "I know things didn't end well last time."

"Because you threw us out," Mom argues, voice rising. She grips her fork like she might need a weapon.

Gramps holds up his hand. "We know. It wasn't right. And we're sorry about that—we really are."

Mom and I look to Gram, whose lips are pressed together like she's holding back an argument. But when she speaks, she says, "You're right—it wasn't the right thing to do. We were upset and shocked and—I didn't—" She keeps starting sentences and not finishing them, like she's not sure how to get to where she wants to be. For a second, she's quiet, and then, without looking directly at us, says, "I don't want to lose you again. Both of you."

Things between my grandparents and me, they're not right, exactly. They turned us out when I needed them the most, and I made a choice that they'll never understand. But over the last couple of years in Hawthorne, I've heard Reverend Wilson talk a lot about forgiveness and grace. How it's not about forgetting hurt. It's about hoping for something better, rebuilding together. And that's something I want to do with my grandparents.

"I know," I tell Gram. "I think, for now, it's better if Mom and I stay where we are. But this, having dinner together—this is something we can do."

Everyone can accept that for now. We finish dinner, and I help Gram clean up while Gramps and Mom watch a Ken Burns documentary on PBS. Gram's scrubbing the roasting pan when suddenly she says, "That group you're doing. The one with all the women's issues."

I pause in the middle of drying a dish. "It's for anyone who wants to join, but, yes, it's mostly women," I say as carefully as possible.

She doesn't look at me as she asks, "You're still doing it?" When I say I am, it's still going, she murmurs thoughtfully. Her head bobs as she scrubs the pan with ferocity, trying to work off the most stubborn crud. Finally, she says, "People didn't talk about that kind of thing in my day. If something happened to you, you carried on as best you could. You know? I don't know. Maybe it's better to talk about it. People have been saying—I've been hearing . . . It's good to talk about these things. Now."

I set the dish aside, watching Gram closely, the way her cheek muscles twitch and her eyes sparkle with tears.

"Did something happen to you?" I ask as cautiously as possible.

She still doesn't look away from the pan, just swallows hard and wipes her eyes with the back of her hand. "No worse than what happened to anyone else," she says dismissively.

But I put my hand on her back and lean my head against her shoulder. She rests her head on mine, and we stand there for a moment, huddled together at the sink, holding each other up.

23.

One morning, at school, I notice the *A* on my locker is faded. It's still there, but less pronounced, like someone has been trying to remove it. At first, I assume it's the maintenance staff, that they finally got more supplies to take off the additional layers of paint. But when I pass Roger in the hall, he lowers his gaze and nods slightly, almost apologetically at me. Maybe he can't say the words yet. Maybe he can't admit that he'd lied to himself, pretending that what he'd done had been all for the greater good, to help force me back on the path to God. But at least he can try to make amends in some small way.

When I see the fading *A*, I think, *That's what this will be someday.* Someday I'll be older and look back and this will all be a thing that happened to me. Choices I made. Paths I took. It won't be all of me, and maybe it won't be something other people will see when they look at me, but it will be something I carry with me. It'll all be a part of the person I am and the person I'm becoming. There's so much more ahead of me, and I don't know what that will be yet, but I want to find out.

♩

When Reagan gets back from college for the summer, we meet for coffee. She already knows about everything that happened at the Spirit Light Festival and the way Alden disappeared afterward. We catch up a little on how the spring semester went for her and how studying for finals is going for me. Reagan tells me about her summer internship with the Parks Department, where she's studying the impact of wastewater discharge, and we laugh over a photo of her in fishing waders and giant gloves. I talk about how I'm spending the summer volunteering at the Wolfwood women's center and phone banking for Planned Parenthood. When she asks if I'm doing anything with youth group now, I say a little, mostly social events. I mention that Reverend Wilson invited me to be on the personnel committee to hire a new youth minister.

"I don't know if it'll mean anything," I admit to Reagan, "but it feels like maybe things are changing."

"I hope so," she says and takes a sip from her cup. Then she says, "I've been thinking. About pressing charges."

She doesn't need to explain what about. I nod, wanting her to continue.

"I'm still within the statute of limitations. Even if we don't know exactly where he went, this could mean that he doesn't have the chance to hurt anyone else." She lowers her eyes, like she's trying to find the right way to say it in the dregs of her coffee. "Because it's not just us. There were others."

Reagan tells me that, after we talked, she did some digging, trying to find parishes and youth groups where Alden had worked before. He'd been asked to leave one church after some "inappropriate behavior" (that was how the minister described it) with a few of the youth group members. Things hadn't gone as far as they had for Reagan or me, but it showed a pattern of abuse and grooming that Alden had practiced years before I'd ever met him. And no one ever stopped him, really stopped him, so he was always able to keep doing it.

Hearing that there were others, more than Reagan and me, makes me shake with anger and sadness. It makes me wish I could reach across time and space and tell those girls that they're not alone.

"You could help," Reagan tells me now. "You need to do what makes you feel safe and supported, but—it might help."

The thought of having to face Alden again, to share in detail everything we said and did in front of a judge and jury, to listen to lawyers question me about what happened and try to make me feel like any of it was my fault—it all sounds exhausting. If we even get to the point of prosecution. Part of me wants to put everything behind me, especially now that Alden is gone. But I keep thinking about Reagan, the other girls she found, Kayla, all the other girls who don't even know what kind of person Alden really is. He shouldn't get to walk away from this.

"I have to think about it," I tell Reagan honestly.

She nods, smiling in a way that's both grateful and sad. "That's all I ask."

♩

I'm at Sunshine Sundaes, getting milk shakes with Chloe, Connor, and Mia one evening, when Kayla comes up to me. She's wearing a Grace Teen Life T-shirt and her blond hair looks brighter somehow in the warmer weather. "Tess," she says, a little shyly. "Can we talk?"

"I'll catch up with y'all in a minute," I tell my friends.

Kayla and I grab a picnic bench a little apart from the rest of the crowd. At first, we sip our milk shakes as I ask about which classes she's taking and which finals she's dreading. She has the same English teacher I did last year, and we commiserate about Mr. Reynolds's fixation on *Great Expectations*.

"I wanted to ask you . . . ," Kayla says, absently stirring her milk shake with her straw. "A little while back I got a text about Alden. How he wasn't the kind of person he seemed like." She pauses and looks at me like she's pulling back a curtain. "Was that you?"

I remember sending that text, not saying who I was. "Yes," I say now.

She nods solemnly. Her gaze moves from me to the long line of people waiting to order, a few other Grace Teen Life kids among them. "He kissed me two days before that," she says. "We'd been talking a lot—my parents are getting a divorce. I don't know if you heard about it." When I shake my head, she continues. "It's been a whole thing. Alden knew and it seemed like he was trying to help me get out of the house, because my parents were at each other all the time." She talks about how they'd go for drives, listen to music, and talk and pray together. He told her she was special, mature. Then one afternoon, he'd taken her for a ride to see the sunset and they'd pulled off to the side of the road where he kissed her for the first time.

As Kayla talks, I see Alden repeating the same patterns, making all of us think we were special. My hands are clenched around the sides of the picnic table, knuckles turning white.

"Then I got your text and at first I thought it was someone trying to mess with me," she says. "But it got me thinking about Alden and maybe I didn't know him, not really."

There are other girls who don't know about Alden. Girls I can't reach out to, not like I did with Kayla. Beyond the parking lot, cars are driving by and all I can think is *He'll never stop unless someone stops him.*

When Kayla goes back to her friends, I take out my phone. My hands are shaking, but I text Reagan: Okay, I'm in.

♩

I keep going to school, work, church, even to youth group on occasion. It gets more and more comfortable, praying with friends again. With the Scarlet Support Project, we keep sharing stories, planning ways to help people in the community speak out and get the help they need. I see more and more overflow between the two groups.

I work with Reagan and the attorney her family hired, along with some of the other girls Reagan found from Alden's old parishes. Reagan and I file reports with the police so they can start an investigation. The lawyer tells us that even if the police end up pressing charges, it can take years to get to court. "I don't say this to deter you," she says, "just to make sure you know the reality of this kind of situation." At first it's disheartening, but I think of Reagan and Kayla and the other girls, maybe some we don't even know yet, and I want to see this through.

When I'm volunteering with the women's center and Planned Parenthood, I meet other volunteers and staff members who go to Grace Presbyterian or other local churches. Every so often, at the women's center, I see a young girl sitting on her own or with her mom, looking so fragile, like she could crack in half, and I pray that she's going to be okay too. I keep praying, for all of us.

♩

I can't go back to the church choir, which feels too raw, even with Alden gone. I sit at church, next to my mom and grandparents now, listening to the choir sing and imagining what it would be like to be up there again. If I could feel safe again. Every week, it seems a little more possible. One Sunday, the choir sings "It Is Well with My Soul," and the voices build on top of each other, *it is well, it is well, with my soul*, and inside it feels like a light glowing brighter, and I think: *Maybe now, yes.*

I keep writing songs, playing the guitar, doing open mic nights at Pammy's. It will get easier and easier to hear the sound of my own voice, to know that others will hear it too.

Maybe one day, I'll fall in love with someone, and they'll want to hear what I have to say, even the hard things. They won't keep me from the people I love, from my faith, from myself. They will listen and they will help me keep moving forward, in love and light and hope. And maybe someday, I'll decide it's the right time to be a mother, and I will give my whole heart to that new person. One day I will tell her *I love you, I'm here for you, I'll always be here for you*, and I will teach her how to sing.

Author's Note

The first time I read *The Scarlet Letter*, I was a senior in high school. I'm sure we talked about major themes from the book, but what I remember most about reading it is how angry I felt. I didn't understand why Nathaniel Hawthorne focused so much on Arthur Dimmesdale, who only admitted his relationship with Hester Prynne at the end of his life. Why did Dimmesdale get to live his life as a powerful religious leader while Prynne and her baby were sent to live in the woods? I wanted Prynne to stand up and name Dimmesdale as the father of her child.

Except speaking out is easier said than done. By the time I'd read *The Scarlet Letter*, I already knew girls shamed for their bodies; guys who got away with improper comments under the guise of joking around; and grown men who initiated inappropriate contact with teens. It happened all around me, and we never said anything because it didn't seem like it would make a difference.

And besides, what would we even call behavior like that? At the time, advice about sexual assault mostly centered on keeping an eye on your drink at parties and carrying your keys in your fist to use as a weapon. That might be helpful in some cases, but it left out a lot of what sexual assault and harassment actually looks like. According to RAINN (Rape, Abuse & Incest National Network), people under thirty are the highest risk group for rape and sexual assault, and among cases reported to law enforcement, 93 percent of child victims know their abuser.[1]

1. "Sexual Assault of Young Children as Reported to Law Enforcement: Victim, Incident, and Offender Characteristics," Bureau of Justice Statistics, published July 2000.

When I first started thinking about *Red*, I knew that an imbalance of power and grooming would be the focus of Tess's story. When Tess joins Grace Presbyterian, she finds a connection to faith she didn't know she'd been looking for—and it's taken advantage of. Sadly, this isn't uncommon in religious groups (or in other organizations that have imbalances of power). I also knew that, unlike Hester Prynne's *A* for "adultery," there was another *A* word that was deeply divisive for contemporary religious communities—"abortion."

I grew up Catholic, and the Church is clear about its negative view of reproductive rights. That, along with other official Church views, didn't sit right with me. Even as I played handbells in my parish choir and joined my college's Catholic student group, where I found some of my closest friends, I was deeply uncomfortable with the blanket condemnation of abortion. As an adult, I still struggle with how I can find a community of faith that also supports my beliefs around these issues.

While I was working on *Red*, the US Supreme Court overturned Roe v. Wade,[2] which had previously made access to an abortion a federal right in the United States. Now, in many states, pregnant people are at risk of being denied health care options, particularly in Black, Latinx, and Indigenous communities, where systemic racism has already caused a lack of safe maternal health care.[3, 4, 5] In *Red*, Tess is fortunate to have a supportive parent and a way to access the care she needs. For many people in the United States, that's not the case.

2. Sherman, Mark, "Supreme Court overturns Roe v. Wade; states can ban abortion," AP, published June 24, 2022.
3. "Racial and Ethnic Disparities Continue in Pregnancy-Related Deaths," Centers for Disease Control and Prevention, last modified September 6, 2019.
4. Merschel, Michael, "After a jump in maternal mortality for Hispanic women, a search for answers," American Heart Association, published September 30, 2022.
5. "UN Body Urges U.S. to Ensure Abortion Access and Culturally Respectful Maternal Health Care in Efforts to Eliminate Racial Discrimination," Center for Reproductive Rights, published September 12, 2022.

It's easy to feel discouraged when seeing this kind of news. But I've also seen groups continuing to organize, to help connect people with the resources they need. Recently, I've seen more and more people speaking out about their experiences with sexual assault or harassment. There's still a lot to change, but there are also a lot of people who want to make a difference.

In Tess's story, I hope readers will find ways to connect with their own voices. To speak out. And to know that they deserve to be heard.

Resources

Sexual Assault and Domestic Violence Resources

- RAINN (Rape, Abuse & Incest National Network): rainn.org
- National Sexual Assault Online Hotline: hotline.rainn.org/online
- The National Domestic Violence Hotline: thehotline.org
- National Sexual Violence Resource Center (NSVRC): nsvrc.org
- There may also be local organizations near you that provide support and services to survivors of sexual violence. For example, in the Boston area, there is the barcc.org.

Abortion and Reproductive Rights Resources

- Planned Parenthood: plannedparenthood.org
- Physicians for Reproductive Health: prh.org
- National Network of Abortion Funds: abortionfunds.org
- NARAL Pro-Choice America: prochoiceamerica.org

Acknowledgments

Writing a book is both deeply solitary and requires so many kind, steadfast, and creative people working together. These are only a few of the people who helped bring my book into the world.

To my amazing agent, Laura Crockett, who believed in my writing and especially this book. It made such a difference to have you in my corner as I worked through multiple drafts, knowing that you *got it* and that you knew it would find the right home. I love how "quick" calls could escalate into hour-long discussions about faith and feminism. Additional thanks to the whole Triada team for their thoughtful collaboration.

To my wonderful editor, Ardyce Alspach, who was the best collaborator I could have imagined for this manuscript. Thank you for truly understanding Tess's story, for digging deep into the hard topics, and for bringing so much empathy and nuance to the editorial process. I'm so glad I had the chance to share this work with you. Thank you also to the phenomenal team at Union Square & Co. for all their creativity and dedication in bringing this book to life. Thanks to Grace House, Jenny Lu, Dan Denning, Renee Yewdaev, Beatriz Ramo, Melissa Farris, and Tracey Keevan.

To my critique group: Annie Gaughen, Allison Pottern, Katie Slivensky, and Tara Sullivan. There is no way I can thank you for all your love and support throughout the years, from your thoughtful critiques to your encouraging texts to the enthusiastic *yay-you-finished-a-draft* dessert party when I didn't know I could keep writing. Thank you for being my people.

To my friends in the writing community, a far from exhaustive list that includes Kendall Kulper, Sarah Combs, Dahlia Adler, SJ Taylor, and, of course, the Fourteenery. You cheered me on and commiserated with me over the tough stuff and always made me feel valued. Special thank-you to Ally Watkins, who championed this book when I didn't know it would ever find a home; I need to find a way to smoosh Massachusetts and Mississippi together.

To my parents, who have supported me as a reader and writer from the time I was old enough to tape pieces of paper together. Thank you for providing me with love, stability, and a strong sense of self from a young age.

To my beautiful family: my children, who are my heart; Bodo the dog for occasionally blessing me with snuggles; and my husband, Walt, who is the best friend and partner I ever could have asked for and a phenomenal writer as well. Thank you for filling our home with love and humor and, of course, stories.